THE BRUTAL WAYS OF A JUNGLE WAR

"Christ, what a real bastard of an area! Everything creeps, crawls, or has thorns on it."

Father Tomkins lifted his sweat rag and wiped his streaming face. Pritchard stood in the normal stance of the laden infantryman—bent forward slightly at the waist to relieve the weight of the pack on his back, rifle balanced on right ammo pouch.

Snapping fingers, the scouts pointed. Section and platoon commander moved forward.

"Who's that over there?"

Green-clad figures with floppy bush hats were visible in the trees on the far side of the grass.

"Dunno, must be those mugs in Bravo. Looks like they're coming over to us."

Both groups waded out into the waist high grass, exchanging waves—hang on, we don't wave like that—their hats . . .

"Skip! They're . . ."

"Hai! Dich! Dich!

"Look out! VC!"

A great burst of firing shattered the afternoon calm. . . .

WHEN THE BUFFALO FIGHT

David Alexander

BANTAM BOOKS
TORONTO · NEW YORK · LONDON · SYDNEY · AUCKLAND

WHEN THE BUFFALO FIGHT
A Bantam Book / February 1987

All rights reserved.
Copyright © 1987 by Lex McAulay.
Cover art copyright © 1987 by Bantam Books, Inc.
This book may not be reproduced in whole or in part, by
mimeograph or any other means, without permission.
For information address: Bantam Books, Inc.

ISBN 0-553-26448-6

PRINTED IN THE UNITED STATES OF AMERICA

O   0 9 8 7 6 5 4 3 2 1

This book is based on the 1965–66 tour in South Vietnam by the First Battalion of the Royal Australian Regiment. While the majority of the incidents related did take place, characters and time have been shuffled, and place names have been altered; in no case is any person who served in the battalion (1965–66) intentionally portrayed as any single character in the book. Apart from the few persons involved who may recall the incidents, and whose memory may present a different tale, as details of events have been altered, no one should be readily identified in the book, nor is such identification intended.

An infantry battalion is a group of about 800 men, whose tasks revolve around closing in on and killing or capturing the enemy and seizing and holding ground, regardless of climate, weather, terrain, and the hour.

It is a complex team. While the commanding officer is the man at the top, no one person can possibly see, hear, or experience everything that the battalion encounters or experiences.

For the sake of simplicity, the experiences of the platoon and company related herein have replaced those on the wider canvas of the whole battalion and its outside influences.

The book is inspired by the Australian soldier, by his matter-of-fact, day-to-day courage, his sense of humor, and sense of comradeship—the last two combining to enable him to keep events and people in perspective. It is dedicated to all those Australians who, regardless of corps, do their soldiering forward of the wire.

Glossary

These are included as explanatory remarks, not exact definitions, for the reader who may not be familiar with the terms.

Ao dai	The Vietnamese national dress: a close-fitting top and bodice, with long flowing panels from the waist, under which long pants or trousers are worn. Pronounced "ow zhy" by the Northerners and 'ow yhy' by the Southerners.
APC	Armored personnel carrier
AATTV	Australian Army Training Team Vietnam
Arc of fire	Each weapon is positioned to fire over a certain piece of ground, which has left and right boundaries. If this is plotted on a map, the area would be represented as an arc at the extremities of the boundaries. There are primary (main) and secondary arcs of fire.
ARVN	Army of the Republic of Vietnam, usually pronounced as "arvin."
AWOL	Absent Without Leave
Back up	With reference to meals, coming back for a second serving.
Base-bludging	Bludging in a base or rear area. Anyone who is farther back from the enemy than oneself is a basebludger. They rarely, if ever, go forward of the wire.
Base up	Make camp
Basic webbing	Generally the minimum harness that a soldier can wear and carry to enable him to perform his basic fighting functions: waist

	belt, shoulder harness, ammunition pouches, water bottles, bayonet, entrenching tool, and whatever else the unit deems necessary. On this "basic" webbing the thoughtful army can build: big and small packs, bedding, radios, etc.
BHQ	Battalion Headquarters. Now Bn HQ
Brass up	To shoot, be shot at, as "they brassed up two VC," and "they got brassed up by a machine gun."
CHQ	Company Headquarters
Chalk	The group of passengers for a single aircraft
Charlie	The enemy: from VC = Viet Cong = Victor Charlie in radio phonetics
CO	Commanding Officer
CP	Command Post
CSM	Company Sergeant Major
Corps	The Australian army is composed of various corps, e.g., infantry, artillery, transport, dental, etc. Everyone belongs to one of them.
III Corps Conference	South Vietnam was divided into four Corps Tactical Zones (CTZ): I, II, III, and IV. These were a means of dividing the country into areas of responsibility in which the various units operated, and had nothing to do with the infantry, artillery, etc., type of corps. The III Corps HQ was almost adjacent to the airbase and the Conference was attended by an Australian representative.
Digger	An Australian soldier
DMZ	The so-called Demilitarized Zone between North and South Vietnam
Dust-off	Radio callsign for a medical evacuation helicopter, the crews of which were renowned and revered for their efforts to lift wounded out of battle and back to the medical facilities despite bad weather and enemy fire. Spoken usage included: "We require Dust-off for six," and "Fred got Dusted-off to Saigon," i.e., Fred was evacuated to Saigon by helicopter.

FAC	Forward Air Controller: a pilot who flies a small (Cessna) aircraft into the battle area to locate, mark, and guide the fighters or bombers onto the targets. A high degree of skill and courage was required.
FN	Fabrique Nationale, the Belgian firm of arms makers
Forward of the wire	Outside the barbed-wire perimeter of the unit or base, i.e., out where the enemy may be met. See "basebludger" and "pogo."
GVN	Government of Vietnam, the Saigon regime
Hutchi	Japanese or Korean word for house or shelter, corrupted to mean the soldier's tent in the field. American: "hooch" or "hoochi."
Huey	UH-1 Helicopter, became Huey
IO	Intelligence Officer
Iron Triangle	A jungle area, roughly shaped like a triangle, about thirty miles west of Saigon, used by the Viet Cong as a base area.
J	Jungle
KIA	Killed In Action
Locstat	Location statement; present location
LO	Liaison Officer
Local Force	The Viet Cong/National Liberation Front organized their fighting forces on several levels. At the bottom was the village guerrilla, then units organized to operate in their home area—but larger than the usual village squad, and given tasks of a more demanding military nature; naturally enough these were called local force units. Above them were regional units and finally the main force.
LZ	Landing Zone
Main Force	Units of soldiers who have graduated from the village guerrillas, local and regional force units, are full-time members of the armed forces, and are now regular troops who can be given military tasks such as those given to regular units of the Western armies.
MASH	Mobile Army Surgical Hospital

Military Region	The National Liberation Front had divided Vietnam into these areas for their own administrative and operational purposes.
MPC	Military Payment Certificate. "Play money" or "Monopoly money" issued by the military authorities in an attempt to halt the flow of dollars into the black market and so on. It is only good in the military system such as canteens, messes, etc. The type or pattern of MPC would be changed at very short notice, and all unchanged old MPC would then be so much paper. There are said to be people throughout Asia with boxes of old MPC, hoping for the day when the particular pattern is again issued, and they will become rich.
MP	Military Police
NCO	Non-Commissioned Officer, i.e., below the rank of second-lieutenant
NLF	National Liberation Front. No Communist Revolution is complete without this title.
Nog	Australian slang term for an Asian: more fully "Nigel the nog." Sometimes, simply "Nigel." Plural is "noggies" and the land is sometimes referred to as "Nogeria."
NVA	North Vietnamese Army. Never admitted by Hanoi to be in South Vietnam, an assertion believed only by the very naive.
OC	Officer Commanding. A company has an OC, a battalion a CO, a division a GOC— General Officer Commanding.
Orders Group	A gathering for the purpose of passing on orders to subordinates.
Political Officer	The communist forces, being the armed effort of the political organization, are always subject to strict political control, which is achieved by placing a political infrastructure paralleling that of the military command, at all levels from company on up. The political officer has the last word in disagreements between the military and political. Called commissars in earlier times, they are a very

important and effective means of ensuring control, motivation, and explanation of policy to the soldiers.

Pepper-pot   A tactic for advancing under fire where one or two soldiers at a time leap up, run forward a few paces, go down, roll away, and fire on the enemy while their comrades are doing the same. The enemy is presented with fleeting targets all across his front, making it very hard for him to take an accurate shot. Like many other things, it requires practice and teamwork.

Pogo   See Basebludging. Pogos are the same, but worse. They supposedly spend their time bouncing aimlessly around the rear areas on a pogo-stick and are thus of no use to the fighting troops, i.e., anyone closer to, or likely to be closer to, the enemy.

PPS   Russian submachine gun of World War II vintage, firing a 7.62mm round.

PX   Post Exchange = US Canteen

Regional Force   Along with a similar organization called the popular force, were part-time troops of the Saigon Regime, used for guard and other light military duties, which could include operations to search for the VC, normally operating in their home locations or areas. Abbreviated to RF/PF, so immediately were called "ruff-puffs."

RPD   Russian light machine gun for section or squad use. The initials stand for the Russian words, the D being for Degtyarev, the designer.

RMO   Regimental Medical Officer, the battalion doctor

RSM   Regimental Sergeant Major, the senior non-commissioned officer in the unit, responsible to the CO for discipline.

RV   Rendezvous

Septics   Septic tank = Yank = citizen of the United States of America

Sheila	girl/woman
Slicks	Troop-carrying helicopters, as opposed to armed versions, the "gun-ships," called "pigs."
Slope	US term for Asian, as the Australian "nog"
SLR	Self Loading Rifle; the Australian-modified Belgian FN, produced at Lithgow, firing the standard NATO 7.62mm round; pronounced "slur."
Twenty mike mike	20-millimeter cannon; from 20mm
VC	Viet Cong; the Vietnamese for Vietnamese Communist
VNAF	Vietnamese Air Force
War Zone D	A term dating from the 1950's war against the French, for a large expanse of jungle about forty miles northeast of Saigon, in which the VC had base camps, training areas, etc., and which was rarely entered by government forces prior to 1965; also called D-Zone or Zone D. Zone C was farther to the southwest, and others were to the north.
Watch your front	Do not stare down your shirt buttons and trouser fly, but pay attention to the area of ground before you, your arc of fire.
WIA	Wounded In Action
Zap	To shoot, kill

When the Buffalo fight, the small animals are trampled.

An old Asian saying

Prologue

October 1964

Battalion commander Ba Thanh ceased admiring the moonlit clouds, checked his watch with a small movement of his head, and said, "Fire."

The mortar bombs chunged up and out, and Ba Thanh's eyes looked down the long grassy slope, glistening silver in the moonlight, to the area of lights, brighter than diamonds, with here and there the rubies of obstruction lights on hangar roofs—the airfield. Fully lighted, figures moving casually, vehicles driving behind their insect-eye headlights, the lizard shapes of sleeping jet bombers . . . and then the sound of giant doors slamming and brief flashes as the mortars ended their journey across the velvet tropical sky.

The casually moving figures suddenly running in all directions, the motor vehicles speeding up and zigzagging madly . . . some of the B57 Canberra jets already slumped on their sides or bellies, their broad wings reflecting the first fires . . .

Ba Thanh's eyes and teeth gleamed in the moon shadow of the bush as he smiled at Bay Chieu, battalion political officer, "That stirred them in their nest, brother."

Bay Chieu barely nodded, his eyes, reflecting the lights, steadily gazing at the scene below.

Dark figures moved quickly back to the left and the right across the moon and shadow-dappled ridge top. Ban Quy reported with a flash of teeth in the moonlight. "All bombs fired and all crews withdrawing, comrade."

Ba Thanh tapped the shoulder of the fourth man,

1

"Nam Dinh, phase three signal now," as the others began moving back.

Nam Dinh's three sharp whistles signaled the escort platoon to begin moving back—the dark-clad, hunched figures gliding quietly and swiftly through the silvered grass and into black shadows.

Now the group fled east under the moon, down the white gleaming paths, for under the scream of the siren was the throbbing hum of the avenging bumblebee helicopters. . . .

At the first halt twenty minutes later, Bay Chieu stared west through the soft tropical darkness to the red glow over the skyline, and the circling blinking red lights of the helicopters searching for any ground assault force.

"So, comrades, the insects are disturbed," one red light suddenly shot away from the circling school and myriad red pinpoints streamed seemingly slowly earthward, "and they expend themselves on brother Can's decoys." A laugh whispered through the watching shadows.

Ba Thanh turned and gestured to the east, "Enough rest. Comrade Tan—the four 'quicks' and one 'slow' —what are they?"

"Comrade, 'quick' approach, 'quick' battle, 'quick' reorganization, 'quick' withdrawal, and 'slow' preparation."

"Good. Now we are withdrawing quickly. Go!"

On the rooftop of his billet in the town adjoining the airbase, Colonel Walter Harvey, Wing Operations Officer, shifted his gaze from the fire glow and the rows of Vietnamese spectators on each roof, rose-tinted by the flames, took, his cigar from between gritted teeth, and said softly, "I guess it's a stupid fucking question Randy, but where the hell were and are the ARVN?"

Randy lifted his shoulders and rolled his eyes skyward. Being an intelligence officer at this base in this country at this time was something that often left him speechless.

January 1965

Mark Raymond, an AAP photographer, shook his head slowly and prepared to record the scene: long decayed stretch of French-built road, bitumen eroded to a filigree pattern over the red earth underneath; long grass encroaching over both road edges, sunlight streaming down as a crushing physical presence—and the regularly spaced silent bundles of clothes lying so still, some half in and half out of the long grass; the bodies of the government paratroopers who had been ambushed, following the young lieutenant searching for the enemy by walking down the road, until he found them.

Their commanding officer had begun his military career with the French and continued with American training. This meant he did not have to go out with the troops but controlled his subunits by radio from a convenient village, in a house or under a shady tree, with maps, orderlies, and radio operators as befitted his rank.

Unfortunately, the VC commanders had not had the benefits of such education and controlled their force from positions much closer to the scene of action.

Raymond reloaded his Nikon and together with Freddie Henson, a journalist reporting in his seventh war (World War II, Palestine 1948, Greece 1948–49, French Indo-China 1950–54, with breaks for Korea, Arab-Israeli War of 1956), walked over to their battered Renault.

"We'll make it in two hours," said Mark, calculating that in three and a half he could be showered, changed, and in the Copacabana on Le Thanh Ton Street with the delectable Huong. As his hand touched the sun-warm door handle, both men's heads flicked around, every sense alert, nostrils flared like a hunting dog's, eyes sharper, as the drum roll of heavy firing crashed out and continued, hardly muted by the distance and intervening trees.

"Christ, ambushed three times in what, a little over a mile? How long can they keep this up? The ARVN are being chewed up along the length and breadth of this goddam country—they can't have many reserves left, Fred."

Fred settled himself into the worn and faded driver's seat and switched on the ignition.

"No, they haven't. You've just been taking their pictures. Come on, it's getting late."

Raymond looked around again at the spaced rows of

camouflaged corpses laying where they had fallen, the yellow-green grass against the dark brooding green jungle, that impenetrable wall covering what? He shrugged and paused to look up at the two propeller-driven Skyraiders roaring down, dark-blue canopies glinting, toward the sound of firing that had now taken on the different note of panicked, uncontrolled blazing at shadows as the ARVN expended their ammunition on the trees—the VC were gone again.

As the Renault bumped back to Saigon, Raymond drummed his fingers in the red dust on the door windowsill, only half aware of the lurching and rocking caused by the neglected road surface, clicking through in his mind who among his contacts could have contacts with the National Liberation Front and who might be worth sounding out about accreditation as a photographer to the NLF to cover the change of government.

February 1965

The small group of Australians stood in the Queensland sunshine, the knee-high grass waving as the breeze from the Pacific whispered up the slope. Bush hats inside shirts and sweat cloths tucked into the open-necked collars, they waited for a helicopter. A lieutenant-colonel, a captain, a lance-corporal with a radio set on his back, and a private— the battalion commander, his intelligence officer, radio operator, and a battalion intelligence section member.

There existed that familiarity among professionals found between people who devote their adult lives to a common calling, and so the group was discussing the various wars going on at the time, training, new techniques, and equipment. The intelligence section private waited for a pause in the conversation and addressed the colonel. "Sir, the Yanks are writing the book on helicopter warfare in South Vietnam, using them as troop carriers and to give air support, but the RAAF say you can't put a machine gun on a helicopter two years after the Yanks started using them. What's wrong with the bastards? That Yank pilot on exchange we had flying us on the last exercise has already done a tour in Vietnam as a gunship pilot."

The colonel's short silver hair shone in the sun as he turned his head and answered, "Remember you said, 'writing the book,' it's still trial and error to a large extent, and we just don't have the helicopters to lift any sizeable body of troops let alone start hanging machine guns and things off them. Now look at Vietnam—despite the Americans there and their helicopters, the VC are winning. It's a losing war, and we won't get involved in it at this stage."

The radio operator tilted the handset toward his ear, acknowledged the message, and looking south said, "Chopper's on its way," which ended the discussion.

1

June 1965

"You will load the twenty rounds into a magazine. That magazine will not be placed on your weapon unless you are ordered to do so by an officer," stated the captain of the 115 men standing in three ranks on the darkening parade ground, equipment piled at their feet.

The quiet twilight scene was a background of pale-painted army barracks around a company parade ground. The 115 green-clad men comprised the majority of the load of a Boeing 707 soon to be en route for Vietnam, and they were now kneeling or squatting to load their twenty rounds into a magazine—from all sides the soft metallic snock, snock, snock, rose into the clear evening air.

"Right, your time's your own for the next thirty minutes. Be back here then, standing by your gear."

The dark shapes of the 115 began moving away, the

buzz of conversation rising and matches flaring as the cigarette smokers fed their addiction.

The regimental sergeant major smiled as he saw the dark shadow figures merge into the ground at the side of the barrack buildings. "There's the Aussie Digger; give him a two-minute halt and he goes down like a pole-axed steer."

Major James Ryder, known as "Red" to one and all, after an American comic-strip cowboy, turned to his officers— Captain Peter Barlow, second-in-command; Lieutenants Bruce Myers, George Benson, and "Speed" Gordon, rifle platoon commanders—"Peter, this will be the last opportunity for these young fellows to buy their seniors a drink in Australia. I'll see you in the mess in ten minutes."

"Right, sir."

Ryder called to the company sergeant major, "Baron," Lord, who was talking to Myers's platoon sergeant, Bart Bartholomew, "CSM."

"Sir?"

"We're going to the mess. We'll be back in twenty-five minutes."

"Right, sir." Turning back to Bartholomew, "So everything's okay with Pritchard?"

"Yeah. It was a close thing though. The bastards."

"Yeah. How often is a Digger buggered around by the pencil pushers in matters we don't have any say in? The Dig, of course, says 'Fuckin' army!' Hmm. Okay, then. How's Private Farley?"

"Moaning as usual. He's all right."

"Yeah. All right, see you back here in twenty minutes."

"Right sir."

Lieutenant Colonel Stan Burrows stood in his office looking out into the autumn dusk, wondering how the children would fare during his absence. Away at school in northern New South Wales, they were just starting to question authority and feel the young blood racing through their veins. Muriel would, of course, have a very busy time with the mass of committees and associated activities. If only she would be careful driving the car. There were so many idiots on the roads.

A knock at the door. He turned, and in a clear voice, commanded, "Come in."

Regimental Sergeant Major James "Razor" Sharp entered, every inch an infantry RSM, executing a faultless salute.

"Good evening, sir."

"RSM."

Quickly, but without appearing to do so, Sharp checked the CO's dress. If it was not up to standard, Burrow's batman would be chastised. the RSM had served with Burrows in one place or another for thirteen years. Looking at the officer behind the desk, he saw a still trim 37-year-old man, of average height, blond, with level blue eyes, faint traces of silver at the temples almost hidden by the blond hair and short back-and-sides haircut. The air of command sat with Burrows always, even in tennis whites, a game he played at every opportunity, and did well. At thirty-seven, Burrows could look back on a career embracing Japan, Korea, and Malaya. His Military Cross was awarded after a vicious action in defense of "The Hook" during the trench warfare stage of the Korean War. Now, his battalion was in the process of moving to Vietnam. Advance party gone, companies leaving by Boeing 707 at regular intervals.

He had said his farewell to Muriel after breakfast. He felt easier knowing the duties of each of them would keep them busy and allow little time for brooding on the separation. His nickname, "Stan-the-man," as well as rolling easily off the tongue, grew from his unwavering grasp of command of the battalion.

Sharp, his five feet eleven inches starched and gleaming, had fought through New Guinea, gone to Japan with the Occupation Forces, fought the North Koreans and Chinese Communists in Korea, and the Communist terrorists in Malaya. His military medal had been won with the bayonet at Shaggy Ridge in New Guinea. He was a firm believer in the saying, "There are no bad soldiers, only bad officers and NCOs."

Burrows and Sharp had served in the same battalion in Korea, again in Malaya, and had also been on the staff at the Royal Military College, Duntroon, at the same time.

Sharp's family consisted of a patient, understanding wife, who supported him in everything he did, and a son, now at Duntroon, in his second of the four years to be spent there before graduation as a first lieutenant.

Together, Burrows and Sharp commanded an infantry battalion of 800 Australians from all walks of life, but which in the early sixties, was composed mainly of Queenslanders, West Australians, and British with only a scattering of representatives of other states. There were so many English immigrants in some units that a current saying was, "This is a good little british army, fucked up by a few Aussies!"

Burrows's battalion was composed of company commanders with experience as platoon commanders in Korea and Malaya and some platoon commanders with Malayan service; warrant officers with battle experience in World War II, Korea and Malaya, and two with previous time in the Australian Army Training Team, Vietnam—AATTV; sergeants with at least Malayan service, and some corporals and privates with service in both Korea and Malaya, but the majority of junior ranks had not been overseas. They were secure in the knowledge that the Australian is superior to the man of every other nation, and while there might be more of the others, with greater wealth, they were definitely inferior. Without realizing it, two of their great strengths were the dry Australian sense of humor and the inborn independence of the Australian male, ingested with his mother's milk, that allowed him not to be overawed by another's appearance and reputation, but to reserve judgment and base approval or rejection on visible performance.

Having dealt with the routine matters, RSM Sharp strode out of the CO's office and along the veranda to the Regimental Police Office, eyes flicking over every soldier in sight to detect sloppy dress, untidy or long hair, or slovenly bearing.

After losing friends in battle against the fanatical Japanese and Chinese, Sharp became a firm believer in rigid discipline—not for discipline's sake, but as preparation for battle. The easy-going Aussie attitude of "she'll be right," if allowed to develop and if tolerated in peace, lead to casualties in war. Sharp knew Australia did not have, perhaps never would have, the manpower to accept needless casualties that were caused by lack of discipline.

With out-thrust jaw and steely eye, he would deliver a short lecture to offenders found below the required standards, finishing with, "Any fool can prance around here with all the comforts! But to look after your weapons, equipment, and personal health and appearance when you're tired, wet, cold, frightened, with mates to bury, *and* be ready to go on—*that's* soldiering!"

The trucks arrived, high square dark shapes against the evening sky, headlights blazing in semicircles, brake lights flaring red, engines rumbling, and airbrakes hissing as the drivers maneuvered their mammoths into line, backs toward the waiting dark rows; drivers swung down and hastened to lower their tailboards. The Diggers pulled themselves up into the dark interiors with practiced ease, the first two up assisting the others.

The inevitable final roll call had been performed in the last few minutes before the trucks arrived; now another count was made before the convoy started for the RAAF base from which the 707 was to take these men on the long flight north under the stars, into the tropics to the "paddies," the blazing sun, the swamps, the monsoons, the leeches, the malarial mosquitoes and the Viet Cong—who, now in June 1965, were roaming the country in regiments with an unending string of victories gained by themselves and their North Vietnamese regular army counterparts.

The usual start-of-journey chatter died out, and the road trip was a silent one in the dark, canopied interiors, cigarettes fiery for a moment, faces dimly glowing in the lights of following cars.

Some family and friends had waited outside the camp and followed the hulking shapes of the convoy to the airbases for farewells. The departure was from an airforce base, for security reasons. Despite the announcement that an Australian battalion was to serve in Vietnam, despite the activity at Garden Island loading stores onto the aircraft carrier HMAS *Sydney*, now a troop carrier, despite the embarking of troops and the night sailing, despite all these activities for days on end taking place under the eyes of thousands of Sydney Harbor ferry passengers, and being visible from the thousands of North Shore windows looking across the Harbor, despite the fact that wives and children must be told, and so neighbors, in-laws, friends, and family doctors, and an ever-widening number of people must become aware that "so-and-so" would be going to Vietnam—despite all this, security people tried to maintain secrecy, to prevent subversive elements and the "lunatic fringe" finding out who was going, when and from where.

Corporal "Father" Rankin's wife, Alice, rang to find out if her husband would be home early or late; packing a battalion for war is one thing, but the domestic matter whether to cook early or late also has a relative importance.

"I'm sorry, ah, er, madam," mumbled Lieutenant Benson, "er, I can't tell you if your, er, husband, is, er, even in this unit."

"What do you mean? I know he's one of your soldiers and you're the officer! All I want to know is will he be home early or late?"

"Ah, well, er, I'm afraid I can't tell you," began the young officer, and suddenly jerked the earpiece away from his head as a stream of fluent English poured out, in which the words "fool . . . commanding officer . . . put up with this . . . simple matter . . . husband . . . idiots for officers" were repeated in varying sequence and increasing vehemence, cut off sharply when the lieutenant's caller hung up. He blinked at the handset.

"Who was that?" queried Sergeant Augie Bennett, looking up from the list of company next-of-kin.

"Well, she said she was Corporal Rankin's wife, wanting to know what time he'd be home," replied the lieutenant.

"But he's on his way now," said the stocky dark-haired sergeant, frowning in puzzlement.

"Yes, I know," said the officer, "but I can't go giving out that information over the phone, you know."

"Fuck me," thought Bennett, anticipating the reaction in the mess when he hit them with the latest one about Benson. Not for nothing did he have the unofficial title of "Jungles"—green and dense.

The convoy rolled through the airbase gate, slowing to the slapping hiss of airbrakes, and halted outside the long marquee. With a minimum of effort the passengers climbed down with their basic webbing and weapons: the long-barreled, self-loading rifle—SLF—called "Slur" by the men, designed by FN in Belgium, and modified and produced in Australia at Lithgow; the US M60 belt-fed machine gun, recent replacement for the beloved Bren; and the Australian Owen submachine gun, famous in the Pacific. Although always popular in Australia, as so much of it could be stripped off and left behind on exercises, the Owen was shortly to be replaced by the vaunted US M16, the Armalite of legend, because of the low muzzle velocity of its 9mm round at 800 feet per second.

When the chairs in the tent had been filled—"fill up from the back!"—and the sergeant major had made a quick headcount, a service corps captain, his rank displayed by a gold wagon wheel on a red armband, stepped forward.

"I will call out your names, and you will be given a boarding pass. Place it in your puggaree immediately; don't lose it, swap it with your mates, or put it in your pocket. In the puggaree! The number must be visible, like this," taking up a slouch hat and inserting the cardboard pass behind the front of the hat band (called a puggaree, ever since the British Army served in India), "and there'll be no messing around getting you on board."

After various administrative notices, he announced, "Right, there's tea, coffee, biscuits, and so on outside. From now until we call you, you can spend the time with your families outside."

Small family groups gathered in the light and shadow rhomboids outside the tent, white polystyrene cups in hand. Those who had said their farewells that morning stood yarning and watching the floodlit 707, silver and white, with the red Qantas tail, perched above its ground crew performing their rituals.

"Well, this time tomorrow night, eh, Smacker?" grinned tall, blond Les Fitzgibbon. Friends for several years, Fitzgibbon and Smacker Riley went fishing together, wangled courses together, and with great equanimity, shared their clothes, boot polish, and money the same way they shared each other's girlfriends. The girls were always placid and affectionate, never seeming to mind the free-and-easy pairing off, sometimes with Les, sometimes with Smacker.

"Yeah, this time tomorrow night," replied Smacker. "Wonder if there'll be anything goin' on?"

"Aw, bloody bound to be, bound to be," put in "Nimbus" Farley, the company pessimist. "Whadya reckon, they're gonna let us get settled in an' do nothing? If you were in their boots, you'd have somethin' set up, woulden ya? They're gonna hit us, mate, you see."

"Aw, bullshit, you silly bastard," from Les, who was in fact recalling the briefing given by the Intelligence crowd, which largely showed how the Vietnamese had run rings around the French, killing 100,000 of the buggers, and beating piss and pick-handles out of them at Dien Bien Phu. Well, so what—that was the French.

Queenslander Tom Pritchard was wondering how his family was settling into the house they had moved into that very day. They had previously lived in a rented house. Ten days ago, the landlord had given them a fortnight's notice: he suddenly needed the house for his parents. If he could find a house in the time available, Tom could not scrape together the money for a bond and removal in the fortnight; moreover, he was on orders to go to Vietnam. He had then gone through the army system and applied for an army married quarter; his company commander and even the battalion commander had added their weight to the request for a speedy allocation, to no avail. The public servants controlling the married quarters maintained their position: "There are absolutely no quarters available."

Even a request for assistance through army channels

to Canberra and to the minister brought the same reply: "No quarters available." There was one final sentence: "But Private Pritchard goes to Vietnam, as intended."

Two days before he was due to go, Tom and a few mates, at their wits' end, were having a lunchtime beer in the Diggers' canteen. Going AWOL was no solution, as his pay would cease, and he would be easily picked up, for no result. "It looks like a caravan park for a year for 'em; Tom said, staring into his beer.

"Excuse me, mate," broke in another soldier standing next to the small group, "are you lookin' for a quarter?"

"Yeah, I'm goin' to Vietnam in two days, regardless, and I can't find a place for the wife an' kids. There's no bloody quarters in Sydney."

"Well, listen mate, I live in Cramer Street, over there, and there's about four or five quarters empty—long grass out front an' all. Been empty six months, some of 'em, I reckon."

"Shit! C'mon Tom, we'll dive over for a look," burst out Corporal "Father" Rankin, "Father" as he was prematurely gray-haired.

"Hey," to the stranger "got time to come over with us and show us?"

"Aw, yeah, wait'll I skoal this."

And there were indeed married quarters, which had been empty for some months, despite direct requests and explanations of the compassionate nature of Tom's request from his commanders and from Canberra. As a result of phone calls that afternoon, Private Pritchard was at last reluctantly allocated a house for his family; a sympathetic commander looked the other way when a truck disappeared with several of Tom's mates to assist in the move.

So, standing staring at the Qantas emblem, Tom drew on his cigarette, past the tightness in his chest composed of equal amounts of worry about the kids settling in and rage against the bureaucrats. Christine was a good, steady type; he had no worries there.

"Fuckin' public servants," he growled, grinding the butt into the grass.

"Pack of mongrel bastards," agreed Father.

*   *   *

Through the long night sky, the 707 rumbled north, halting to refuel at Townsville, and on to Manila. Major "Red" Ryder, the officer-in-charge of the group, spoke over the aircraft announcement system, telling them the stop would be for several hours and that they would be confined to the transit lounge. The aircraft door slid back, the men walked down the steps and across to the transit lounge. The route was indicated by two lines of unsmiling Philippine soldiers, all armed with submachine guns, all facing inwards. "Don't the bastards trust us?" from Father Rankin.

After "breakfast" for those who wanted it—'It'll be a long time till lunch," moaned Nimbus—the bar and tobacco counter was crowded. San Miguel beer revived memories for those who had drunk it in Malaya and expanded the experience of those who had not.

"Hey, ya wanta go for a leak in there," grinned Blue Barnes, a machine gunner, to the rest of the section. "There's a nog in there with a vibrator he wacks onto ya shoulder blades while you're havin' a leak."

"Yeah, you shoulda seen 'im leap!" laughed an interested spectator. "Ever seen a bloke leap into the air, tryin' to stop pissin', put his dick back in his pants, not wet himself, and turn and punch a nog behind him, all in midair? Thought the dreaded Asians had 'im!" and held his sides at the memory.

Meanwhile, three other travelers decided to go to the door for a look out at the surroundings. A lone Philippine soldier stood about ten paces away from the door. As it swung open he moved one foot forward, cocked his Thompson submachine gun and went into a firing stance. The three paused and took in the leveled gun and closed Asian face. "Oh, welcome to the Philippines, eh?" one of them observed as they retired.

"I wonder why the bastards don't like us?" mused Frank Gardiner.

"Yeah, if *we* acted like that, they'd be screaming bloody 'racists' in the UN," growled Barry Reimann, "you'll learn it's only us white men who're racists; never any of these little bastards."

"Never mind, when they get into the deep shit, they'll scream for us white men to get 'em out," said Geoff Bates, from the depths of his three years' military experience. "They can get rooted; let's have a beer."

The group walked back to the aircraft through the silent rows of Philippine soldiers, either ignoring them and chatting, or striding along and looking them up and down. Secure in their knowledge that Australians are superior to every other bastard, they took their seats for the final leg to Vietnam, timed to arrive at dawn.

With their usual forethought, Father, Tom, and Nimbus, sitting in the cabin rear, spent their last Australian cash on a bottle of Philippine rum. A word to the stewards, and they were comfortably seated in the small compartment in the very end of the cabin, ready to drink their way to Saigon. Liberal dashings of Qantas orange juice helped disguise the taste—"Dunno what part of the bloody sugar cane went into this piss. Christ, it's crook stuff." By steadily working away at it, they were able to place the empty brown bottle in the rubbish sack as the long fuselage tilted down for the descent into Saigon.

2

The wet blanket of the tropics wrapped itself around each man as he climbed down from the air-conditioned fuselage, the last link with Australia, the wife and kids, the footy, the club, sheilas, the Cross, the beaches... now, they really were there; sweat rushing to the skin's pores and the peculiar smell of Vietnam in the nostrils. That circus smell of animals and sharp animal urine, straw, perfumed blossoms, and the scent of tropic grasses and leaves mixed with the kerosene stench of jet fuel and motor car exhaust.

"They're not gonna put us in those bloody things, are they? If we get ambushed, we've bloody well had it," moaned Nimbus, mournfully gazing at the US Army olive-drab buses, with wire mesh over the windows to prevent grenades lobbing in.

"Come on yer whingin' bastard, they're probably waitin' till tonight."

"Yeah, yeah," and he climbed in staring distrustfully at the onlookers, his hand resting on the pack holding his twenty-round magazine, thinking, "I'll never get the thing on and cocked in time. Christ almighty . . ."

The buses rolled out of the Tan Son Nhut airbase into the teeming Saigon traffic: a rushing honking beeping mass of trucks, vans, cars, jeeps, motor cycles, motorized bicycles, farm wagons, converted Lambrettas, bicycles on "pedal power," cyclos—a chair propelled by the driver from behind and its motorized version, all trailing a plume of blue smoke, all honking at each other, and with much arm waving by the drivers, weaving, overtaking, turning left and right, or suddenly pulling over and halting—an ever-changing mass of mobility in a blue haze, peopled by thousands of Vietnamese whose only common feature was black hair and slant eyes. Vietnamese with round faces, thin faces, square faces, oval and triangular faces, dressed in drab pajama-type clothes—uniforms of green, khaki, white, and camouflage; western suits and ties, western dresses, and the elegant ao dai and dainty parasols for the women; and the universal school uniform of white shirt and dark shorts or white ao dai. The women and girls who walked elegantly, ao dai tails fluttering, or balanced demurely and expertly on the pillion seats of motor scooters and motor cycles, were in a class of beauty of their own, as a chic Parisienne or slim Indian woman in a sari are in their own class.

The convoy left the city behind, and its escort of US

paratroopers took up position ahead and behind on the highway leading east from Saigon. Young soldiers with brilliant markings on their green uniforms—white parachute wings, white name tags, "US Army" in gold, gold rank badges on sleeve and collar, and the universal white T-shirt visible at the open-neck of the shirt.

"Look at 'em—like show ponies in field dress—every bit of color gives 'em away. A sniper's delight."

Driving east along the highway the men were confronted with the flat landscapes of Asia—smooth water-mirror surface of paddies reflecting the peasants walking along the dividing earth "bunds"; brilliant green of rice plants, subdued green of shrubs, dark cool green of fruit trees, and strips of jungle; thatch-roofed houses; flocks of white cockatoos starting up and circling; children everywhere running, playing or tending younger children, jumping up and down at the roadside to attract the attention of the foreigners for the always popular cigarettes or sweets; adults gliding with the smooth jogging step under the balanced loads at each end of the yoke; in the distance the timeless Asian presence of the small man under his conical hat trudging through the mud behind the round-bellied patient buffalo. Overhead, the birds—both feathered and steel. Against the blue sky and clean white puffy clouds paraded all types of aircraft from buzzing Cessnas to roaring Skyraider fighter bombers. A dozen dragonfly shapes of the famous "Hueys" threshed their way along, two F100s climbed steeply, underwings laden with streamlined shapes, and circling around and down in all directions were the fat transports—the four-engine jets and their chubby propeller-driven brothers; the sky filled with silver birds. Later, they would be camouflaged, but now they all glistened in the sun.

The buses trundled through the airbase gate and turned onto a zigzagging red dirt road that followed the perimeter, past the hangar, past the parking area for the Vietnamese Air Force Skyraiders and Cessnas, and the scrap heaps of aircraft destroyed or damaged beyond repair by enemy action or accident; mingled in the pile were the carcasses of the B57s destroyed in the mortar attack.

Standing alone to the east of the main complex was a
building with a square tower on one end like the figure *L*
on its back, an old French post that became known at once
as "the fort." The Vietnamese airfield defense soldiers—a
nondescript group in various stages of somnolent ease,
ranging from chairs tilted back and feet on the parapet, to
hammocks slung under the roof—occupied a series of
pillboxes. Beneath the "growth" that had occurred since
the French built them, the original pillboxes could be
seen: concrete, narrow firing slits and barbed-wire de-
fenses. The Vietnamese had added sandbag parapets around
the roofs supporting jerry-built structures to keep off the
sun and the rain. The larger ones included chickens,
ducks, and families. None gave the appearance of alertness.

Nguyen Thi Ba sat under her umbrella at her dusty
mobile cigarette stall, a smoking incense stick casting
fragrance down wind, along the street leading to the
airbase gate. Ba casually began to restack her wares, and
only the most astute observer would have noticed that the
number of packs she moved equalled the number of
olive-drab buses in convoy that entered the gate. When
comrade Trinh came later to purchase his cigarettes, she
would inform him how many Australians had arrived.

The buses halted and the men climbed down to find
themselves on the inner side of the huge grassy rim of the
airbase. Not a tree or bush existed for almost a mile in any
direction—and there was the first problem: since the
bunkers and trench systems of Korea, the Australian army
had operated in jungle which, if nothing else, had plenty
of trees to which one could tie one's waterproof shelter, or
trim saplings to assist in the erection of a comfortable
sleeping area. But to be dropped in an expanse of grass
with not a tree! They stood there, sweating under the
blazing sun, straight from the Australian winter to Saigon,
baking in the huge frying pan formed by the great grassy
depression, no shade and no prospect of any.

The position was a recently abandoned US artillery
area, liberally covered with debris of all kinds. Ingenuity
in the form of split ammunition boxes, sandbags, iron

sheeting, and Australian entrenching tools soon formed a basis for a variety of two-man tents.

The afternoon rainstorms circled the town—not a drop fell on the Australians watching the gray curtains descend from dark cloud bases to mask trees, villages, the airbase buildings, the Vietnamese pillboxes: everywhere, but where it was longingly awaited.

Military matters take precedence over personal comfort, however, and defense against the VC had to be organized.

"Okay Father, you'll be on the right here—hop over and find out where their left-hand pits are and tie in with them," ordered Bruce Myers.

"Right oh." Father turned, jerking his head in the direction of the US area. "Frank, you, and Tom come over as well."

The three strode off through the long grass, rifles carried from habit, balanced on the right ammunition pouch, grasped around the forward woodwork with the right hand. The camouflaged helmet covers of US paratroopers were visible above the grass, marking where the Americans squatted or sat looking out over the area to the east. The closest, alone and with an M79 grenade launcher across his knees, looked up as the three approached, faces shadowed under the broad brims of their hats.

"G'day, how ya going?" greeted Father.

"Hi there. Guess I'm okay."

"Listen, we'll be in the right-hand pits of our crowd over there," gesturing behind, "and we want to tie in with your mob. Where are your left-hand pits?"

"Huh? Pardon me?"

"Where's your trench, weapon pit, fighting position?"

"Ah, I dunno."

"Well, look . . . where would you go? What would you do if the VC attacked now?"

"Ahh, look. Ya better go see that sergeant, he's sittin' under that tree over theah."

"Never mind," smiled Father, "come on, let's get back," to the other two, and all three walked back, highly amused at their first encounter with the legendary US paratroopers: a man sitting in a grassy field, now knowing what he was doing, what his arcs of fire were, what to do if the enemy arrived, and seemingly not interested.

"D'ja see that bastard? Parachute wings, name tags, shoulder patches, rank badges, and knows bugger-all," marveled Frank Gardiner.

"Forget 'em. We'll have to put Barnes's gun around facing back that way, that's all," calculated Father, stopping at the location. "Frank, you link up on our left and I'll be in the center."

"Right," said Gardiner.

"Okay, c'm'ere you blokes. This is what we're doing tonight, at least. Those Yanks over there don't know what they're bloody well doing, so we'll have to spread out a bit and this is how we'll do it. . . . His voice rolled on, flat Australian accent, voice low-pitched from habit after years of training and the long weeks patrolling in Malaya.

The evening meal was provided by American cooks, from the kitchen set up in a half-dug gun position. For the Australians, it was a hopeful sign of good things to come, despite some items on the menu a little strange to their palates. The unbelieveable sight of bins filled with chilled cans of milk in various flavors and assorted fruit juices was greeted with grins between mates and awe in general at the US standard of feeding the troops. The Australian supply system was born in the bottomless mud of France, 1916–18, and bred over the Kokoda Trail; in both places what could be delivered to the front line had to be carried by another man, and so every ounce was grudged. Such niceties as chilled tins of milk never entered the heads of generations of quartermasters, catering staff, or the front-line soldier. For basebludging air force, yes; for the army, no.

After the evening meal, at dusk the ritual "stand-to." Don basic webbing, weapon in hands, occupy the fighting position, and watch your front while the clearing patrols move out from three points on the perimeter and sweep in a predetermined direction—clockwise or counterclockwise— to the departure point of the patrol on their left or right, and reenter the perimeter. Any enemy with evil designs for an attack would be preparing during the last light, or at dawn; hence the "stand-to" at dawn and dusk observed for decades by British Commonwealth forces all over the world. How many millions have lain behind rifle and machine gun as the last light seeped away below the rim of the world, watching the replacing blackness rise up over mountains, deserts, fields, hedges, towns, rivers, swamps, forests, sand dunes, jungles, paddies, cornfields—over every type of terrain and in every climate, and watched the next morning the darkness gather in on itself and retreat as the returning light spilled over and another day began.

And at stand-to, further awareness that the US Army has its own ways: Americans regarding with curious eyes the Australians silently extinguishing cigarettes, carrying webbing and weapons to shallow pits, and watching the grass in front.

"Hey, what's goin' on, youse guys? Charlie gonna attack?"

"No, just stand-to."

"Stand-to? Oh, yeah." Going on with their unmilitary activities: transistors blaring, car and truck doors slamming, wearing of white skivvies and everything that is taboo during stand-to.

"No wonder the bastards get the shit shot out of them," whispered Tom Pritchard, turning side on, so his gaze took in Nimbus, peering into the gathering gloom at the American contingent cheerfully and noisily clearing up after the meal, and in the distance the fully lit airbase.

"I thought these bastards were paratroopers—their best. Just fuckin' look at 'em."

"Yeah. I was talking' ter one today—here he is overseas, nineteen, a paratrooper, a truck driver, and only been in seven months. They can only be half trained, cob. Jumpin' outa planes might prove they're brave, but it doesn't make 'em better soldiers, for heaven's sake."

Around the perimeter, dozens of other eyes looked over shoulders at the noisy, unconcerned Yanks, and the fully lit unconcerned airbase, and wondered at the commonsense of these very confident Yanks.

As the night secured its grip on the world, from all around the flares rose into the sky as men in their barbed-wire posts fired the parachute-borne lights to disperse the shadows for a minute or two and bring a different light to the heart, oppressed by the heavy blackness outside the wire.

The tiny blink as the flare ignited in the sky, then the rapid silent blossoming of the minute sun, smoke trail visible for a short distance as the wind carried the flare and its parachute along, without noise, across the deep inky night sky. So every night, all night, all around, the flares silently flowered and drifted across the sky.

After stand-to, sleep, cigarettes inside the two-man tents, or yarns, until time for the two-hour stint on the machine gun, gazing out over the moonlit grass, glistening silver and ink-black, ignoring the dark figures moving quietly across in front—not "Charlies," as the VC were nicknamed, but Yanks sneaking into town for a drink and women.

The clean-cut american brigade commander decreed that his clean-cut American boys would have no beer or spirits—and nothing more could be knowingly done to incite every self-respecting paratrooper and Australian to begin planning immediately how to get some of the forbidden fruit.

So across the sights of the guns drifted the dark figures, following twin wheel marks in the grass leading to the promising land. "Let the VC come, fuck 'em. We're gonna find us booze and broads in that mother-fuckin' town, man."

Thus was Day One.

3

The days passed, baking in the grass under the white blazing sun, digging trenches, cleaning the area of rubbish left by the Yanks, eating food cooked by the Yanks—

"Okay Aussie; how many eggs ya want boy?"

"Er, can I have two?"

"Ya can have as many as ya want, just eat all ya take!"—and watching the constant aerial activity: groups of forty Hueys in files of ten buzzing along like strings of giant dragon flies, curving around and down to earth, crouching, and then lifting slowly with their load of soldiers, climbing singly, gaining speed and formation as they flew off to the east.

"In one glance we can see more helicopters here than there are in all of Australia," observed an impressed Bruce Myers.

"Yeah," from his fellow platoon commander, George Benson, "but no one knows what's going on, despite all the show."

Sternly from Myers, "Are you trying to flout tradition, Mr. Benson?"

As each company arrived to expand the perimeter, muttering soldiers filled in the pits they had dug and began a new one—sometimes only thirty yards from the old place.

The *Sydney* arrived on the coast, and the road convoy from it drove in at stand-to one evening. Then all the things from *Sydney's* great hull began to appear—tents, Land-Rovers, trucks, M113 armored personnel carriers, telephone cable, and the inevitable typewriters and paper.

A tent city sprouted; showers were erected and latrines dug. Deep storm-water drains crisscrossed the area, claiming their share of the unwary, probably the noisiest being one of the battalion characters, Sergeant "Moose" Morrissey: a soccer player, six foot four, loud of voice, and direct in action. Stomping forcefully into his tent one pitch-black, night, he puts a size eleven boot into an ammo box used as a cigarette-butt tin, and instead of halting and removing it by hand, tries to shake it off in the best Moose manner—stomp, thump, off balance in the pitch black, one flailing arm catches in a mosquito net, net wraps around body now pirouetting out of control, into camp table that goes over with a crash, the whirling

160-pound body reeling in the dark, hits a camp stretcher, crashes onto it, falls out the back of the tent, a roaring mass wrapped in mosquito net and tropical sleeping bag rolling across the six feet of ground into the yawning blacker mouth of the drain. The eruption of clanking, crashing, and thumps accompanied by the distinctive roaring voice halted all conversation for 200 yards; heads popped out of tent flaps:

"What the hell's going on?"

"How the devil do I know? The Moose is gettin' stuck inta somethin'."

"Bit early for the big bastard ta be pissed, ay?"

"Infiltrators!" muttered Nimbus, reaching for rifle and belt, eyes peering into the black.

Augie Bennett, one of the occupants of the tent, ran to the front calling, "Moose! Moose! What's goin' on? Where are ya?"

From the darkness, a muffled curse and "I'm in 'ere, Augie," and Augie blindly plunged into the Stygian darkness, hands outstretched meeting upturned tables, disarrayed beds, clothes once neatly stacked now on the floor; all the while, the muffled curses and sounds of struggle so close in front in the pitch black.

"Arrumph . . . bloody thing . . . Augie, come on!"

A slowly gathering group in the blackness outside wondering what the hell has happened, imaginations starting to flare.

"Moose," plaintively, "where are ya? I can't find ya!"

Moose jerked his head free of the mosquito net folds, and his roar was plainly heard 400 yards away in the soft black tropical night.

"In the fuckin' storm-water drain, ya great nog!"

Bob Edmondson, the intelligence officer, hung his bush hat on the corner of the mirror fixed to the tent pole, sank into a canvas field chair, spread his extended legs, and slapped his open palms onto his thighs.

"Well, active service and travel is said to broaden the mind, and I think the III Corps Conference will live in my memories of Vietnam."

"Oh?" from pudgy, rugby-loving Captain Reg Waterson, the adjutant.

"Yes, I've never seen anything like it. It's held in a large room, about sixty by thirty feet, no ceiling, just the roof of galvanized corrugated iron. The chief staff officer sits at the top of the table and calls on people from the units and so on to report.

"If you don't have any interest in what's going on, you talk to your neighbor or just get up and walk over to the window with a couple of others and have a yarn and a smoke. When the rain starts on the roof, no one can hear anyway. The leaks make life interesting as well. Lieutenants just turn their backs on a full colonel and talk about where they were last night. Incredible. Come on down and broaden your experience, young Reg!"

"Wouldn't miss it for quids, Bob."

The first patrols went out: three Australians as members of American patrols to familiarize themselves with the area before the battalion patrolling program began in earnest. The first groups of three returned with accounts of American patrolling that gave much cause for snorts, laughs, and contemptuous sneers at Yank professionalism.

"We turned up over there, met the Yank patrol commander, and he took us down to the company. He just walks in and says, 'Okay, youse guys,'" said Tom Pritchard with a Yank accent, "'who wants to go on a patrol?' an' a couple of the wackers sort of act real indifferent, say 'Okay sarge,' grab their M16s, and stand up. The sergeant says, 'Okay, we're gonna head out a piece an' try and get us a buncha Cong' and that's all the patrol preparation there is! No briefing, no map, no check of gear, no chain of command, no arty, no action on contact, just 'who wants ta go?' and 'we're gonna get a few Cong!' Ya get out there and they are crashin' along, one has a transistor, they're coughin', and spittin', and fartin'. No wonder we never saw any bloody thing. They dunno the first fuckin' thing about it!"

After the night on which two groups fired on each other and the third was collecting one lot of Land-Rovers from the small battle, enthusiasm for patrolling with the Yanks all but disappeared.

Shortly after, the Australians began their own patrolling program, and until the battalion left, there was never a day or night without patrols out in the area to the battalion's front, extending to the major river flowing east to west. The VC had used the area as their own, approaching to attack the airbase and retreating through it. Now, after several small patrol battles, they could no longer roam at will. Their couriers, food supplies, resting places were all in danger, and VC activity ceased.

After several months, fallow ground that lay some distance from the towns was again cultivated. Virgin ground was broken, some forestry work began; the market became livelier, and electric street lighting was installed.

The market places were to provide a point of comparison later, when operations took the Australians into areas controlled by the VC; there the market places were deserted, overgrown and not used. All produce was taken by the National Liberation Front. However, in areas under government control, the markets were thriving, bustling centers of activity.

Meanwhile, in other areas of the country, the VC were very active, continuing their series of successful battles, smashing the government forces, demonstrating their superiority.

The Army of the Republic of Vietnam had a garrison some miles away on the edge of the large river. Part of the garrison consisted of 155mm howitzers employed to fire into the huge expanse of jungle known as War Zone D.

One night soon after the Australians arrived, tropical rain poured down, clouds covered the sky, and the inky darkness was complete. Softly but distinctly through the night came the thuds of explosions; the word flitted around:

"The VC are hitting the camp at Xuan Thanh, and the wheels are worried they might get the 155s and turn them on the airbase."

"Sounds like a problem for the pogos in the US Air Force, eh, mate?"

"Yeah, but they've turned out a lot of lights—look,"

and through the streaming wetness, the glow from the airbase was greatly reduced.

"The pricks must be worried. Anyway, there's not much we can do against 155 rounds in the air."

Ten-feet underground, in the humid command post, the two captains on duty decided to send a situation report to brigade headquarters. Ignoring the radio and telephone, as the fiendishly cunning VC had been known to listen to radio transmissions and tap telephone wires, young Captain Reg Waterson, as adjutant, decided the best thing to be done was to send the report by messenger. A happily sleeping driver was awakened and a not very impressed "Fred" Fredericks—who better to go, being a Vietnamese-speaker?—given the sealed envelope:

"To be delivered by you to the duty officer at the brigade CP. Understand that?"

"Yessir."

Outside, Fredericks spoke earnestly to the driver. "Listen mate, apart from being woken up in the middle of the fuckin' night, you better realize we're in a prick of a position. We have to take this friggin' envelope to brigade headquarters—fair enough—but in this pissin' rain, pitch-black night, past all those noggie posts, and through the trigger-happy bloody Yanks. Okay?"

"Fuckin' hell."

"Yeah. Now listen—go real slow, convoy lights only, and for Christ's sake, stop and go when I tell you. Those bastards out there will shoot us as soon as they look at us. They think the VC are comin' as well, so we gotta be really careful. Okay, let's go."

And so began a trip in pouring rain and pitch black, along a road with no directions, past nervous Vietnamese and American posts, getting lost among the vehicles and conex containers of the supply unit, calling out loudly and firmly: "Australian" as each post announced its presence by a "Halt! Who is there?" simultaneous with the click-clack of machine gun bolt. After forty-five minutes, brigade CP was reached; the rain had ceased and the reflected glow from the town lights dimly showed the white MP helmets and building. To the north, the explosions had ceased.

The American duty officer looked up in surprise at the appearance of the wet, muddy Australian, producing an envelope from his pocket. "Message from the Australian battalion, sir."

With a questioning glance at his radio and telephones, the American opened the envelope, read it and looked up, a light in his eyes composed of weariness, "another-illusion-destroyed, nothing-can-surprise-me, you-Aussies-have-them-too, eh?" And with the tiniest shake of his crew-cut head, asked, "Do you know what this says?"

"No, sir," as it was proffered for reading under the field lighting—"Sitrep. Nothing to report."

"Fuck me! All the way at night in this weather, through the trigger-happy bastards out there—Jesus Christ!"

"Okay, take care."

"Right, sir."

Out into the dark for an equally careful return, fuming at the stupidity of the officer class.

The arrival of the entire battalion meant the departure of the American cooks and the American scale of food. Back were the traditional Australian cooks, traditional Australian rationing of food—"one slice of bread per man, per meal" rumbled the huge bulbous warrant officer caterer, at the dismayed, resigned infantrymen filing past.

"Look at these bastards," muttered "Charger" Seymour to his mate, Pete Sanders, both "known to have a beer on a hot day."

"Look at the difference between the Yanks and these bastards. The Septics were happy and proud to serve the food they cooked. These bastards are serving shit, and they know it. It took a lot of fuckin' imagination and effort to serve bloody spaghetti again—third meal in a row. And they're gettin' the food down the hill exactly where the Yanks got it."

"Hey," butted in the Digger behind them in the queue, "didja hear about Ollie Casey? Went in with that fat bastard of a caterer Porky to pick up the rations. He has a list of what he wants and starts reading it out. The Yank is a bit surprised at the low number of eggs—Porky says it's a third of an egg a meal per man, but the Yank doesn't understand that means one egg a day—he says, 'Shit man, whyn't ya give 'em a whole egg?' Anyway, when it's all in the truck, the Yank says, 'How about some fruit juice and stuff like that?' Ollie pipes up and says, 'Yeah, let's have some.' Porky tells 'im, 'Shut up you. I'm the caterer here,' and tells the Yank that Aussies only eat what he's got on his list!"

The queue moved forward till Charger and Pete were being served. He turned to Pete and said loudly, "Ya notice the difference between those Yank cooks and our cooks?"

Porky, hands on hips, surveying his empire, perks up and moves a pace forward, eyes anticipating a compliment; the cooks and queue in earshop pay attention, "No, Charge, what d'ya mean?"

"Well, Yank cooks go to cooking school for fourteen weeks, fair enough, but they only learn how to cook."

Porky leans forward, all ears, as Charger says, "Our cooks go to cooking school for fourteen weeks too, but they're mainly taught how to catch blokes coming for a back up."

A roar from Porky, glares from the cooks, grins and chuckles from the queue, and the two walk off under a hail of threats from the irate Porky.

"You two bastards won't be fed again!"

And so, in a daily round of erection of tents and marquees, digging trenches, drains and latrines, putting up barbed wire, clearing the ground in front of it, scrounging ammo tins as lockers and wash tubs, laying telephone wire, digging command posts, reminding anyone with a vehicle going outside the area to bring back some beer, waiting for mail, buying the only two items available in the canteen (brilliant purchasing—seventy-cent biros and warm American soft drinks), getting a tan but avoiding sunburn, extending the patrol boundary, watching the incessant air activity, becoming accustomed to the sudden nerve-crunching crash of artillery being fired from the rear (new arrivals started and dropped things; older ones started less until the crash had no effect), gluing maps together and requesting air photos from brigade, and relating tales of American lack of professionalism, the battalion grew acclimatized, and, most of it, waited to begin real operations.

In the officers' mess, "Red" Ryder nodded to the barman and repeated the question put to him by a class-mate from military college now on the staff in Saigon. "How do we find the Yanks? Some are very good, very switched on. But in general, half trained and inexperi-enced by our standards. I think they are relying on a combination of shouting 'Airborne' and courage to get them through. They are very confident but have nothing to base it on since World War II and Korea. They'll learn the hard way about decking themselves with bright name tags, para wings, and so on. You'll notice the fashion is to bleach the helmet cover as pale as possible. This is to impress with the length of time in the tropics—sun and rain, and so on, making the wearer 'an old Asia hand.' How do you reckon those bleached helmet covers will go in the jungle?"

"Ah," said his friend thoughtfully. "Well listen—the M16 now; we look like being able to acquire enough to . . ." and the conversation moved on to the eternal Australian problem of enough modern equipment.

During stand-to, the men sat watching the scrub in front, and the clearing patrols sweeping past. Friends exchanged yarns in low tones, waiting with the patience of experience for the word "stand-down." A silence settled over the Australian area, through which floated the shouts, revving engines, transistors, and hi-fi gear of the neigh-boring Americans.

Suddenly, one evening, to the rear of the rifle compa-nies, from the area of the administration company, a submachine gun fired one long burst . . . a few shouts . . . silence.

"Wonder what the fuck that was?"

"Dunno, sounded like an Owen, but funny."

"Yeah. One of those administration company wackers."

Next day, the story went around: the bloke had suddenly run into his tent and fired a whole magazine into a photo of his family, screaming, "The commies won't get 'em, the commies won't get 'em," which added continuance to his upset manner and performance on the cruise over on the *Sydney*.

As the Australian force lacked the medical and psychiatric facilities, the deranged man was flown to Singapore the next day, and thence to Australia by RAAF. Six feet tall, weighing 168 pounds, a member of administration company (back from the perimeter) and unlikely to go on operations, his "nerves" cracked after less than a month in a war zone. Months later, soldiers coming up from Australia related the story of a chap who had been sent back because he got fed up with the way the battalion was being run, and with his own gun, held the assembled officers and sergeants while he lectured them on the correct way to run an infantry battalion; then "someone crept up behind me and hit me."

"Well, eh?" grinned Father. "Now we know what really happened that day in administration company."

"Yeah, makes a good yarn though. He couldn't say he had stomach problems, could he?"

"You mean, no guts?"

"Right."

"Wonder when we'll get leave in Saigon?"

"Coupla cathedrals ya haven't seen yet, eh?"

And so the subject was dropped.

For those whose stand-to positions faced north and northeast over War Zone D, beyond the crest of the slope, the dusk patrols by helicopter provided some entertainment: the flashing red dots of the light on top of the choppers blinking their way across the velvet tropical sky, sometimes with a big yellow moon rising over the horizon— the red dots, always in pairs, blipping low across the sky, sometimes circling as the crews examined something below, then flashing along on another course. Several times, when the red lights were visible against the black but were so far away that no noise reached the watching Diggers, a trail of tinier red dots streamed up from the ground. Immediately, the two helicopter lights, like hunting fish in a dark underwater world, began a circling dance—arc around, straighten into a shallow dive, silent red arrows flare, flit forward and down, and a short red rain spurts slowly after as the rockets and machine guns are fired—all in silence against the backdrop of the soft black night; the blinking ruby turns aside, circling around, and the second begins its shallow dive—before it can fire, the stream of tiny dots leaps up again at the first circling fish; the red shower from the second; red dots rising again until the circling fish, by common consent, veer away, and their blinking red dots grow larger and brighter as they speed in a straight flight back to the airbase to rearm, the soft drumming engine noise growing to a roar of clattering blades as they streak overhead, circle, and land—home amid the galaxy of lights and their fellow hunters. Out in War Zone D, the soft blackness is complete.

Tom Pritchard pushed the final roll of maps along the floor in the rear of the Land-Rover, slammed up the tailgate, and perched his floppy bush hat on the back of his head.

Hands on hips, he glanced into the dark interior of the map store where the American storeman was going through the ritual of getting signatures from Father for the quantity of maps issued.

Tom turned, lifting one red-dusted boot onto the rear bumper of the Rover, forearm across knee, and surveyed the scene across the road. The airbase PX sprawled in its air-conditioned comfort, streams of green-clad US Air Force and US Army entering and leaving, with here and there a couple of Australians.

Tom's eyes fastened on a lone Vietnamese standing outside the PX, near the access road to the side door. Small, dark-skinned, clad in a decrepit Vietnamese air force shirt and trousers—once blue, now gray—neglected black shoes, and a dilapidated, grubby blue cap, skinny arms disappearing into huge canvas protective gloves, he silently stood in the sun by the rear of the garbage truck, watching the streams of casual, tall, laughing, clean, well-dressed Americans striding past into and out of the doorway. His face was expressionless, eyes unseen in the shadow of brow and cap, ignored as a post would be ignored by the men who were visitors to his country. In their pockets and wallets were sums of money he only dreamed of; in the cartons and bags they carried were riches, treasures, and wonders he had only heard of and could not hope to earn as a lowly private.

Through the windows of the cafeteria could be seen Americans eating the varied luxuries endeared to the Yankee palate: hamburgers, french fries, creamed potatoes, potato salad, roast potatoes, hot dogs, chili con carne, baked beans, bean salad, lima beans, lettuce, celery, cucumbers, ham, roasts, ice cream (flavor after flavor), and all the drinks—Coke, Pepsi, 7-Up, tea (iced or hot), coffee, chocolate, milk (homogenized and pasteurized) in a dozen flavors, and a dozen fruit juices—all forbidden to the small, thin, scruffy garbage man. He was a free Vietnamese whom the Americans had come to help fight Communism—at tremendous cost in technology, treasure, and blood; assistance which would provide him with any instrument of destruction but would not give him one chocolate bar.

The small onlooker, seen as a figure casting a small shadow on the far periphery of their own awareness of the scene, did not exist for the Americans. Cartons of cigarettes and drink, radios, tape decks, turntables, speakers, cameras, binoculars, watches, soap, large fluffy towels, sweets, yards of dress and suit materials, all the outpourings of *Cornucopia americana* flowed past the man who did not exist.

Tom looked up as Father came out of the map store and swung up into the front seat.

"Look at this, Father, it's bloody wrong."

"What is?"

"That nog there—arse out his strides, staring at all the goodies. No bastard knows he's there. Even a fuckin' dog would get some attention. How d'ya reckon they *all* feel, seeing this stuff and not able to have it, just because they're not Yanks or allies, in their own bloody country, too!"

Father absorbed the comments, took in the scene, thought for a moment, and turned to Tom.

"And one thing you better realize right here, mate, is if this was in Australia, the garbo could be *you*," emphasized with jabbing forefinger, "standing there in *your* own country, ignored by the Yanks, with all their goodies. Think about it. Now, we gotta get back and drop these bloody maps at BHQ. Hop in."

"Well, it never struck me before, ya know. Do the Yanks really need all this stuff? Can't they do their job without all that milk and ice cream, and stereo gear?"

"Aw, ya know, they're a strange mob," said Father, flicking glances left and right as he edged onto the road surface, "but Tom, as the bishop said to the actress when the elephant came into the bedroom, 'It's bigger than both of us,' so don't let it get ya down. Your worries are Chris an' the kids."

"Yeah, I know, but that sad lookin' little bastard really got to me, old fella."

The first weeks passed in a rush of digging, getting used to the heat, erecting tents, moving them, observing the Americans and commenting on their methods, and establishing domination over the area to the north by patrolling and ambushing. Then the move out into jungle believed to be held by the VC.

4

The long semitrailers halted on the road, and the rows of green-clad infantry clambered up onto the flat, walled-in backs, looking like puppets with the packs, water bottles, and ammunition pouches as artificial sectioning of their backs and hips.

At the helicopter pad they clambered down and broke up into their small groups for each Huey. Immediately, the long lines of soldiers slumped to the ground, backs against packs. Cigarettes lit, paperbacks out of pockets, the Aussie Digger was at ease.

Over 100 helicopters squatted in rows along the sides of the old French runway, made of pierced steel plate and now relegated for use as an aircraft parking area and helicopter pad. Silent, the sun glinting off the large perspex windscreens, main rotors secured fore and aft, crews lolling inside or completing some minor adjustment, the huge assembly of robot insects squatted.

On the noses and sides were painted plunging eagles, tigers, red birds, a cave man's axe, a dean's mortar, a top hat, gloves, cane and champagne glass, hornets, a highwayman's mask, a bull dog, a coiled ready-to-strike rattlesnake—the only sign by which any of these mass-produced machines could be distinguished from any other.

Then the stir of movement—pilots donning large bulbous helmets with blank dark-green visors that turn the men also into faceless robot insects; crewmen releasing the main rotor blades; infantrymen heaving themselves upright, bending at the waist to relieve the weight of packs containing clothing, food, ammunition, radio batteries, and water; using rifle and machine gun as a third leg to take some weight; huge Moose with a rucksack so heavy some men could not lift it, and he bearing it as a feather; the rotors turning slowly at first, then faster, to a rising, whining, roaring chorus of a 100-jet engine, prickling the hair on the nape, quickening the blood: the prelude to the first airmobile operation, an air assault into a jungle area to the south, then moving north through it, seeking the enemy believed to be there.

Those in the first wave, or "lift," are in their helicopters—the man on each side sitting on the floor, legs dangling outside; the helmeted gunner holding an M60 in his lap, long smooth coiling brass ammo belts lying in the box under the seat, gleaming, alert to the command of his finger.

The roaring note changes, taking on a deeper more purposeful tone, as the first lift raises a few feet, hovering, blades great blurring circles, then like ballet dancers, the lead machines dip their noses, and long tails pointed up, begin moving forward, rapidly accelerating and curving left, followed by each of the other nine in the elements of ten.

Half a mile away in the town, Phuoc leaned forward slightly on the thick beam under the roof to follow the direction of flight through the gap in the tiles and called down to Binh, "60 UH-1-B loaded with infantry flying south."

Binh nodded and spoke into the handset of his radio. The aerial masqueraded as a clothesline running out to the tall, old mango tree in the rear of the house, then up to its highest branch.

Forty miles away, the information was received, recorded and marked on the map in the headquarters of the military region. No great excitement was evident, as the staff had received a copy of the operations order thirty-six hours before.

Many other indications of a helicopter-borne operation had been evident to the NLF reconnaissance teams in the town: the American and Australian camps were visible to the naked eye from the town, and telescopes in roofs were put to constant use; weapon test-firing increased greatly and was easily heard by paddie- and rubber-workers on the river side of the airbase; fuel was ordered and arrived; maps were picked up from the map store, and it was relatively simple for the Vietnamese sweepers to ascertain which sheet or sheets had been taken; as the time drew closer, observation aircraft intensified their activity over the target area; the helicopters arrived and refueled; the long green trucks trundled to and from the infantry camp; the soldiers sat or lay along the sides of the landing zone, shortened to "LZ"; Skyraiders took off to bomb the edges of the jungle clearing selected as the next LZ.

Most important, within eight hours of the ARVN receiving their copies of the operation order, at least one was in the hands of the NLF, and the objective had been passed to them in any case in two hours.

So all Phuoc and Binh were doing with their reports

was confirming the detail of the pages on the camp table of Hai Quyen, chief-of-operations in the NLF military region.

He briskly rubbed his crewcut black hair and turned to Bay Dinh, signals chief, "Have you contact with our comrade in the target area?"

"Yes, comrade; through two relays."

"Very good." Hai Quyen smiled slightly as he thought of the massive operation in progress to sweep an area he knew to contain nothing except jungle and a few reconnaissance elements he had ordered deployed to test the foreigners' fire discipline and tactics.

Meanwhile, the troop-carrying Hueys, the "slicks" in US slang, were gaining height to the south of the airbase, and those looking forward could see the Skyraiders diving and climbing, and the flashes and gray smoke marking the bombing of the LZ clearing. Off to the sides thrashed the escorting gunships, known as "pigs," noses down, machine guns or banks of rockets on the sides, looking like aggressive fighting fish in the clear gray light under the rain clouds.

The lift began descending in a left curve, moving into line astern, and the gunships moved forward and below—lower, the trees rising, the river below passing to the rear—now at tree top—over a large grassy area, smoke rising from the edges—explosions; only delayed action shells—slowing—nose up—grass flicking below, around the landing skids—gunner leaning out watching the tail rotor and its closeness to the ground—leveling out—skids touch the earth—out and run—down—cock rifle—what's in the trees in front? Gunships weaving, snarling, overhead—slicks lifting, nose down, gunner waves, wave back, there they go, climbing into the gray sky, turning left for the second lift.

Right, where are the others? Here they come, all grins, pulling hats from inside their shirts, moving fast off the LZ, get away from the open as fast as possible.

Now, secure the LZ for the second lift. Twenty minutes later; here they come—slicks nose up—touching down—gunships streaking down the sides, door gunners leaning out staring forward and down—infantry piling out of the

slicks—down—up and away they go with a great roaring of
blades—the twentieth-century war machine that enables
the infantrymen to travel at 100 miles an hour, effortlessly
vaulting the backbreaking, gut-busting hills and mountains.

In forty minutes, a fresh infantry battalion has been
positioned twenty miles from its last location, hopefully
behind the enemy. Now to sweep through and flush them
out. And so began the real infantry work—forward scouts,
section and platoon commanders, machine gunners and
riflemen moving forward, ever searching for signs of the
enemy, see him before he sees you, or . . .

Now the helicopters are gone, the jungle reverts to
quiet. The animals and birds are silent, aware of the men's
presence.

The green-clad figures move quietly through the silent green light, sleeves down, sweat rag of green cheese-
cloth around neck, floppy cloth hat on head, its irregular
outline breaking up the distinctive shape of the head, the
rifle and machine-gun muzzles pointing wherever the eyes
look. Overhead, the trees extend their leaves—upper
ones, lighter; lower ones darker—against the sun and sky
between the clouds. Patches of dappled sunlight move
gently on bushes and tree trunks, but mostly it is dim
under the trees.

And apart from trees and a few huts, nothing was
seen, no shots fired.

At night, lone VC fired in the direction of the Australians
trying to provoke some reaction, but discipline held and
Hai Quyen was informed that the Australians at least had
fire discipline.

With no significant contact, the battalion swept north;
its only results being three people captured and released,
simply leaving them on the side of the landing zone, an
area near a railway station from which the battalion was
extracted in pouring rain. Even though no concrete results
were seen, morale rose.

Then a few days later, sudden alert. Committing a
tactical error that was to be repeated, the American
artillery was deployed and set up a firing position, without
infantry protection, some miles across the river into the

jungle expanse of War Zone D. Such a target was not passed up by the VC who began harassing the gunners at night with quick mortar bombardments, small infiltration parties, and sniping.

Into the trucks, down to the helicopter pad. This time, even Vietnamese helicopters were used: big, blunt-nosed H-34s, the pilots sitting up in their separate cockpit. Waiting for the rain to clear from the jungle-clearing LZ, final cigarettes and yarns, the inevitable paperbacks.

"Saddle up!" And the rising metallic whine of the first turbine turning.

Flight past heavy gray rain clouds, some trailing their long curtain of water, north over the river in the dull gray light, dark green jungle stretching away to the north as far as the eye can see, lighter green of abandoned paddies along creeks and smaller rivers breaking up the solid green mass. The slicks in a great curving turn to the west, descending, moving into line astern; there are the ones in front, looking like a line of tiny fish in the gray light—they're down—black dots pop from the sides—moving toward the trees—the slicks lift off—getting closer—lower—grass is very short here—there are the VNAF H-34s behind, still high, noses up, fishtailing—slowing—stopping, gunners wave us out—splash into waist-deep water—that was why the grass looked so short; only a couple of inches show above the surface, and the dull light did not show the water—H-34s sliding past, still ten or fifteen feet up—they're up in front of everyone—H-34s settling—splash, splash, splash out they come—all the slicks are lifting—gunship roaring low along side of LZ—splashing, wading, to the side of the LA.

"Wait you bastards—we're stuck! Give us a hand!"

There are two fellows who have jumped in and sunk in the mud, just their shoulders and head above water; a roar of laughter rolls across the LZ and the rescuers splash out.

George Benson's platoon arrived in the H-34s. At the rendezvous off the LZ, he spoke to "Red" Ryder.

"Sir, if we're using VNAF choppers again, it might be well to be careful. When we were coming in just then, the gunner waved us out—I was just going to leap out when I saw we were still twenty feet up. They wanted us out then so they could piss off. I shook my head and pointed down. That's why we landed where we did."

"Okay George. I'll keep it in mind for the orders group."

Move up and dig in around the guns. The sudden arrival of infantry was audible to the enemy in the area whose only activity was some mortaring that caused the first Australian casualties—all light.

Next day, a long hot walk and a truck ride back to base. Still no decent contact; no VC have even been seen.

Stan-the-Man, standing by the road, watched the companies striding down the overgrown, neglected road surface. Despite the savage heat and sheer physical effort needed to carry the packs, weapons, radios, and ammunition, there were enough wisecracks and alert eyes to show that the battalion was in good shape.

Tregonne, the second-in-command, who had come out to the RV with the urns of tea and who would fly back to ensure that meals and showers were ready for the returning companies, was standing by Burrows's side. He turned to Tregonne and asked, with raised eyebrows, "Any bets going on which company is going to get the first kill?"

Tregonne's teeth flashed in the sun, "Well, there are some, strictly unofficial, of course. Personally, I don't know who it might be."

"Razor" Sharp, a few paces away, turned, hands on hips and growled, "It'll probably be a cook or someone firing blindly, and won't that upset 'em!"

"Hmm," mused Barrows, "I know they'll do well. What we need are a couple of successful contacts to get our fellows' tails right up. We're bound to get into it any time now."

But it was another two weeks before the next operation. Then, in conjunction with the US paratroopers and Vietnamese troops, they flew north again, across the river into D-Zone, watched and counted by Phuoc and Binh, in the house in town.

Down into the paddies, off to the sides, reorganize and move, searching for the elusive enemy.

Nguyen van Hoa paused behind the bamboo clump, avoiding the hooked thorns, and peering under the long fronds, carefully examined the area in front. Sometime earlier, from the regimental camp, he had seen the small dark shapes of the helicopters climbing in long strings up over the trees under the gray clouds. They had obviously landed troops, and Hoa, Nung, and Kim had been allocated this area to reconnoiter and report on enemy activity. Hoa knew Nung and Kim were behind, carefully observing to the left and the right; they had worked as a team for almost two years and were one of the most experienced teams of the Regimental Reconnaissance Company.

Nothing moved, the bushes and grass showed no unusual signs, no boot prints were visible on the sandy path they were following, no noise of radios, clanking of metal on metal, voices, coughing or any of the other signs of government soldiers. Hoa tapped his index finger knuckle twice on the stock of the Russian PPS M1943 submachine gun and, knowing Nung and Kim would follow, trotted forward.

Herb Knowles frowned, wrinkling his nose to try to get rid of the sweat running down between his eyes onto his nose. As forward scout, he knew his life and the lives of the rest of the section, and possibly the platoon, depended on his eyes and brain. His entire purpose in life was now to see the enemy first, and inform "Tommy" Tomlinson, the section commander, so the section and platoon could be maneuvered to engage the enemy.

He halted, kneeling beside a tall shrub. Twenty feet away, a sandy path, gray-white against the foliage and dark shadows, ran toward him from his left and swung away through 90 degrees, disappearing behind some huge trees thirty yards away on his right.

Knowles turned to look at Tomlinson, knowing the second scout was watching, and gave the field signal for "obstacle." Tomlinson quickly and quietly moved forward, hunched over, and squatted on Knowles's left.

Behind them the signal was being relayed. "Dwarf"

Palmer, the big machine gunner, moved up, obedient to Tomlinson's pointing hand, and lay behind the gun at the track bend, where he could fire up either stretch: his Number Two on the left, next belt ready in the plastic bag inside the green cotton carrier.

Tomlinson placed his scouts to fire to the left, his four riflemen to the right, in less than fifteen seconds from his first sighting and assessment of the track; he turned to find Bruce Myers striding toward him, his attendant radio operator trailing behind.

"What have you got, Tommy?" in a low voice hardly more than a whisper.

"Track running in from the left and going out there, Skipper," equally softly.

"Ah yeah?" pulling out folded map from the thigh pocket on the side of the trousers. "Hmm, it's not on here." Turning to the radio operator, "Call 'em up, tell 'em we found a track running from the northwest, turning to the northeast." And to Tomlinson, "Right, I'll send Ferdy across for a look."

He turned to give the next section the "corporal to platoon commander" signal, and saw the second scout click his fingers for attention, clench his fist, and give the "thumbs down" sign—enemy!

Following the scout's gaze, they saw the black-clad figure trotting toward them: round-crowned black cloth hat with stitching-reinforced brim, checkered neck cloth, submachine gun and canvas magazine carrier, sandals on bare feet. A random ray of sun placed them in a shadow, and Hoa did not see them till he was fifteen yards away. Without breaking stride, he lunged sideways but felt the thump in his right thigh and knew he was falling onto the track. He fell on one shoulder and had time to register a fan of sand leaping in front of his face. Before any grain reached him, the M60 machinegun burst hit his shoulders and chest, shredding his rib cage and organs, and Hoa died wondering who shot him. They did not look like Americans.

Knowles fired at the second man to appear and saw his black shirt leap under the impact of the 9mm rounds from the Owen: the man went over backwards, feet kicking up; then he rolled over and disappeared behind the bush that had hidden their approach.

"Quick 7 Section, sweep through this side of the track!" yelled Myers. "Tommy, keep that gun going up the track!"

Palmer was already firing ten-round bursts up the track. The four riflemen continued to watch their section of track on the right. The signaler was saying into his handset, "Contact one enemy KIA details to follow," as Myers called to his third section, "Nine Section: Jeff, quick, go left, shake out and sweep through on Ferdy's left"; to the platoon sergeant, "Bart, one KIA on the track—we'll sweep through on the left."

"Right, Skip!"

Despite his wounds, Nung was on his feet and running; Kim, holding one arm. Fear injected speed to their feet, and they flew back up the path that curved gently left and right.

Myers soon realized that despite the blood trail visible, he was being outdistanced by two lightly clad men, and not knowing what he might run into with only two sections in an unknown area, halted his men, and returned to the scene of action.

The pulse-quickening tang of gunfire hung in the air, and Bart Bartholomew knelt by the side of the black-clad body.

"Company HQ is on the way, boss," reported the signaler.

"Okay. Tommy—across the track, gun to fire up it on the left. Ferdy, on the right, gun down the track at the big tree there. Jeff, back the way we came. Now Bart, anything on him?" Bart, hands bloody from searching his shirt remains, leaned back on his haunches.

"Well, what he had in his shirt is ruined with bullet holes and blood. Wallet in his back pocket though; got a coupla photos, letters, and some of these certificates or something in it," displaying the sole remaining solid evidence of Hoa's life.

"All right. Headquarters will be here in about five minutes. The Intelligence bloke can have a look."

Company headquarters with its attendant platoon arrived. The OC, "Red" Ryder, walked over and looked down at Hoa.

"Good going Bruce. Who got him?"

"Private Palmer in Nine Section, sir, but Private Knowles, the scout, hit him in the leg as he tried to jump into the bush. Palmer finished him off. Knowles also hit another one. From footprints, there were three. I followed the blood trail for 200 yards, but they were moving too quick. He's got some documents on him, and we got this, . . ." holding up the PPS, "and a Yank M1 carbine where the second one went over," holding up the carbine.

"Good." Turning aside, "Anything there, Acorn?" to the attached Intelligence Section linguist.

"A fair bit about the man, sir. He's a Recce Company member from Q965 Regiment. Joined in 1960, worked up from local guerilas to a main force unit. Been there two years. Been in a few battles; got these certificates: 'Determined to Win Hero, Third Class' and 'Brave Destroyer of Armored Vehicles.' The letters are to a girlfriend, no indication of where she is, but this looks like a photo of her. If it's okay with you, I'll hang onto the stuff with military info and give the rest to Mr. Myers to split for souvenirs?"

"Good. Do that. Thanks."

He turned to the signaler and dictated a message containing all the relevant information of time, location, enemy casualties, weapons captured, documents captured, and unit identification for transmission to battalion headquarters.

"All right Bruce, you've done well, but I'll give young Benson a turn. His platoon is almost dancing to get out there."

A thousand yards away, Kim finished bandaging, as best he could, Nung's wounds in his right arm and shoulder. Nung lay silently, eyes closed. Kim glanced up at the sky, as the first drops of rain splattered on the leaves.

"Nung, now is our best time to move. The rain will

wash away any blood and our trail. Come on," heaving Nung to his feet, looping his good arm over his own shoulders. "Let's go. We must report. Hoa has laid down his life for the revolution."

Under the dark trees, soaked by the pouring waterfall of rain, the two made their way back, another 2,000 yards to the company RV. There, Nung was attended by medical personnel and Kim made his report.

"The enemy are on the southern side of Mango Hill, about 1,000 yards from the six coconut trees by the mahogany tree. They must be the Australians. I only saw them for a moment, but they are dressed differently from the Americans, or the puppet troops. No helmets, different packs, and the long rifles the Australians are said to have, not the black ones of the Americans. They made no noise. Hoa almost walked onto them. I don't know how many there are. I heard more running to trap us on the left; I think at least one platoon."

"All right, comrade," said the platoon commander, Xuan. "Tran and Bi have also reported. There is a battalion of them spread along Angry Buffalo Creek."

Other fleeting contacts occurred and caution increased on both sides. The Australians discovered many camps and supply dumps recently vacated. These were burned.

Truong, Van, and Nanh crept carefully forward—they could hear the foreigners talking—and peered through the entangled mass of branches, vines, and leaves. There, the foreigners had found Camp 16 and were discussing it. One carried a radio. Now the others left, and the radio man sat in an old shallow trench, but he was visible from the waist up; the others were searching the building and bunkers. So be it.

Truong carefully looked to the right at the other two, through the intervening leaves and vines. He intensified his gaze on Nanh and gave a slight jerk of the head in the direction of the foreigner. Nanh gave the tiniest nod and slowly began to raise his 1944 Mossin-Nagant carbine to his shoulder—gently rest it on the branch, taking care not to jiggle the leaves: foresight on the green shirt, in the center of the chest; the foreigner is paying more attention to the radio handset than watching the jungle. Inhale, hold it—squeeze...

Jim Kennedy was slammed back against the dirt wall of the trench as the 7.62mm round passed through his chest from left to right. The handset and Owen gun fell from his hands, and as he looked down in surprise at the hole in his shirt front, blood rushed from his mouth.

"Fuckin' hell, I've been shot," he realized as he slid sideways into the trench. He recognized the platoon sergeant against the fading light—"It's dark in this bloody trench," was his last thought.

Truong, Van, and Nanh were running as fast as they could and halted 600 yards away, chests heaving.

Nien loped along at the head of the squad, eyes in his round face alertly peering forward. Close behind came the other eight members of the squad, ready to fight if the foreigners or puppet troops were met. All were very confident; they had taken part in many attacks against government posts and units, and knew they had superior spirit to any of the puppet troops, despite the presence of the tall US gangsters, the so-called advisers. This squad's weapons were all captured and of US manufacture.

The squad was to locate the foreign troops in the area and harass them: snipe, ambush, delay, make them uncomfortable and then afraid of this jungle, War Zone D, which had been almost impenetrable to the French colonialists.

Suddenly, there were four or five green-clad figures ahead through the trees, one standing near the path. Both groups saw each other and fired.

As he turned to run, Nien saw the man in the open stagger. Glancing back after a few steps, he saw the foreigner on the ground, alone, clumsily trying to cock his weapon with one hand.

"We could take him prisoner!" The thought flashed into Nien's head. "The others have disappeared; run and lift him!" He cried to the others, some of whom had hardly begun to turn away. "Wait! Wait! There is one wounded we can seize! Come with me!"

A second glance showed the lone foreigner shouting and trying to fire his submachine gun with one hand. The eight, after some jostling, turned and began running toward the wounded enemy.

Then, from their right, through the trees, came the other foreigners. Nien realized too late that they had not run off, only to one side, and now were sweeping his squad away: Chau was falling, brains spilling from his head; Tien, staggering back against a tree, clothes leaping under the impact of the bullets; Phuong, thrown down by the burst that shredded his lower stomach and groin. Nien fired frantically without aiming and leaped sideways into the bush; doubled over, he dodged under bushes and branches, heart pounding, empty M1 carbine in one fist. Finally, he halted, reloaded, and caught his breath. Where were the others?

All seemed quiet. He gave the whistle signal, but no answer. Where had those foreigners come from so quickly? They had suddenly appeared on the flank and not opened fire until very close. Perhaps no one else had survived? They must have been Australians: green clothes, green cloth hats, long rifles, and the submachine gun with magazine on top. They had good spirit for mercenaries and lackeys of the US imperialists.

Nien whistled again, got no answer, rose, and quickly but carefully made his way to the company camp where it was confirmed that Chau, Tien, and Phuong were dead. He also found that Minh had been seen to be hit and had fallen, and that Canh, Trieu, and Anh were wounded. Only Nien and Can were untouched. The only known casualty to the enemy was the one at the beginning.

The other platoons came in, leaving squads to harass the enemy, but all carrying dead and wounded. Not one enemy had been captured, alive or dead, and no weapons or equipment.

Nien, cleaning the M1, watched Sau Ly, the political officer, talking to Mot Dan, the military commander.

After the evening meal, the unit gathered for the political instruction period. Sau Ly spoke briefly of Vietnamese history and the long, drawnout struggle against the French. He explained again the Geneva Accords of 1954, by which elections were to be held in two years to decide the government and unification of Vietnam; he described the refusal of the Diem regime to hold the elections, and its increasing corruption and oppressive measures against the population, until in 1960 the National Liberation Front was established to struggle against the Diem regime and its US masters. Now as a desperate measure to prop up the Saigon regime, as the system of "advising" had failed, the US and its lackeys were sending soldiers to intervene in Vietnam, first by air strikes over north and south, and second by ground forces. Sau Ly concluded:

"So comrades, remember, these foreign soldiers cannot save the Saigon regime. They can only delay its fall. This is not their country; they cannot stay. We fought the Chinese for one thousand years, and won. We fought the French for ninety, and won. The Americans and their lackeys will also have to learn their lesson! We are the Armed Forces of the People's Front for the Liberation of South Vietnam! Ten thousand years to the Front!"

"Ten thousand years to the Front!" responded the assembly, clenched fists raised. "Ten thousand years to President Ho!" roared out into the darkened jungle.

"Now, Comrade Mot Dan has plans and orders for the next few days," and Sau Ly handed over to the military commander.

Nien and Can had recovered their morale and resolved to "strike the enemy wherever he is."

Again their tasks were to harass and delay, not to engage in battle, however. The enemy methods and tactics, strong and weak points, must be learned before decisive action could be taken. Both sides skirmished, but neither would allow the other to get in at a disadvantage; and when finally the helicopters appeared in their long gently rising and falling lines to lift them out, neither the VC nor the Australian unit had been really hurt.

The quiet dusk settled softly and quickly over the area. The machine gun pointed down the track, first man on shift behind it, chin resting on folded hands on gun butt. Then down the track came the sound of pitter-pattering feet, closer and closer.

"Di duong nay, di duong nay," in the high Asian chatter.

"Ay? What'd yer say?" in Australian accent.

Scuttling noise, pitter-patter of feet running back along the track.

On the final day, the companies strung out in the heat, making for the landing zones. Myers's platoon was snaking its way around the impenetrable clumps of thorn and bush. As distance from the head of the column grew greater, so attention and interest grew less. The very last two had given up hope of anything happening and had relaxed, strolling along, talking in low tones, inaudible more than a few yards away. The line curved away around the bushes and most of the platoon was out of sight.

Frank Gardiner reached back and slid the aluminum water bottle out of its carrier on his hip, held his rifle between his arm and his body, and unscrewed the top. Barry Reimann, in front, halted and followed Frank's example. Frank also halted, and in the act of raising the bottle to his lips, casually turned to look behind and saw the VC aiming from twenty yards. His shouted warning spoiled the VC's aim, and the round snapped between the two amazed Diggers, weapons held uselessly. They leaped backward around the bush, dropping their water bottles and bringing their SLRs to the ready, as the remainder of the platoon came charging back down the track.

The VC were fifty yards away on the far side of a bushy clump and making good speed toward the safety of the solid jungle. "Tryin' to drown the bastards, were yer?" as the water bottles were recapped and returned to their carrier.

So the operation continued to its end: small contacts involving five or six people in all—the VC breaking off as soon as they could and carrying away the dead and wounded if it was possible.

The echoes of the small battles had reached far beyond the jungled creeks and hills, into all the lamplit houses where the news was delivered that Hoa, Chau, Tien, and the others had sacrificed their lives for the Front; and parents, brothers and sisters, and wives and children stared sadly, or dumbly, or proudly, at the bearer of the tidings during his short visit before he slipped away into the night.

Away to the south, a thousand hearts stopped, and the white icebolt thumped home into each stomach as the radio or TV announcer spoke:

"Army Headquarters in Canberra announce that two Australian soldiers have been killed and three wounded in operations in South Vietnam. No names will be released until all next-of-kin have been informed."

Muriel Burrows paused reading the minutes of the meeting of the Ladies' Auxiliary, then continued, forcing herself to concentrate on the next line, pushing down, back, and away the little black demons that leaped up, ready to dance across her mind.

Jacqueline Myers bounded across to the TV, switched it off, and quickly selected a Beatles LP, drowning herself in the sound. "It can't be Bruce, not Bruce!"

Christine Pritchard stood turned to stone—not hearing the following news items or the children's chatter as they sat in their pajamas—her unseeing eyes on the suds-filled sink before her, one thought filling her entire being. "Tom, oh Tom."

Two duty officers read the messages before them and began preparations to break the news: check the address of next-of-kin, check the religion, contact the minister of religion, telephone for the duty vehicle . . .

5

Leave in Saigon. The Pearl of the Orient. The small parade in the first rays of the sun. The condoms given to those who wanted them: "It's a self-inflicted wound, remember," grinned the medic. Then rolling down to the brigade area to join the rest of the leave trucks from the other units, and forming a convoy to barrel down the highway, past the sprouting US camps.

"There's one place I don't want to see," from one rifleman, voicing all their thoughts as they sped past the MASH on the southern side of the highway and the rows of ambulance helicopters, universally known as "Dust-offs."

The Dust-off pilots were greatly respected for their bravery and expertise, flying in if there was the least chance of extracting the wounded, in terrible flying conditions, through rain, cloud, wind, mist, over mountains and tall trees in almost zero visibility, often under intense and accurate enemy fire, as the VC or NVA seldom recognized the Red Cross.

All eyes in the truck studied the helicopter pad and the network of buildings into which some of them would go, muddy, wet, dripping blood, trailing bandages...

The momentary silence was broken, conversation resumed, and eyes looked ahead over the cab-roof to where the silhouette of the Saigon skyline appeared through its own layer of pollution.

The trucks rolled through the tree-lined streets to the river, halting at the base of a high three-legged pedestal from the top of which had been removed the statues of the Trung Sisters, legendary heroines who had fought the Chinese.

The impatient Diggers listened to the final words of advice, which concluded with, "and the convoy leaves at 1700. Be here."

So they scattered into the sunny streets and dark bars. Those who had done some preliminary work, knew of places to go; the majority walked on, "playing by ear, mate."

At the end of the day:

"Anyway, Harry an' me just sat down and ordered a beer, an' this bird sits on the next stool and grabs me by the dick..."

"D'ja ever see such bloody filthy arrangements for

toilets? Built by the bloody *French* though. Rather have a shit in the J, at least it's a lot cleaner out there, eh?"

"Bloody kid grabbed my watch, twisted it to snap the band, and was gone, the little bastard!"

"Yeah, we tried this French restaurant, really good *and* air conditioned; ya betta believe it!"

"These bloody shoe-shine kids came in and put cream on our shoes before we could stop 'em; little buggers. Have to pay 'em to polish it off then."

"I had this bird who'd been workin' since the French days. Jesus, talk about movement—like the bloody proverbial Swiss watch. I'm goin' back there next time, no risk, pal."

"Hey, ya tried those little bowls of soup, meat, noodles, chili, everything in it? This bird I was with talked me into it, at one of those little stalls on the street. Not half bad."

"Well, you oughta know the noggie bastard is gonna swindle you. Christ, never change money without a mate there. Bloody hell."

"I dunno. These sheilas don't turn me on. The one I had didn't know fuck-all about it. Just bloodywell lay there like a great log. Give me Singapore any day."

"Hope the photos come out okay."

"There's 160,000 of the bastards in the J tryin' to kill us, and the rest tryin' to bloody well rob us. What a country."

"What'd ya buy that bloody monkey for? Ya know there's no pets allowed in the battalion lines."

"Yeah, it seemed a good idea at the time, Col. . . . Hey, kid, want a monkey?"

"Whatja mean, parades? We came here to do operations, not fuckin' parades!"

"Shut up and listen. 0800 every morning, company parades. No bullshit, for real. Dress: bush hats, shirts, shorts, personal weapon, boots. Ya thought the army had forgotten, ay? Never."

"Yeah, stands to reason: The CSMs have been lost

since we got here. No parades, just work parties. Jesus Christ, ay?"

"Well, ay, parades in the middle of fuckin' Vietnam. Notice the CSMs were in their element? New men. Hear the baron when we went past 'im on the way? Looked happier than I've seen 'im since we got here, muttering 'left, right, left, right' under his breath."

Second-class Private Nga leaned idly on the sandbag parapet built on the roof of the old French defense post, watching the vehicles driving around the perimeter tracks; dark blue US Air Force, olive US Army, green ARVN, and olive Australian.

An open Land-Rover appeared around the bend, splashing through the puddles from yesterday's storm.

The driver nudged his hat back off his brow and spoke over his shoulder to the three passengers,

"Listen, if our story is gonna hold up, we better stop here and put some water in the tank, because they're a monty to check."

"Yeah, we couldn't spend the night in Saigon because we got water in the petrol, then turn up back here with no water in it, ay?"

"Hey, there's a big pond near that pillbox."

"Good, that'll do. Anyone got a canteen cup?"

"Here ya go."

Nga watched the Land-Rover halt, the passengers get out, unscrew the petrol cap, and scoop up a cup of rain water. His eyes widened as the water was poured down the chute into the petrol tank.

"Nien! Than! Quickly! Look at these Uc Dai Loi!"

"What, what?"

"They're pouring rain water into the petrol tank—see, see."

One of the Australians noticed the sudden arrival of two more heads over the sandbags, and the intent stares.

"Listen, don't look up, but the nogs in the pillbox are taking this all in, and I bet they're buggered trying to work out what we're doin' here. So, when we take off, drop yer foot and see if we can throw a bit of gravel with a fast takeoff, okay?"

"Yeah, fair enough," with a sly grin.

"Nien, why are they putting water in their car?"

"I don't know, maybe it's special water. There they go. Look! They're going fast! The wheels are throwing gravel! Come on!"

"Hey, hey—look the three of 'em have disappeared—bet they're heading for that pond! Ha, ha, ha!" and the US MPs wondered at the mad Australians driving in roaring with laughter.

Back down the road, around the bend, three little figures were squatting and carefully tasting the pond water with all the inhaling, palate-tasting, and spitting of expert wine judges.

6

"Look at the names of all these bloody laundries, tailors, bars, carwashes—the whole lot: San Francisco, Texas, Manhattan, Golden Gate, bloody monotonous. I'd rather see Jade Dragon or somethin'."

"Feel more Asian, ay?" said Les Fitzgibbon, looking up the street.

"They're only out to make a quid. If the English were here, it'd be London, York, Penzance, or Hero of Sherwood. Don't worry about it," replied Smacker, as they turned into the New York tailor shop to pick up the shirts ordered previously. This would be their last opportunity to shop for weeks to come, as an operation was due to begin in two days.

An American was ordering a safari suit, and the sleek owner of the shop looked up from his order book.

"Okay, be ready for fitting in four days," holding up four fingers to emphasize, "You come back Monday, okay?"

"Uh, no. Saturday, we're all goin' to Cat Ben. So, how about I come back when that's over?"

"How long you go?"

"Well, 'bout three weeks, I guess."

"Okay, I have ready for you."

The American strode out, and the owner turned to the Australians.

"Yes, Uc Dai Loi? What I can do for you?"

Later, outside, Smacker turned to Les.

"Listen, we'd better report that Yank to our intelligence officer, even though it's too late now. No wonder the pricks know what's goin' on and before we do. Loudmouthed bastard told him where we're goin'."

"Yeah, let's get on back."

Bob Edmondson, battalion intelligence officer, looked up after reading their statement. "So, that's a true account of what happened? All right, I'll take this to the CO, but don't expect anything. Thanks for coming in with this."

Stan-the-Man sighed, placed the signed statement on his field table, drummed his fingers on its blanket-covered top, and looked at his intelligence officer.

"Well, all I can do is bring this up at the next conference. Christ knows it won't change anything. Those bastards are blinded by 'airborne' shining in one eye and 'America' in the other. Their pride was hurt enough when the reporters printed our lads' remarks on their lack of patrolling expertise.

"Despite the stomping back and forth around the area, there have been no big battles, and that means no legends, no medals, and no future. We both know they've been claiming great kill figures but have damn-all bodies and weapons. Now, if we push this to attack their sense of security, we know there are little beggars in town radioing everything that happens on the helipad, let alone leaks in III Corps Headquarters. The best we can do is not let them point a finger at us. All right then," in dismissal, "thank you Bob."

"Goodnight, sir."

Chuong and Thien pedalled their bicycles along the red dirt road, past the defense post—solid black against the softer night sky. The cyclists knew there was no danger from the occupants. Isolated here, almost two miles from Cat Ben, linked by one road across the paddies, the regional force soldiers in the post were content to fly the red-barred yellow flag of the Saigon government and do nothing to annoy the NLF in the area.

Up in the post, Trinh leaned forward, peering down at the road. He could just make out two shapes against the lighter road surface and hear the tires crunching on the dirt and the tinny rattle of the mudguards. Two of *them*. He released his pent-up breath. They weren't going to attack after riding bicycles past. Anyway, the night noises were as usual out there in the jungle.

The pair cycled to the straggling collection of small buildings that housed the farmers and their families, making their way from one to the next with no need for stealth.

Tap on the door.

Inside, the knowledge that at this time of night it can only be the NLF.

"Greetings, comrade. How is your family? Good. Now listen. In a few days the US imperialists will be here. They will want you to leave the area and go to Cat Ben while they are here, to make their job easier. Protest: say you cannot leave your fields now; it is too far for the children; how will you live in Cat Ben? You are afraid of the VC," with a broad grin, "you have no travel documents. Understand? Good, now here is comrade Thien to collect the taxes," repeated in each house.

The sky was paling as the two cycled back to the town and entered by paths they knew to be unguarded by the government troops: Thien to his small restaurant, Chuong to his carpenter's shop.

*   *   *

The long "cattle trucks" halted at the helicopter pad, and the green-clad mass climbed down: an anonymous green horde to the casual observer, but to the initiated, a whole consisting of individuals of different size, height, coloring, manner of carrying the weapon, hat shape, and posture.

The men split into their individual aircraft loads, or chalks, and subsided to the ground until the order to board.

"How many choppers d'ya reckon there are?" asked Les of Smacker, "I counted over ninety slicks plus gunships, and command and control must be well over a hundred, ay?"

"Yeah, a few dollars worth," replied Smacker, settling down with his pack as a backrest and closing his eyes.

"Saddle up!" and the rising whine of turbines.

The first lift rising, noses down, moving forward over the grass, fences, houses, gaining height, closing on one another with escorting gunships on the flanks, turning north under the gray sky.

Phuoc clambered down to Binh.

"All quiet now, comrade."

To the north, the lifts shook out into the familiar line astern landing formation and settled, troops leaping out, running, down, slicks lifting, nose down, churning up and away, off the LZ before the next lot arrives in thirty seconds.

Lift after lift, wave after wave, three battalions are flown in. While the third battalion is arriving, the road convoy rumbles up and past: armored vehicles, trucks, jeeps, artillery—with their own tale of driving through a gun battle en route.

"Well, dunno if it were VC or ARVN or two lots of ARVN shooting it out. A little town back there with some canals in it—every bastard blazing away across the road at each other, ignoring us driving through the middle. Now I know how those little ducks feel in the sideshow shooting galleries. Never hit anyone that I heard of."

"Christ, what's that?"

"Will ya have a look at *that!*" Heads turned to regard

a strange pair—she slim, blonde, camouflage shirt unbut-
toned far enough to reveal the beginning of magnificent
breasts, the nubile hips and slim legs in tailored trousers
and US jungle boots; over one shoulder hung a writing
pad in a case, and over the other, a high-fashion black
leather handbag, incongruous in the center of this airmobile landing operation; he tall, Errol Flynn-swashbuckler
in tailored camouflage clothes, hung with photographer's
impedimenta and topped by a bright red beret.

"Hi there. Where can we find the US paratroopers?"

The blonde, aware she is the center of interest for
every man in sight, hand on hip, one knee flexed, stomach
in, shirt front opening and closing, carefully scans the
cloud base as if expecting the US paratroopers to come
drifting down.

"Uh, US paras? Haven't seen any here," said Smacker, turning to the others. "Seen any Yanks?"

"No, they're all back at base," in the faint hope the
two would decide to stay.

"No, they're here. C'mon," to the blonde, "we gotta
find 'em," striding off to the road, the blonde's hips the
focus point for two hundred pairs of eyes.

"Christ, I could sit here all day watchin' that blonde
breathe in an' out."

"How's Julie an' the kids, mate?" in an unctuous tone.

"Get fucked, bastard," hurling a water bottle and a
grin.

"Well, there they go," and perched in the back of a
jeep, blonde and red beret disappeared down the road.

"Did you notice something besides that sheila's tits?
Here they are out in the J to get a story, and they haven't
got a drop of water or a bite to eat, nothing to sleep in or
under—completely unprepared. They'll be a burden to
everyone."

"She coulda been burdening me, no worries," from
the group.

"Yeah, yeah. Here it's okay. When we get into it
though, you'd see. They'll do their thing—he'll photograph, she'll write; they'll get back to Saigon all dirty and
have a few drinks in the top bar of the Caravelle, to be

seen as combat types. Trained military observers, my arse."

"Well, don't let it get you down, mate. They won't last."

"Yeah, but it worries me. Wackers like them, instant experts, write absolute crap, and that's what is printed back home. Like those bastards who went around the battalion, interviewing anyone they wanted to. All they sent back was who hadn't got any mail, who didn't know if his wife had the baby yet, and who didn't know what was going on. They can print any crap at all!"

"What are ya gettin' so excited about? There's nothin' you can do about it. They don't give a damn for what's goin' on—they just want to see their name in print. 'Our man in Vietnam.'"

From a prone figure under a bush, "This whole thing is a career booster. The Yanks are gonna get medals and promotion, and so are we. The reporters are gonna make names for themselves, and even the North Vietnamese and VC are gonna do okay, win or lose. Hang on, hang on," as a chorus of "What bullshit, ya mad, come on" rose.

"Think about it—look at the Japs and the Germans. Bombed flat in 1945. Now where are they? Win or lose, I said, and I'm right. The Yanks will come along and offer 'em a hundred million and away they go."

"Moving in one minute," and the green figures rose, puffing the last drags on their cigarettes, clipping their belt buckles, swinging their packs onto their backs, friends holding heavy rucksack frames loaded with the radio as well as the normal pack for the radio operator, the signaler, to slip his arms through the straps. Pick up weapons, arrange sweat rag around neck, and stand, slightly hunched forward, waiting the last few seconds before moving.

As the head of the column disappeared behind the dark green and black of the jungle edge, a rising roar from the south swiveled heads, and fifteen silver Hercules, fat whales under the gray sky, roared low overhead, rear exit doors open and the figure of the jumpmaster visible, looking down.

"Looks like someone's gonna jump in," as the silver

shapes in line astern flew away north, toward the darkening sky on the horizon.

"Look at those bloody black clouds. We're gonna get a wet arse an' no fish tonight."

"Come on, you're gettin' as bad as old Nimbus. Just think of that blonde and take your mind off things."

"Aw, she's probably got the jack anyway."

"Jesus, brighten up, for Christ's sake. Here we go," and they moved behind the first tendrils of vine into the trees. Under the gray sky and the leafy canopy, the jungle floor was dark with no breeze, and the cathedral-hush enveloped them; silent shapes, alternately staring left or right down the line, all messages passed by hand signal, treading carefully, weaving under vines with thorns to catch in their hat, shirt, or pack. The only sound breathing, leaves rustling on their clothes or pack, and soft noise of wet leaves underfoot.

The signal comes back: left forearm crossed over rifle barrel, then one hand making a rippling motion: an obstacle, a creek.

George Benson moved up to the leading figures crouched behind the trees or bushes, looking up and downstream. There it is, a creek about ten yards wide, flowing left to right and, on both sides, six to ten yards of knee-high grass.

"Okay, I'll put Two across, then Three, Headquarters, then you. It'll be Two on the left, Three on the right, you fill in the rear."

Two section's scouts separated and on the quiet "go," quickly moved out of the dark, into the light, covered the open space to the water's edge and carefully but rapidly entered. Despite the narrow width, the creek shelved steeply, and both men went up to their chests in the cloudy water. They heaved themselves up the far bank, water streaming silver from their pack, webbing, and clothes now black after immersion and moved rapidly to the trees. Already, the machine gun group and section commander were in the water, and as they hauled themselves up the far bank, the rifle group began moving across, and the shots came cracking down from the left, thumping into one rifleman's pack, toppling him, rolling him over and over. As the answering fire lashed at the trees and bushes upstream, the man got to his feet and plunged across the stream.

Sergeant Augie Bennett, waiting for orders from Benson, saw him lying motionless.

"Christ, he must be hit," and taking command, gave his orders:

"Right, pepper-pot up the banks and flush 'em out. Three first, one keep up firing," and shouting across the noise and stream, "two section, you okay?" and on the shouted, "Okay," responded "Right, we are going up this bank; keep up on your side."

"Okay Augie."

"Right! Three on my left, One on my right, let's go."

The jungle quiet shattered by the crashing machine guns, rifles, and crump of M79 grenade launchers, the figures, two or three at a time leaping up, running forward, down, fire to cover the next couple moving up; never presenting more than a fleeting target, but always advancing and under constant covering fire.

Under the pressure the enemy on the far bank withdrew, leaving several pools of blood. As the VC fire ceased, Bennett held his sections, swept the area, and returned to where the action had begun. The radio operator and Benson, staring silently into the canopy, waited.

"You okay Skipper? Thought you'd had it."

"Yes, thanks; don't know what happened. I couldn't think."

Noticing the looks exchanged among the nearby Diggers, Bennett turned. "Come on, stop standing around like harlots at a christening. Quick now—Three section get across—one straight after," turning to the signaler, "what are the others doing?"

"Five has seen people in gray uniforms, no contact though."

"Okay, tell 'em we're crossing here, only three blood trails, lost 'em."

As the sections crossed, Benson struggled to control his racing pulse, remembering the huge black paralyzing wave that surged up from somewhere at the back of his brain as the first shots cracked past.

"Christ, what happened?" He knew he couldn't have moved or spoken whatever happened.

Bennett turned to the radio operator, "Right, over you go. Come on Skip," and in a lower voice as they walked to the jungle edge, "You'll be okay. It's just the first time; don't worry about it."

"Thanks Augie." But the ink-black rivulets of that bottomless wave were still draining from the crevices of Benson's mind.

Further east, Lieutenant "Speed" Gordon put away his map, passed the radio handset back, and waved his section commanders close in. "Okay, Mr. Benson's lot over on our left have bumped a few. Nothing either side, a few blood trails. They might be heading our way down the track, so we're going to prop here a while. The OC and Mr. Myers are to our left rear about 500 yards. So, absolute quiet, aimed shots and we'll get 'em."

Old Phat trotted down the track, gray uniform trousers flapping around his ankles, Remington rifle in his right hand down at arm's length, parallel to the ground. He grinned as he thought of the foreigner he had hit trying to cross Singing Water Creek. Phat's great-great-grandfather had fought to clear the Cambodians from the area; his great-grandfather had fought the North Viet dynasty; and since then, they had fought the French and the Saigon regime, who were not even southerners, but Catholics from the North!

Phat did not care about elections, religious differences, or democratic procedures. He would defend this area against all strangers and that meant anyone who did not speak his local variation of South Vietnamese dialect. Now, these foreign strangers were here. They must be those Americans or the Uc Dai Loi from the Great Southern Land. The political officer knew many things, but even he was something of a stranger—after all, he came from Thai Phuoc and that was a day's journey.

"Humph." Phat looked over his shoulder as he jogged around a bush—nothing behind—and then saw in front of him one of those Uc Dai Loi. Long rifle coming up. Phat ducked and ran but a charging buffalo hit him in the chest and everything went black.

Speed Gordon lowered his M16 and grinned at the machine gunner.

"Good shooting Wilkie."

Phat's body lay stretched out, face up, not six feet away, the blood from his wounds trickling down the small slope to puddle around the bipod legs of the M60 machine gun.

After a minute, Gordon rose from his prone position, scanning the direction from which Phat had come.

"Well, looks like he was the only one. I'll see what he's got on him."

Phat became aware of the gray light above him through the mottled layer of leaves, dark green lower down, medium and then lighter against the sky. A green weight was pushing on his chest; it was hard to breathe: flashing into his brain—those cursed foreigners! Where are they? Phat sat up as Gordon knelt by his side, avoiding the pool of blood; Phat glared, blood spraying from his lips as he cursed, shook his fist in Gordon's face, and seized his Remington. Gordon leaped back, falling in surprise as the dead man became very much alive but was blasted back along the track for two feet by the second M60 burst.

Gordon looked at the grinning faces, knowing he had presented a ludicrous spectacle leaping back from the blood-spraying spectacle at his feet.

"All right, you bastards," with a grin, "only Dracula could love a face like that."

"Give us a look at yer fangs, boss," from the anonymity of the bushes.

Captain Reg Waterson was a bright young man of inquisitive nature. Ever since he was old enough, he had pulled to pieces, examined the workings, and reassembled (with improvements) clocks, watches, radios, bicycles, motor cycles, cars, televisions, steam irons, and anything else he could attack with a screwdriver and wrench. For some time his interest had centered on finding quicker ways to strip and assemble the infantry small arms.

Now, in the quiet of the afternoon, he sat on the edge of his four-foot-deep weapon pit, his Owen gun pointing up at an angle, wondering if he could use the power of the recoil spring to speed up the disassembling process.

"Hmm. Bolt to the rear, spring compressed. If I simultaneously lift the retaining pins for the bolt *and* the barrel, the bolt will travel forward free and push the barrel out, following the barrel itself. Then there's only the magazine to come off. Let's see: Bolt first, then . . ."

The twenty-eight rounds went off in one long burst as the bolt flew forward, pushing a round into the breech, the fixed firing pin doing its job, bolt blown to the rear, nothing to retain it, forward again.

The leaves and bark shot off the tree above drifted down, onto, and around the prone figures of Stan-the-Man and the HQ group.

Momentary silence.

"What happened? Anyone hit?"

Waterson, with great presence of mind, was at the bottom of his pit, out of sight, and, he hoped, out of mind.

"If I'd taken the magazine off first . . ."

Myers's platoon had found an unoccupied staging camp and were looting the packs and belongings of torches, fountain pens, biros, writing paper, hammocks, and any other useful items.

"Tommy, get one of your blokes to take one of the empty packs and whip around with it, collecting any documents or paper with writing on it."

"Righto, sir. Here Herb, away you go."

Company headquarters and its attendant platoon arrived. The company intelligence representative began photographing the installations.

"Look at the way these bastards are set up: latrines dug, kitchens dug, chimneys running along the ground to dissipate the smoke, Hutchi spaces cleared, ridgepoles set up. All they have to do is roll in, throw their plastic over the ridgepole, sling their hammocks, and put on the rice.

Talk about organized. Each one has a pit dug for shelter from air and arty."

"Yeah, they're organized, the little bastards."

"Notice this place has been shot up recently? By gunships, I'd say—rocket craters and M60 holes in the trees. I haven't seen a single pit with damage to it, either."

"Hey Smacker, you're always working out chances of winning on the dogs and horses. What do you reckon the chances are of getting hit in one of these?"

"Well, how big is this camp?" with a calculating glance around, "say 200 by 200 yards, ay? That's about, er 40,000 square yards. Each entrance to the pit," indicating the narrow entrance to the pit, vertical then branching out at right angles in an *L* shape, "is about, say one quarter of a square yard. If a helicopter puts forty rockets into this area, there's one in a thousand chance of getting near the pit, and one in four thousand of getting the edge of it. The rocket, or bullet, is traveling on an angle, but the pit is vertical. So, what do you reckon? You could be having a root down there and not worry about anything important getting hit."

Snapping fingers attracted their attention. All around in the green gloom dark figures were shouldering packs.

"There ya go. It's gonna rain any minute, and we move out of this nice camp into the uncivilized J."

The darkness and silence enveloped the battalion, staring into the trees, waiting for stand-to to end—pow! A single shot.

From RSM "Razor" Sharp, the low command, "Whoever that was, charge him," and around the pits it went.

"Whoever it was, charge 'im," from one to another in the dark.

"Whoever it was, charge 'im."

Back came the reply, muttered up the line of dark pits, "It was Lieutenant Turnbill: shot himself in the foot."

From the RSM: "God help us."

The farming families were removed without much effort into a large abandoned church, standing alone in its peeling yellow wash in a huge, empty, overgrown area. The church had been built as a central point to which it was hoped small shops and houses would concentrate. However, the plan failed. The priest could not journey the six miles from Cat Ben: one of his predecessors had been shot dead, and the second had disappeared. The farmers lived in seclusion.

So, determined to enjoy the enforced holiday for the few days necessary, the families moved into the church: old men, women of all ages, and about five children for each adult. No young men. They were either in the government forces or with the VC.

Edmondson, the intelligence officer, and Fredericks, one of his linguists, stood surveying the scene.

"They're all Catholics, you say?"

"Right, sir."

"Well, we'll send the padre down and the RMO to have a sick parade. All pills or medicine must be consumed on the spot. Otherwise, the VC will get it."

For the first time in two years, the Latin words rose over the green jungle.

The rain streamed down, a silver-gray curtain, running in torrents from the leaves, reducing visibility to a few yards; trees nearby were indistinct shapes and, farther away, everything faded into a green-gray dark opaque mass. All other sounds were absorbed into the noise of the rain on canopy and ground.

Thuc, Bien, and Nha squatted under a huge tree, patiently waiting for the rain to end before making their way home—not to stay, but to watch and observe the foreigners in and near the hamlet by the church.

Thuc smiled at Nha, thinking of slim Tuyet, Nha's sister. Tonight, they would visit their families, and he would give Tuyet the photo taken of the three of them standing before the wreckage of the puppet airforce airplane. A movement caught his eye, and Thuc looked up, eyes widening at the two dripping foreigners who appeared, one on either side of the tree ten paces away. He saw the orange flashes from the muzzle as one fired from the hip, the fountains of earth and leaves spraying near his feet and hips, and leaped up, trying to bring his French MAS36 rifle up to fire:

"It is very hard to stand . . . the foreigner is trying to put a fresh magazine in his black rifle . . . it's so dark," and Thuc fell back as the second scout fired aimed shots into his body.

Bien and Nha, despite their wounds, tried to recover Thuc's body, but after the third time, and when in danger of being surrounded, they escaped under cover of the driving rain that had concealed the approach of the Australian platoon.

"Look at the size of this bastard," grunted Tom Pritchard.

"Yeah, he bloody near got Frank too. Stood up with all those hits in his legs and tried to zap him. Then Reimann hit him and the bastard went down for good."

"Not much on him. Photo, couple of letters. We'll hand 'em in tonight. Okay, bury him."

"Can't we throw him down this old well here? Fuckin' hell, we do enough diggin' as it is!"

"Red" Ryder leaped up from where he had been studying his map, "That's enough! There'll be no nonsense with enemy dead in this company! He'll get a decent burial, the same as we'd expect for our men. Now get digging!"

The cluster of green dripping figures around Thuc's body stood motionless and silent, scorched by Ryder's evident anger. Then one took up his entrenching tool, and the sound of digging rose under the roar of rain. In silence, the hole was dug to three feet, the body dropped in and covered, and the dark figures moved off in the dark dripping trees.

Benson's platoon crept forward, soaked to the skin, ignoring the rain streaming down.

A sudden scattering of rifle shots, snapping sounds as the rounds flew by; lead section returning fire; remainder of the platoon closing up through the dark, bottom-of-a-green-bottle watery gloom; section commanders giving orders; Bennett finding Benson prone behind a tree, eyes staring and blank, unblinking.

Frowning, Bennett shook him by the shoulder, "Skip! you okay? Skipper!"

With an obvious return to awareness, Benson shook his head, looked around and up at the stooping dark figure in the gloom, as the black mass flowed back from his mind, and the light came in again. "Uh-uh, yes Augie. Yes, I'm okay."

"Come on then. I think they've gone through."

Benson stood upright in the mud, glad of the gloom concealing his blushing.

Now by every move and action, Bennett indicated that he was at all times, even more so than normal, prepared to take over the platoon. The platoon itself, in a dozen small ways, also showed their acceptance of the fact that it would be necessary for him to do so next time contact was made.

Bob Edmondson stood dripping inside the church. "How is it going, Corporal?" to Alan Fredericks, the linguist.

"Not bad, sir. Want a bit of this brew?" offering the steaming canteen cup.

"Thanks."

"I notice everyone seems to look to that woman and bloke over there, despite old Mr. Binh here being the official government headman. They never give orders or anything obvious, but they're the leaders. Mr. Binh is very respectful to them. Whenever I say 'VC,' she gets a broad grin on her dial. There is a father and brother in her family book unaccounted for. In Saigon she says, but no letters or cards or anything to back it up."

"Here's a photo from that kill this afternoon—let's compare it with the book."

Opening the family book, Edmondson and Fredericks compared the photographs, Thuc's sister and Bien's father peering over the edge of the book.

"Don't look at the book, watch their faces. There, they recognize them. Ask them who these three are."

Shrugs and denials, the Asian inscrutable mask dropping over the normally animated faces. Where did the foreigners get the photograph?

"Okay, we'll tell 'em this one here was killed this afternoon, the others wounded. Also, his MAS36 was captured. That ought to convince them."

The inscrutable masks never flickered, but the eyes grew more unreadable.

"Well, that's taken the grin off her face anyway. Make a note of their names and personal particulars; we'll pass it on to the authorities in Cat Ben, for all the good it'll do. The bastards will never come out here."

"Sir, did you get the exchange of looks between the woman and that young bird over there—round face, holding the kettle? The young one was watching it, the photo business, and now she's not happy at all."

Tuyet sat there, concentrating on pouring the water into the bowl to wash little fat Chen, knowing in her heart that Thuc was dead and never again would she see his shy, quiet face against the evening sky as he recited love poems, timidly holding her hand. How proud she had been when he had gone with her elder brother Nha and Bien to be soldiers of the Liberation Front to struggle against the absentee landlord who sat in Cat Ben and collected half their crop in taxes and rent. She bent her head, long black tresses hanging to hide her face, washing the laughing baby brother.

Why could not all these people with guns go away? First the French and Viet Minh, then the government, now the Liberation Front and the government and also those strangers who had killed Thuc; and all she wanted was to be Thuc's wife.

She looked up and saw Thuc's sister watching her. Looking away, there were the two foreigners, one who spoke her language, quietly regarding her.

What are they going to do? She must not cry. Laugh with little Chen. Concentrate. And with her heart breaking, Tuyet sat in the peeling church under the gray sky, laughed, and splashed baby Chen in the water.

Under the trees, Thuc's blood washed from the leaves

and the pool of red gradually subsided into the ground, washed clean by the downpour.

While the rain fell from the gray afternoon sky on the church and jungle, it was night in Sydney and the announcers were before camera and microphone.

"... announce that two Australians have been killed and four wounded in operations in South Vietnam."

Click! The off knob twisted so hard in her hands it snapped off, and Jacqueline Myers flung it into the far corner of the room, away from the now silent TV.

"Damn them! They didn't tell me it was going to be like this. Not knowing if he's dead or alive or mutilated. The bastards!"

If she'd known this part of it, she would never have married Bruce. But no one ever speaks about it—the stomach-grinding wait after the announcement, fearing a knock on the door, and if it is a friend calling, the instantaneous thought, "Is there a padre and strange officer there, come to tell me with a friend to comfort me?," and the fast flick of the eyes searching the hallway behind the visitor.

After those terrible announcements, it was an effort to hold coffee down, let alone anything else, and cigarettes flared and died, mashed and bent under restless fingers, until the next morning the impersonal voice released her from the torture.

"... the names of those killed were Private Keith James Anderson ... Anthony Peter ... Travers. ... All next-of-kin have been notified."

Then a great weight seemed to drain away from her. Appetite returned, the sky was blue, the sun shone, the harbor sparkled, and Martin Place was cheery as she walked through it from the office to Wynyard.

Bruce was unhurt.

But even in those bright times fear lurked in a deep recess in her brain, ready to crawl out and spread its dark wings whenever Vietnam was mentioned: newspapers, magazines, TV, meetings of the wives' associations—all of which she avoided as much as possible.

As the weeks passed, Jacqueline had found she could

not bear the wives' meetings and their social events, where she was surrounded by women chattering away with such brave faces, women whose husbands might at that moment be dying or maimed.

One evening, sitting before the mirror opening a jar of face cream, she paused, noticing in her reflection the dark patches under her eyes and the faint but distinct lines between her brows and from each nostril to mouth corner. Her resolve flared: blast them! This is a year out of our lives, and I have a life of my own to live. I'm not going to bury myself in that tribal cluster of wives. Jackie, get out of this cocoon and live!

Rather than finding strength and comfort in the company of people in a like situation, she found it in isolation from them—in work and in friends unconnected with the army.

Stan-the-Man and Tregonne sat inside an APC, speaking loudly to be heard over the noise of the rain.

"Well sir, we're lucky that while everyone is wet, they're not cold. Thank Christ we're not in Korea; we'd have a real problem. We have enough socks back there to provide three pairs a man. Greens don't really matter, I think. The MO is starting to get concerned at the prospect of foot problems if this wet keeps up."

"Yes, I know. God knows we're not finding much: base camps, supplies, the odd brave young local chap, but no contact with their major units. Our Intelligence people report the locals were told two days before we arrived that we'd be coming." He lapsed into silence.

"The brigade commander is convinced there is something here, so we're staying for a few more days. Maybe his S-2 people use a different crystal ball from our Intelligence staff. Personally, I think we're wasting our time."

And then both men's heads cocked, they frowned; out of the darkness, barely audible, came the chung, chung, chung of mortars, then the slamming of giant doors, boom, boom, as the bombs arrived.

"They aren't going to do much good in this mud," said Tregonne, eyeing the steel roof overhead.

A distinctly different whistle and explosion drew down the eyebrows of Stan-the-Man. He climbed through the back door of the APC and stared as a red comet flashed across the darkening headquarters camp.

"Where is all that firing coming from?"

"From the bloody village, sir," shouted "Razor" Sharp, running up through the mud. "We're all set to return fire."

"No, no," growled Stan, "wait. They're not hitting anyone, and we don't want to cause unnecessary destruction," diving behind a convenient pile of ration boxes as another salvo of mortars exploded, splashing mud over him. Razor and the APC crew entered by the small door.

Just as he was about to order return fire, the mortars and recoilless rifle ceased, and peace returned to the dark night. The villagers huddled in the shelters required by law in each house, and the headquarters personnel breathed in relief.

The two groups finding amusement in the event were the VC crews, happily trotting away over secured paths, and the rifle companies, halted for the night and chuckling over the news—BHQ has been mortared and shot at by recoilless rifles.

"Pogo bastards—serve 'em right, sitting for four days outside a village."

"Bet the bastards are still digging."

Tom Pritchard sat, in the lap of luxury, writing home:

"... after all this slogging along in the wet, we're reserve company at last. Time to take off our boots. You know how your hands and feet wrinkle after a long time in water? Well, that's how my feet look. Here I am sitting under a hutchi airing my feet, with Father with a brew on. Dry socks to put on after and a letter from you. Sheer luxury, my darling.

"Life has different meanings over here. Remember the Snoopy cartoons? 'Happiness is ...' Well, over here, 'Happiness is sitting dry in your hutchi watching someone else go out on patrol' and 'Happiness is sitting with a pair of dry socks to put on!'"

*　　*　　*

With minor clashes, the operation wound on, ending on a light note. The platoon lay in ambush along the track with a good field of fire. Cycling steadily over the skyline came eight VC, armed and uniformed. Clicking fingers alerted the ambushers; safety catches were thumbed down, M60 belts quickly checked, rear sights adjusted, and grins exchanged. Eight sure kills.

"They're pedalling right into the killing zone...twenty-five yards to go...what the hell is *he* doing?"

Do-gooding, nonsmoking, nondrinking, nonwhoring, Albert (always "Albert" in full) Goodrich, steps out into the killing zone, hand held up as a "halt" sign: bicycles going in all directions, VC running and ducking and disappearing into the bushes, and the huge figure of Moose Morrissey rearing up, one huge hand grasping Goodrich by the collar and lifting him off the ground.

"And what were you doing? Playing traffic cop, son?" he growled.

"I was going to capture them alive, Sergeant."

The fleeing VC went to ground as the roaring voice rose to a piercing scream. "You were fucking *what?* Do you think we're running a fucking circus?"

Jacqueline Myers watched the beach god going through his posturing, muscle-flexing routine—his rippling muscles gleaming under the film of suntan oil. She lowered her book and looked from behind her sunglasses at the other sunbathers. Some ignored the peacocking male, others regarded him with boredom, envy, or amusement. How she and Bruce would have exchanged smiles, had he been here. Instead, he was miles away up there...

"Excuse me, you're turning very red. Would you like to use some of this?"

She looked around and into the friendly blue eyes of the man reclining a few feet away, his hand outstretched, offering a plastic bottle. She glanced down her bikini'ed body that was turning a scarlet hue. Should she?

"Oh, that's very kind of you." She began rubbing the lotion over her legs.

"Hope I didn't spoil your enjoyment of the show,"

grinned blue eyes, with a tiny nod past her, toward the bleached-blond god now artistically reclining, one leg flexed on his beach towel.

Jackie smiled. "I find them incredibly self-centered. Not my type at all."

"Oh, there's hope for we lesser mortals, then?"

"Yes, surely *all* men don't have as their ideal the pneumatic Hollywood creation? They're as unreal as his type," nodding toward the reclining figure.

"True, true. I'm Harry Brandon, by the way," extending a slim hand.

"Oh hello. Jackie Myers. Do you come here often?" with a broad smile.

"Well, not really. You can see I'm not *that* well tanned. I can get down here about once or twice a week. I have a small gallery in Paddington that takes a great deal of my time."

"That must be very interesting and rewarding."

With a flash of white teeth, "More of the former than the latter, I'm afraid."

And as the afternoon stretched away into the west, pushing the lengthening shadows behind, they lay on the warm sand, chatting about art, politics, films, and books.

Brandon lived alone above his gallery, in a comfortable complex of rooms he had redecorated, and where he entertained. Jackie declined the invitation to drinks but promised to pop in during the week to see what the gallery offered.

The following Wednesday she parked the Mini and walked up the short flight of stairs to the door. A discreet sign announced Jaralee Gallery. The door swung open soundlessly, and she stepped in. Brandon noted her entry and flashed a brief welcoming smile over a client's shoulder, eyes flicking over her summer-dressed figure.

She smiled back and strolled around the small, well-lit rooms, losing herself in the paintings till a soft touch on her arm startled her.

"I'm very glad you came. Can I offer you a drink?" smiled Brandon, looking neat, suntanned, and alert—blue eyes looking deep into her brown ones. She felt the tiny electric spark flare at the base of her spine. . . .

Later, she relaxed the grip of her thighs around his waist, sliding her legs down onto the cool sheets, waiting for their breathing to regulate. He raised himself on one elbow, smoothing his hair back from his brow, smiled into her eyes, "What say you to a shower, then a few drinks at Double Bay and dinner at a very good little cellar in Elizabeth Bay?"

"Wonderful." Jackie arched her back, brushing one nipple against his chest, placing both arms around his neck, and drawing him down onto her, "Can't think of a better way to spend an evening in Sydney. But first, I'd like you to explain and demonstrate one of my favorites."

"Oh?"

"Yes," with oh-so-innocent wide eyes, "it's a French term, soixante-neuf. I can never get it right. Am I soixante or neuf?" smile breaking through.

"Ah, mademoiselle," curling an imaginary moustache, "eet depends whethair you are left or right handed, ze phase of ze moon, and whethair you are in ze nord or ze sud hemisphere, comprenez-vous?"

"Show me, monsieur."

7

The Saigon leave truck rolled out of the area, to the brigade and onto the highway. Sitting in the back, Alan Fredericks flicked through in his mind what he planned for the day: look up an old friend working at the Australian embassy on the seventh floor of the Caravelle, down to the market area to do some photography, and then a few drinks before going back.

He had already decided on the bar for his drinking—La Popotte, off Tu Do Street. There, the lovely Xuan worked as cashier. On their first leave to Saigon some weeks ago, Fredericks and a couple of friends had casually walked into just another bar, with just another set of bar girls. But behind the bar was every man's dream of the Asian woman: gleaming black hair, beautifully set, to complement the lovely features—high, clear brow, arched eyebrows, slanting dark eyes, peach bloom cheeks, cupid's bow lips, and a firm, delicate chin. Xuan's voice was low, so one had to strain to hear her perfectly spoken Vietnamese, and her laugh was like tinkling silver bells. Her dresses were always beautifully cut ao dais in lovely colors. She worked in La Popotte solely as a cashier to pay off a debt her parents had incurred against the bar owners, chubby, smiling Mr. Hao and his wife, happy "Mama-San."

Xuan immediately invoked the "big brother" feeling in the Australians and Americans who came to La Popotte, to admire her, drink, and eventually go with Mai, Huong, Kim, Jennie, or one of the other girls. There was a great roar of laughter one day when a huge black paratrooper insisted on buying Xuan a Saigon tea, the cold tea the customers bought with their own beer or whisky and that was credited to the girl. With cries of encouragement from the girls and customers, smiling Mr. Hao and Mama-San nodding, and the big black man standing there, Budweiser in one upraised hand and a tiny Saigon tea glass in the other, blushing, smiling Xuan wrote out the ticket for the drinks, inscribing a delicate Xuan on the tea ticket and, greatly daring, eyes downcast, the paratrooper thrust the girl's half down the front of her high-necked ai dai, clapped and cheered by the entire bar, the huge black booming out, "Ain't she a little honey!"

Beautiful, delicate Xuan—a lovely flower in the midst of the garbage heap of Saigon.

After lunch in Hai Ba Trung Street, and his photography, Fredericks strolled into La Popotte, fairly sure of whom from the leave truck he would find there.

Slightly under the weather, grinning cheerfully, the happy gum-chewing Mai on his right, sat Frank Gardiner.

"Hey Freddo ya bastard! Where ya been? Come an' have a beer, old mate. Hey, garcon, mot bia pour mon ami ici," in a potpourri of Vietnamese and French.

"Garcon" appeared with a cold Pabst Blue Ribbon, and Fredericks slid into the booth opposite Frank, smiling at Xuan and greeting Mai.

"Hope you been behaving yourself, you old bastard," to Gardiner.

"Course I have, mate. Mai and I went to lunch at a very suave little street stall, then up to her room to work off the dreaded D-Zone dirty water, and here we are. Thommo and Jacko just left, an' they'll see us at the truck. Hey, isn't that one of them Yanks who came out with us before?"

"Yeah, so it is. Bob Sayce, I think."

"Hey, Yank! Bob! Come an' have a beer!"

"Hey Aussie. How's it going' man? Hi there, Fredericks. How you goin' honey?" to the toothily smiling Mai.

"Sure can squeeze in one itty bitty beer," as garcon placed a can of Falstaff before him.

The three chatted easily for some minutes, oblivious of the crowd, then gradually became aware of a loud voice dominating the room. They looked up to see a corpulent, squat, red-faced, crew-cut, gray-haired American civilian, dressed in a Hawaiian shirt and checked Bermuda shorts, ankle socks and Hush-Puppies, with a saturated cigar in one corner of his mouth under a prominent, purple-veined nose, brandishing a roll of notes at Mr. Hao.

"I got the money and I want her," pointing to Xuan. "None a these others! Her! That little one!" jabbing a broad-nailed finger at the shrinking Xuan. Mr. Hao and Mama-San weakly protested, "She no bar girl. She cashier only," eyes fixed on the roll of piasters, US "green" dollars and Military Payment Certificates, MPCs, only good on military bases.

"Bullshit! How much you want? Makes no never-mind to me, goddamit!"

The bar girls were watching, inscrutable masks over

their faces; the customers frowning, trying to understand
what was happening.

Frank began to comprehend when he focussed on
Xuan standing against the wall, tears rolling down her
cheeks, muttering, "Khong, khong, khong . . ."

He began to rise to his feet when Mai caught his arm,
"Please, you no can do nothing! Xuan parents owe much
money Mr. Hao. Xuan here to work. That man, he give
beaucoup dollars for Xuan. If Mr. Hao say go, she go.
What you do? Hit American? Police take you. Take Xuan
away? Mr. Hao make trouble her parents. You pay more
than American? Today you go. Tonight he come again. You
think find Xuan job another bar? Where? It *here* parents
owe money Mr. Hao! She must go. Anyway, it no big
thing. Time she have man. She can make beaucoup money, very beautiful."

Frank subsided and looked at Fredericks. "That right,
Freddo?"

"Yeah, Frank, and I feel like a real mongrel just
sitting here. But anything we do will only make it worse
for her. That's how it is in this fucking place," and in a
spasm of rage, he crushed his beer can.

Bob Sayce turned from staring at the fat civilian, at
the folds of red skin bulging over the Hawaiian shirt collar,
"Fellas, this is one time I'm goddam ashamed to be
American. That mother-fucker has probably done more for
the VC in his time in-country than a dozen of their
propaganda teams."

The civilian took the sodden cigar from his mouth,
spat into an ash tray, and coldly and triumphantly pierced
Hao and Mama-San with his glass-chip eyes, "Well, c'mon
goddamit! How much?" secure in the unquestioned power
of the dollar.

"Okay, okay, she number one virgin. Never go with
man. Thirt' t'ousand p. okay?"

"Thirty thousand p? Okay, okay, here," and began
peeling off 500s from the roll.

Xuan's wide eyes followed each note from the roll to
the mounting pile on the bar, and she moaned, dropped
her face into her hands for a moment, took a deep breath,

and looked up and around the bar in a last appeal for help, with the swimming eyes of a frightened doe. Fredericks dropped his gaze, clenched his fists, and said through his teeth, "There are good men on both sides out in the J dying for what they want this country to be. Both sides want it to be without rotten bastards like him and the corrupt swine running it at the moment. They're out *there*, and the scum are in here making fortunes, grinding everything down with the sheer weight of their money," and as the squat shape strode out into the sunlight with the weeping resigned girl held by one arm, "C'mon Frank, let's get out of here. Coming Bob? That prick ruined her life and my day off, today and for some time to come. See you, Mai. Hao, if you were burning in the gutter, I wouldn't piss on you."

"Oh, good day, good day, Uc Dai Loi," busily counting 500 piaster notes.

On that morning, 6,000 miles away to the south, Christine Pritchard delivered the kids to school and was steering the Morris Minor into the driveway when she noticed the huge removal van, all yellow and red, at the end of the street. Gloria O'Reilly moving out.

Christine knew very few people on the street, as they had moved in with such haste, and Tom had gone immediately, and people were wary of inviting a lone woman, a stranger, and a grass widow to boot into their home.

The children has been unsettled and puzzled by the rush to move into this strange house and by the disappearance of their father. To them, this house was not home; home was where they had been before, with dad as well as mum. This was something different, from the inexplicable world of the grown-ups. However, they soon found that Johnny O'Reilly was a classmate whose father was also in Vietnam—whatever that was—and linked by the children, Christine and Gloria had exchanged greetings when they met in the street or at the shops.

Bringing the children back from school one afternoon a fortnight ago, Christine had seen the green army sedan outside the O'Reilly gate and realized what it meant. She

took the children inside, turned on the TV, and made a
fuss of them with ice-cream, Coke, and cake—as much to
keep them away from the O'Reilly house and what was
happening there, as to lavish good things on them in some
blind offering to the gods to demonstrate how she did love
them, petitioning the gods, please don't make them
fatherless.

She had stood watching the children, their eyes fixed
on the TV screen, lips covered with ice-cream, spoons
clinched in chubby fists, and knew more strongly than
ever that they and Tom were all she lived for, and prayed
again for his return, but not a gentle Christian plea: "God,
even if you have to kill them all, please let Tom come back
to us, you can let all of the others go, take them all, but
not my Tom!"

Now, in the driveway, she saw down the street the
men carrying a wardrobe out of the house, and Gloria
standing in the yard with an elderly couple who looked as
if they could be her parents. She drove into the carport,
calculating how much was left of the chocolate cake and
the biscuits in the tin—she'd pop down and invite Gloria
and her parents up for a cup of tea when the movers had
finished.

8

In the long, dark dining tent there was little conversation: 5:30A.M. is not the best time for lively chatter and
hearty appetites. The eaters chewed their ritual bacon,
the smokers sat half asleep, hand cupping the steel canteen mugs.

Outside, another colorful tropic sunrise gradually

blossomed over the eastern horizon, the rose and pink pearl-shell sky brightening, lightening, and suddenly the day was there.

"All right, fall out on the road."

Silently, the platoons formed up, sergeants' and officers' dark shapes standing slightly apart.

"Okay Herb, lead off."

Down the dirt track through the grass, the first sun's rays casting elongated shadows, striding out, settling quickly into the old familiar pace, past the battalion HQ area, down to the armored personnel carriers. Steel aluminum boxes on tracks, great slab sides as high as a man's head. Everyone rides on top: being caught inside one blowing up on a mine is what everyone wants to avoid. Riding on top means a chance of being thrown clear.

The Australian ones are diesel powered, while the US ones are gasoline driven; gasoline ignites more easily than diesel, and who wants to be trapped inside a burning steel box?

So climb aboard and establish yourself on the top deck, sitting on pack, or on the open slab of top hatch. It is cooler, there is a view, and it is much more comfortable, anyway.

The engines begin their growling, the first squat shape rumbles out, the second, the third, and then there is a long line of them, "tracks," rumbling along the bitumen-surfaced road, through towns and villages, past the early morning market-goers, and then the later traffic— vegetables loaded in bullock cart or van, children going to school, and people going . . . who knows where?

In the cool of the morning it was a pleasant journey, despite the tiring vibration and engine noise, and steel corners to gouge hips and sides,

At last, rumbling through the streets of the district town of Cat Ben. Last time, the helicopters flew over, the sky was gray. This time, it is a sunny, cool morning. Roaring, rocking, pivoting through the narrow dusty French colonial streets, flanked by rows of wooden, tile-roofed shops, houses, and offices: the rare brick or stone building of two or three stories, balustraded and shuttered, in a peeling coat of yellow or white, dirty, moss-streaked in vertical strokes where guttering has leaked for months. The shrubs are hibiscus, bougainvillea, poinciana, and frangipani; hydrangeas are the most prized, proudly displayed, and lovingly tended.

Through the central square, halting on the edge of town; ahead the river, bridged by a steel affair, then an expanse of bright green paddie, and on the far side, the rising ground covered in the darker green of bush and scrub. On the very skyline, next to the road climbing the rise, a small defense post, tiny yellow flag fluttering bravely against the blue sky, defiant in its isolation.

The Diggers, by training and experience wary of large open spaces, begin to mutter about the halt. Over there is the enemy. Why halt this side of the river, this side of the open space?

As the wait becomes longer and longer, several of the inquisitive get down to stretch their legs. Fredericks, relying on the rumble of engines starting to warn him in time to get back, walks to the market and buys bananas and grapefruit, returning to the track to share with the Diggers and Yank crew.

"Why are we waiting?"

Next to the M113 is the rice co-op, floor and outside platforms dusted white, the rusted corrugated roof and peeling cement walls contrasting with the palms and shrubs in luxuriant spread around it.

Suddenly out of the sunny, cumulus-dotted sky, great rolling beats of thunder. Where is the storm? Heads turning . . . and over the skyline, in the bush and jungle, long strips of upflinging billowing gray . . . and again . . . a giant's footsteps.

B52s: there, away up in the blue, so far away that *they* could not be responsible for the great rolling, drumming thunder those innocent silver specks sailing backward and forward.

"Well, there you go, ay! Twenty trips like that and an Air Medal! You're in the wrong outfit, Yank," tapping the smiling M113 crew commander on the shoulder.

"Hey, hey, you buy? You buy?" Down below, a flat

basket full of bananas and pineapples, stands a smiling aged lady; the ever-present trading spirit has decided to take advantage of the long halted line of potential customers.

"Yeah? Okay, how much banana? Er, Christ, er . . . bao new chewey, hey?"

"Chuoi, ha? Okay, fi'p.," holding up five fingers.

Soon, the long line of tracks was flanked by fruit and drink vendors doing a roaring trade.

"Hey, mama-san—chewey, hey bao new?"

"Chuoi, ha? Ten p."

"They were only a bloody five a couple of minutes ago!"

"Ten p."

"Okay, get down, we're securing the bridge and this bank. Company HQ in that building," from the company sergeant major "Baron" Lord.

"Hey, that's a bloody pigpen, CSM!"

"Yeah, yer'll be right at home," from a rifle platoon member.

"Don't take yer webbing off, we won't recognize yer!" from another.

"Smart bastards!"

The remaining companies marshaled themselves and rolled across the bridge, along the raised road and began the climb to the skyline. Undismayed, or perhaps stirred up by the B52s, the local guerrillas opened fire on the advancing armored vehicles, wounding two Diggers. Return fire sprayed the trees, the carriers roared up over the skyline, and silence fell.

The battalion settled into the rubber plantation on the right of the road, dug in, cooked, and waited for what promised to be an interesting night.

The clouds dissipated, leaving a clear velvet sky and bright moon. Under the rubber trees was inky black; beyond the edge of the plantation the fence wires gleamed, running left and right. Behind it, the road shone gray-white, and the jungle on the far side spread a moon-illuminated backdrop. Under the trees, kneeling in their pits, the men waited silently in the friendly darkness, until the whispered "stand-down" began the succession of two-hour sessions behind the machine gun, awake in case of attack.

Trinh, Nuong, and Cat met in the shadow of Nuong's house, whispered for a moment, and set off up the path that would bring them out into the road that skirted the rubber plantation. They had carried out similar harassing actions against ARVN units several times and were among the most experienced in their unit. At the rendezvous, they exchanged grins in the night with the other twelve, all keen to show those foreigners what it meant to enter the "Iron Triangle."

Binh, who had fought the French, adjusted his US M1 carbine as he spoke quietly, "Comrades, you are our vanguard," touching Trinh, Nuong, and Cat lightly on the shoulder, "and we will exploit your scouting. When the enemy seeks to rest, harass him, and that is what we shall do again. The puppet Seventh Battalion of the Fifth Regiment has learned it is better to sit in their base camp than to go outside. We shall reconnoiter these foreigners and report to our comrades in the district committee."

Nuong felt a great surge of élan pump through him as he looked around the squatting figures in the moonlight and shadow. Together, they had carried out many tasks for the Front. Tonight, he, Trinh, and Cat would again do well.

Footfalls soundless in the dust, the three walked with the speed of long familiarity up the track that shone softly under the moon. Their black-clad figures cast moon-shadows over the dark grass with its silver filigree edges and spines painted by the moonlight. Under the inky shadow-blob of the old mango tree on the crest, then out onto the road, now onto the path following the plantation fence, Cat, in the lead, turned and indicated the fence—the place to cross it. Helping each other with the bags of grenades and M1 carbine, they quickly, but without any effort at stealth, climbed over and walked toward the rubber plantation's darkness.

Having operated many times against the puppet troops

with their Yankee advisers, they knew no enemy was near: no cigarettes glowed, no smoke hung in the air, no radios crackled or spoke, no transistors mumbled faintly, no coughs, no hawking and spitting.

Cat was almost into the shadow when he saw a faint glistening in a patch of moonlight and leaned forward to peer at it as the world ended in the soundless orange flash. He never heard the machine gun that killed him from ten feet away. Nuong and Trinh turned to run in the moonlight, perfect targets in its beautiful light, and died so close to Cat that the three bodies overlapped, outflung arms and legs intermingling.

Silence. Overhead, the moon continued its impersonal journey, and its light moved off the tent it had found through the gap in the leaves, painting it with the silver that had caught Cat's eye in his last two seconds of life.

Binh and the others at the mango tree waited for the sounds that would advise them the "vanguard three" were alive—grenade bursts, flat M1 cracks, and return fire—nothing.

"Harh! Uyen, come with me. Trac, wait with the others here. We must locate the enemy and our brave comrades."

More carefully now, keeping to the shadows, Binh and Uyen crept forward. Binh's sense of survival told him to remain out of the moonlight near the fence. Halting behind a huge bush, he put out one hand to stop Uyen, took out a grenade, pulled the pin, and threw it as far as he could toward the inky dappled area under the rubber trees—*bam!*—silence.

"Have they gone?" Binh was too experienced to accept that. Another grenade, and again silence. Nothing moved under the rubber trees. Creeping to another position, Binh and Uyen carefully scanned the area in front. What was that unnatural thing at the edge of the rubber plantation? A strange tangle of light and shadow. Binh heard Uyen's sharp intake of breath, and he leaned closer, placing his ear to Uyen's mouth.

"There," pointing finger silhouetted, "the three of them together."

Binh concentrated and suddenly the odd tangle of light and shadow resolved itself into the unmoving bodies, arms, and legs of their three comrades.

Binh felt the hair lift on his nape; under the cloak of the rubber-tree shadow lurked death: implacable, impersonal, final.

Though he knew now it was useless, they threw their remaining grenades into the silent, unresponding trees, returned to the waiting group under the mango tree and dispersed.

The dawn light crept up over the sky, seeping under the rubber canopy, and gradually the occupants of the other pits became visible: first, dark shapes, then the difference in texture of earth, leaves, shirts, skin, and hair became apparent. The brown wood and black metal of rifle, brass of machine gun belt, dark shadow pools of eyes in stubbled faces, quietly, patiently waiting for "stand-down." The clearing patrol quietly drifts around its arc, files in, and sinks into its individual pits. Nothing.

Three paces from the machine gun lay the stiff bodies—Trinh face up, eyelids drooping over cold glass eyes staring down that long distance.

"Hey, look at this bastard," nudging Trinh with a red-dirt crusted boot, "he was selling bloody pineapples back in town yesterday!"

"Yer fuckin' right, cob. Little prick."

The "Baron" looked up from searching the bodies, "Private Grinnell, don't touch those grenades! We don't know how they've been treating them, or what condition they're in. The Pioneers will look after them. Unload the M1 and take it over to CHQ."

Graham Prentice lay on his stomach, shadowed by the broad-leaved bush, staring out at the expanse of jungle. Nothing stirred under the hot sun. The rich green tropical growth was motionless under the blazing sun.

"Fuckin' hell. There's no bastard out there," Faintly behind him, he could hear the chunk of digging at the company position.

"No bloody nog is gonna scrub-bash through that shit."

Fumbling at his thigh pocket, Prentice pulled out the American paperback he had bought at the PX. Opening it, he began to read the exploits of the hard-fisted, hard-drinking private eye. Lying like this was uncomfortable, so gradually Prentice drew himself into a sitting position, webbing hanging open, rifle across knees, book open. The sun slid around, and Prentice was sitting in a patch of sunlight. A shadow moved across the page, and he looked up, frowning, as Binh pushed the M1 muzzle to within inches of his eyes and fired. Prentice's head snapped back, but his body remained upright, blood and brains running down his shirt and across the pages where . . .

"Cleve Harkson drew his fingernails gently up the length of one firm white thigh, looking deep into her blue eyes now dark with passion."

"In-fucking-credible," snarled Razor Sharp. "Reading a fuckin' stick book on sentry. A complete waste. His parents raised him. He joined up. He's been trained, paid, fed, clothed, and brought here to soldier. All he had to do was lie there and stay awake. Commonsense should have told him. What's the use? He's dead because of his own stupidity, his mates have got to do more now, the army has to send his body back and bury it, his parents and friends are going to grieve, and we've got to fly another Digger up here because that boy lacked self-discipline. A complete waste, just a bloody waste!"

Seizing his entrenching tool, he expended his anger on the rich red soil at the bottom of his pit. The surrounding Diggers of BHQ discreetly remained quiet, watching the red soil fly up out of the excavation.

Benson became aware of Bennett shaking his shoulder, face frowning with concern.

"Skip! come on! Skip!"

As the black treacle surged back into that bottomless pit under his skull, Benson sighed and resigned himself to the inevitable interview with the CO and medical officer. Whatever this darkness was that overwhelmed him when shots were fired in the real thing, he would have to speak of it.

"Okay Augie. It's all right."

And with the words, Bennett understood what was meant, what Benson had decided, and relief and compassion mixed in his gaze.

Not knowing of Prentice's death or the RSM's rage, Corporal Andy Barker of D Company led two of his soldiers out to the position selected as the company sentry place; on the edge of the minor growth under the older trees lying fallow, the position commanded a good view out over the lower, sparser growth extending to the road. The two privates settled down in the growth, observing the sunlit scene before them. Nothing moved; nothing happened: the sun beat down.

"Hey," whispered Steve Carruthers to Kev Crowe, "wish to Christ I was back in Aussie on a day like this. Down to Maroubra or Coogee . . ." His voice trailed off, eyes blank, mind visualizing the golden sand, surf, blue sky and sea, bikinis, cold cans of Reschs.

"Hmm, bloody terrific," agreed Crowe.

"Christ, all those hawkers around the town yesterday, not a bloody one to be seen. I could really have a fresh pineapple, Crowey."

"Shut up, fuck ya, Steve."

"Look, there's no bastard around here. There hasn't been a thing since we got here. All these nogs are in their hammocks at this time of day. Let's have a cup of coffee, ay?"

"What, here?"

"Yeah, come on."

"I dunno, bloody hell, Steve," voice trailing away in doubt.

"Come on," Carruthers opening his small pack and removing solid fuel, folding metal burner, coffee and sugar, tin of rations and opener.

"I'm goin' out here in the clear ground."

Crowe followed, and the two picnickers sat comfortably against adjoining trees, fires flaming merrily under metal canteen cups, opening tins of rations and chattering about leave.

Binh and Uyen, cautiously threading their way through the growth of jungle, caught the whiff of the distinctive fumes from the solid fuel. They exchanged glances, crouched lower, and crept forward.

Peering up the lane that had previously been an access road but was now growing over, they saw a lovely target. Two foreigners, backs toward them, busily cooking.

The Vietnamese crouched and very carefully scanned the area, bush by bush, shadow by shadow, open dirt areas, inch by inch, to find any sign of a trap or other Australians: nothing.

Binh smiled at Uyen, tapped his own M1 and pointed to the man on the right, reached out, tapped the barrel of Uyen's PPS M1943 and pointed to the man on the left. Uyen nodded and began to raise the Russian submachine gun, perforated barrel-jacket edges gleaming in the sun where the blueing had worn off.

Carruthers leaned sideways to stir his coffee and Binh fired; the rounds hit him in the shoulder instead of the head. Uyen saw dirt and leaves leaping around his target, then both green figures were gone into the denser growth.

Binh and Uyen were already running, dodging through the bushes and trees.

Back under the rubber plantation, in its cool, muted green light, CHQ and the remaining platoon were seizing weapons and tumbling into pits. Through the rubber trees, two hatless, weaponless figures came running, staggering, and collapsed at the CHQ pits. The medic was up and examining the prone, gasping figures before the first question could be shot at them.

"Don't know—what happened—ow! We were—quietly there, and they shot us—ow! Bugger yer, Blue, go easy!"

"Baron" Lord stood, looking at the wounds, eyes narrowed, "Private Carruthers, how is it you're shot in the back of the shoulder, and you, Crowe, are shot in the arse? Come on!"

"Er—ouch—they musta got behind us, sir."

Turning to "Red" Ryder, "Baron" snapped, "I think they've pissed off. I only heard one M1 and the burp gun.

How about if I take a section out and check the area?"

"Hmm, okay, CSM. Take the platoon radio. Mr. Gordon," raising his voice across the intervening fifty yards, "the CSM will take one of your sections and your radio to sweep the area," pointing in the direction from which the two bleeding figures had come.

"Right, sir. Corporal Cole, saddle up. Bill," to the signaler, "you too."

The section climbed out, buckled webbing belts, gave weapons a last check, and moved into a dispersed line, silhouetted against the light seeping under the edge of the rubber-tree canopy.

The medic examined the wounds in Crowe's buttock, took a scalpel from his medical kit, and sliced along a dark swelling. He placed both thumbs alongside the cut and pushed: out popped a bloody black blob. He picked it up with tweezers, sloshed water over it, and placed it in Crowe's hand.

"There ya go, Crowey, souvenir. Seven-point-nine-two burp gun slug. The Yanks will dig out the other back there."

Turning to "Red" Ryder, he asked, "How about we get 'em moving up to the pad, sir?"

"Red" Ryder glanced towards the area "Baron" was sweeping, frowned and nodded, "Okay, Private Carruthers, you can walk. Two of you take Crowe over on a stretcher."

Saplings were quickly cut, trimmed, and pushed through the sleeves along the edge of the li-lo cover. Crowe was placed face down, bandaged bare buttocks ignominiously displayed under flapping shirt tails—white flesh contrasting strongly with green cloth—and carried away with Carruthers walking alongside, out of the life of the company.

Captain Gerald Lomax stepped inside Tregonne's tent at the main camp. The second-in-command was shirtless, seated at his blanket-covered field table, fingers tapping on a sheet of paper on the table top,

"You want to see me, sir?"

"Ah yes, Gerry, sit down. Smoke?"

"Thank you sir."

"Your Pioneers did a good job with the battalion sign;

it's the biggest and best in the area. What I want now is the tallest flagpole in the area. The engineers will build it; you put it up. Look at this; it will show you where and how big to construct the bases for the pole and the guy wires."

"Ah yes. You're having it made of waterpipe, sir?"

"Yes. We've got it, haven't we?"

"Yes sir, but . . ."

"I don't want any buts, Captain. This battalion is going to have the tallest flagpole."

"Very good sir."

"Well, RSM, here's our flagpole."

"Big one, sir."

"Hmm-mmh. The tallest in the area."

"It looks as if it's made of waterpipe. It won't support its own weight, you know, sir."

"RSM, I don't want to hear why it won't do this, can't do that. We'd get nowhere if I listened to all the negative thinkers around here. Now get those Pioneers busy."

"Yes sir."

"Well, there she goes, RSM, what did I tell you," as the tall, slender white flagpole with its cross bar rose elegantly against the blue sky and stood with the sun gleaming on its freshly painted surfaces, then gracefully curtsied—bending at ankle, knee, waist, and neck—and subsided into the red dust of the parade ground.

The RSM stood silently, knowing he would never utter one of the several witty, scathing remarks flitting through his mind.

"Humph. Well yes. RSM, get that truck up here and get it removed. A shorter one will still be taller than the one at brigade."

Claudia Ryder put down her novel as the doorbell rang, rose, smoothed her skirt, and opened the door.

A man stood at the bottom of the two steps that lead up to the entrance to the ground floor flat rented by the Ryders in preference to an army married quarter. They had no children and preferred to live in town.

"Yes?"

"Mrs. Ryder? Wife of Major Ryder?"

"Yes." Had something happened to James? No, the army would inform her; the visitor in that event would be wearing uniform. Or it would be Muriel Burrows. Or a padre, or all three.

The man lowered his head into his shoulders, looked up from under his eyebrows and gave a small smile, "Your husband's a murderer. He's killing women and children. He's fucking Vietnamese harlots. You married a monster."

"What? Who are you?" Hand at her throat, Claudia stepped a half-pace back. Seeing this, the creature placed one foot on the bottom step.

"A monster, a murderer. He oughta get what he deserves."

"Get out. I'll call the police!"

"You haven't got a phone, Mrs. Ryder, I looked in the phone book."

"You despicable little man! I'll scream."

"Goodbye." Turning, he walked quickly away and was lost in the night.

Claudia shut the door and sank back into the chair. Who was he? What did he want? What did he mean about James? How did he know the address? Had he checked the phone? Was he still out there?

Switching on all the lights, she examined the window latches: nothing. Then rage ignited at the rear of her brain. Who the hell did he think he was coming here, spreading his sewage on James and herself? But how did he know? Would he come back?

The neighbors? In the year that they had been there, she and James had become acquainted with, and friends of, several other couples in the building. Mostly childless or with one small child; the other people were either under thirty or over sixty.

She made coffee and sat, brows knitted, trying to make sense of the visit.

Next day, from her desk at the office in the city, she telephoned the police, the army security branch, Muriel Burrows, and her own brother, who also lived in Sydney, so that evening she had several callers. The police and security men departed to compare her description of the man with their records; Muriel and her brother Rod settled back with their second coffee.

"Look Dee," said Rod, knees crossed and fingers drumming on the chair arm, "it's no real problem for Diana or me to stay with you or for you to stay with us. You're very welcome."

"Or with me," offered Muriel. "Now that the children are at school, I'm going mad trying to keep busy on those committees."

Claudia thought for a moment, then raised her eyes to each in turn.

"That's very very kind. Thank you both, but why should I run and let that little worm win? No! And please don't suggest a phone. All that means to me now is obscene phone calls. He's talking rubbish, but somehow he knows who I am. I want to find out how he knew."

"Now look, don't go doing anything silly. I'll be over tomorrow to put a deadlock on the door, and a bolt and chain."

"I'm not going to do anything foolish, but somehow he has access to information about me: where I live and what James does, for a start. Perhaps he could do the same thing to some poor woman who can't stand it as well as I. Now, don't worry. I'll be all right. Have you heard from the colonel?"

"Yes, they're all doing magnificently," and the talk turned to other subjects.

9

Les Fitzgibbon stood on the cleared hillside outside Cat Ben watching the gunships make strafing runs to the south, listening to the conversation between the ground forces and the helicopter crews blaring over a radio loudspeaker.

Suddenly he knew, as sure as the sun rose in the east, that the enemy would be met down there to the south. He frowned, shook his head, and glanced at the other company members sitting or lying around the slope. The inevitable cigarettes were curling blue-gray smoke, the green clothes were red-tinted from the soil, the faces laughing or tired, and he knew in his bones that some of these men would be killed and wounded in a short time from now, when he sat on that cleared slope, in the sun, overlooking the red-tiled roofs of Cat Ben.

The trucks rolled roaring into view and halted at the foot of the slope, engines rumbling and snorting with puffs of blue exhaust. Rear ramps dropped and lay open like great Ubangi lips.

"Right, saddle up."

The battalion was moving to an area south of Cat Ben to search for VC thought to be there; it lay directly to the east of the Iron Triangle, which had been well covered.

With the speed they had come to expect, a mass of black clouds roiled and rolled over the puny cumulus, blotting out the sun, dragging with it the wind and an opaque skirt of rain. The storm struck as the vehicles grumbled along the road—the rain cascaded down the wind, and in minutes the ground was covered with sheets of silver-gray water flowing down every slope, filling every dip and hollow. The dark foliage lashed to and fro in the howling blast of air and coconut fronds; twigs and leaves tumbled end over end down the wind.

"Jesus," thought Fitzgibbon, perched on top of a carrier, "this is just like a Hollywood scene: wind, rain, leaves, water, dark sky—the lot."

Looking down, he saw puddles formed in the folds of his shirt and trousers; the water had not been able to run away fast enough. Conversation was halted, the men sitting hunched under the sheer presence of the dark clouds, and the brute force of wind and rain beating on them.

The tracks pulled off the road next to an ARVN unit

that to the Australians strongly resembled a Beau Geste Hollywood cavalry fort into which a band of gypsies had moved with all their animals. The ARVN battalion was surrounded by a dirt wall six to ten feet high; inside could be glimpsed a conglomeration of buildings and tents, washing hung out to dry, radio masts and aerials, flags, shelter halves, sandbags, boxes and crates in which chickens and ducks cackled and quacked. On the parapet sat and stood assorted ARVN soldiers. Across the road was a straggling collection of cafes with open fronts, shops and houses, in and around which lounged more ARVN and the usual civilians, children, chickens, and dogs.

The ARVN commander and his entourage stood in a small group on the side of the track leading into his domain. The US adviser towered over the Vietnamese, yet another of the mass-produced US Army captains: tall, slim, twin bars of rank on collar and baseball-type cap, white teeth, thin-framed glasses, crew-cut, and innocent "I want to be your friend" eyes.

As the leading Australians walked up the slight slope and halted before what was obviously the ARVN command group, Fitzgibbon found himself not more than six feet away as Ryder introduced himself and told the American the rest of the battalion was following.

Water was still flowing in small rivulets down the slope between the blades of grass, dripping in crystal chips from the leaves of the bushes dotting the grazing area on which the ARVN fort was built.

The tall American introduced himself and the ARVN commander, and went on to say Major Tinh spoke very good English and had completed several courses at schools in the US.

On cue, the major nodded and stepped forward with a lieutenant who held the mapboard so the commanders could see it. Tinh pointed to their present location and said, in accented but easily understood English:

"Here is my unit. My men control all this area here," and the pencil indicated an area encompassing the ridge on which they stood, ground to the north and south, and out into the paddies. "There are no VC in this area," with an arrogant glance at the Australians standing in platoon groups, his tone indicating resentment that foreigners should be in his area.

Ryder replied as diplomatically as he could, "Thank you very much, Major Tinh. We'll sweep through then, into the area here," pointing to the western end of the ridge.

"Well, if there's nothin' here, what are we all doing here, soaked and more rain on the way?" thought Fitzgibbon, looking at Smacker and raising his eyebrows to indicate his feelings. Riley gave a slight smile, shrugged and lifted his eyebrows to mean, "the bastards don't know what they're doin' at the best of times."

The company moved out past the earth walls of the fort, shook out into a dispersed formation, and began to sweep forward under the gray sky, over the relatively open land: the only growth being saplings and bushes in clumps and lines, cut by small creeks and runnels. Water still trickled along these creeks and lay in pools in the holes, hollows, and dips, reflecting the gray underside of the clouds and the dark green shrubs.

An explosion: a voice shouts "contact front," the signal to close up and move forward; CSM "Baron" Lord calling to the HQ support section, green-clad shapes jogging forward.

Fitzgibbon took a firmer hold on his rifle; on his left strode Smacker. The section advanced across a clearing with a wall of bushes on the left, ground sloping away on the right through clumps of shrubbery.

"Where are you, Snowy?" from the platoon commander on the far side of the left-hand wall of shrubs.

"Over on this side," from Snowy Peters.

"Right, come over to me."

"Okay." Snowy turned and waved the scouts through the green mass, turned to follow and gestured the remainder to follow him. The scouts passed through the gap; Snowy, Blue Barnes, with the machine gun, and Smacker climbed a small bank and stepped into a narrow parting of the bushes; Fitzgibbon stopped, obeying the old training slogan—"don't bunch up"—and turned to follow the lines of bushes to find another gap.

The flat slam of an explosion: smoke, twigs, leaves, and a bush hat fly into the air. Smacker and Barnes roll screaming back through the bushes down the bank into the gray puddle there.

Christ, the bastards are in the bushes, down—peer in—fire—rifles forward—no! The rest of the platoon is only feet away on the other side. Grenade? Can't see any VC, any diggings, any sign—Smacker and Blue still screaming: "Les! Les!"

"Hang on, Smacker, hang on!"

The "Baron" shouting, "What's going on over there?"

"Two wounded over here, checking the area."

"Righto."

Turning to the other three, "Okay, be careful, watch that way," waving out over the slope falling away to the north, the smoke still hanging over the blasted area, a few leaves still twisting toward the ground. "It's only seconds since it happened, I'll see to Smacker," he thought.

Pack and webbing off, run over, he's lying in the puddle, now red with the blood pumping through the tears in his clothes. Christ, blood everywhere, where is he wounded? Legs, groin, shoulder, arms.

"You'll be all right mate," remembering the first aid lectures—"bullshit baffles brains, reassure the patient" —"We'll have you fixed up in no time."

The eyes full of pain, fright, bewilderment. This is my mate, Smacker, what have they done to you? Field dressing out of pocket, tear it open, sense of helplessness surges up, what fucking good is this little pad in the palm of my hand when he's got wounds bigger than this all over him? Where, which one am I going to put it on?

"Les! Les!"

"Yeah, mate," in tones for a hurt child, "you'll be okay, you're all right, we're gonna fix you up, no worries."

Then, literally jumping through the bushes, leaping and bounding over them, come two medics with all their gear: one kneels alongside in the red water.

"Hey Les, what are yer doin'?"

"G'day, Slim. Stupid bloody Smacker's copped it; silly bugger, ay, Smacker?"

"Well," unzipping the medical satchel, "bludging again, you bastard, Smacker? After a couple days light duties, so you can sneak off early and see Sharon, you shonky bastard. Okay, let's have a gander."

Chrome-gleaming scissors snipping away trousers, "Undo his webbing and pack, but don't move him, Les."

Unbuckle, unfasten, unstrap, so Smacker is lying in a nest of belt and straps. Scissors cutting the other trouser leg, now the shirt, peeling away the grimy dark green cloth impregnated with red dirt, water, mud, and blood, peeling it away like a skin, and there he is, pale flesh like a peeled fruit. Slim looks up.

"Both legs, groin, collar bone; give me a hand with these," pulling out of the satchel a clear plastic sleeve, "We pull it over the leg and blow it up, air pressure holds it rigid and tight."

"Fuckin' hell. Slim, who thought of that?"

"A Yank, I guess. Good idea, ay?"

Holes all over his legs, bone, flesh—Christ, all up around his crotch, I can see the inside of his balls—white tubing coiled round and round. Oh, Jesus, Smacker . . .

A figure standing over them in the gloom: the "Baron."

"Dust-off on the way, be here in three minutes. Get him over to the LZ. Make sure he's tagged, Private Fitzgibbon."

"Yessir. There you are, you lucky bastard. You're on the way—beautiful nurses waiting and all."

Slim looks up, "He's going into shock. Tie the tag on the dog-tag chain and let's get 'im over there."

Snowy, Blue, and Smacker were carried over to join the two casualties from the first explosion: five quiet prone figures, tattered remnants of dark green on arms and legs, bundles of pack and webbing tagged at each man's head, all ammunition and grenades removed before going under the Red Cross.

"Who the hell yelled 'contact front'? If we'd known it was a booby trap, we'd have taken care, and Snowy wouldn't have his feet blown off, and Blue and Smacker wouldn't be chopped about."

Whoever it was will never be known.

Here it comes—distant throbbing hum growing into a chopping roar, red and green lights burning so brilliant, so clean against the evening's dark clouds: pop—fizz—zz—zz, the yellow smoke boiling up marking the LZ. Huey circling, white background to Red Cross, helmeted heads peering down, level out, settling nose high, the attendant whirlwind beating at bushes, leaves and twigs curling up and away, wind pressing wet clothes against tired bodies, fluttering tags on packs, whipping loose ends of bandages; the skids on the ground, crew men leaping out, sliding stretchers out of the runners, handing each one to two Australians who run up, bowed under the the rotors whipping around, kneeling by each casualty for quick professional assessment of in-flight attention needed, and information to be radioed ahead to the waiting surgical teams. If the helicopter can get to the man, he can be taken from the battlefield to surgery in forty minutes at the most, which is far better than the victim of a city peak-hour accident can expect.

Okay, here he comes: bend down, squeeze uninjured shoulder, grin, grab stretcher handles, up, over, in he slides like a lifesize toy with those grotesque plastic legs over which the last drops of red muddy water are being driven by the rotor blast. Move back, standing braced against the wind, rotor note changes, machine lifting against the dark sky, nose dips, and they're away, silhouetted dragonfly-shape against the western light, red glowing eyes on the flying thing: one burning steadily on the side over the door, one flashing brightly on the roof, gaining height to the south.

Okay, back to the section, walking carefully, how can you see a booby trap now? Fuck it. Dig a shell, scrape just deep enough to get you below ground level. Don't want to eat; force something down. Sleeping in bloody wet clothes again, bugger it . . .

And so began the purgatory.

The company went out searching and found nothing;

the explosions slammed out across the bushes, and the Dust-offs flew in, lifting away the two or three grimy figures trailing their tattered clothes and bandage ends in the wind. The rain washed away any traces of the emplacement of the mines and booby traps: one, five, ten, or forty men could walk past or over the thing, until one man brushed the twig or put his foot in the necessary place and . . .

The locals, knowing the area like the back of their hand, and covered by the wind and the rain, wormed in to emplace new devices. The patrolling, probing Australians rarely saw them—why wait for battle? The foreigners are killing themselves on our traps.

As blood flowed, so it began to boil.

Hard faces with tight lips and icy eyes stared toward the ARVN fort and the indolent shapes on the wall and in the cafes across the road.

"We oughta go back there and round those bastards up and force them out across here. They never patrolled here in their fuckin' lives, the noggie bastards!"

Les Fitzgibbon related the words of Major Tinh, adding outrage to outrage. Weapons were tapped and stroked, and the talk spread, from savage man to savage man, from section to section, platoon to platoon, and company to company. The frustration and hate sown by each explosion during the useless searching focussed on the ARVN, who were a visible presence. The disgust and hatred was deeper and more implacable than that held for the VC, who were not deeply hated, only disliked as the enemy.

"We're losin' blokes here for nothing. We're doing their job while the mongrels are lyin' back in hammocks watchin' the Dust-offs" snarled Frank Gardiner, jawline rigid, nostrils flaring, tears of rage trickling down his cheeks as he watched the Dust-off thrum away south with the corpse of Barry Reimann and the wounded body of Geoff Bates.

Two sobbing women were brought in: they had been seen leaving the village and making their way across the top of the area, furtively scuttling from bush to bush.

Bruce Myers's platoon saw them, followed them, and were interested witnesses to a meeting between the women and five armed men. The women began to return.

"Okay quick." Myers lowered his binoculars, turning to "Tommy" Tomlinson, "Get Dwarf to engage the men," turning to the sergeant, "Bart! Stay with Tommy, I'll take the other two sections after the sheilas."

"Right Skip. C'mon Dwarf, here's yer chance. Five of the bastards standing near the fan-shaped bush . . . see 'em? Range: 300; try ten round bursts when yer ready."

Dwarf estimated the distance through slitted eyes, adjusted his rear sight, checked the belt of gleaming brass rounds, snuggled the butt into his shoulder, placed the foresight on the group of tiny manikins, inhaled, held it, and squeezed.

The belt wiggled like a live thing up into the slot in the left side of the feed-plate cover and from the other side spewed the smoking shining empty cases and the black hooded-links that held the belt together; the tracer streaked out along its invisible path, and the five figures were flung down as the long foresight wiped them away.

"Down a bit, Dwarf!" shouted Tommy, between bursts, peering through his binoculars, "put a whole belt into 'em!" and the gun rattled on, dirt spouting amid and near the writhing bodies trying to stand up or crawl away but being remorselessly driven down by the magic, terrible fist that was all around them.

"You bloody beauty!" The frustrations of the day lifted, were dissipated by success. "C'mon, let's get up there!"

The five lay like abandoned puppets, arms and legs at awkward angles, weapons scattered, bags of food split, and great fans of rice flicked over the bodies and grass by the impact of the 7.62mm rounds arriving at 2,800 feet per second. All the corpses had multiple wounds: brains and entrails mixed with rice, fish, oil, and bread.

They were quickly searched, their weapons collected, and the two sobbing terrified women hustled back to the battalion area where they were held in the company.

"They probably think they're gonna be raped," said

Bartholomew. "Different game now, ay love?" Grabbing one by the hair and forcing her to look at him. "You and yer boyfriends lost this one." Teeth bared in a ferocious smile, pitiless eyes and tone of voice gave the meaning of the words even if the women could not understand.

It was dusk when the company area was reached. The women were tied and placed under a bush; their moaning and wailing never ceased.

"They're gonna give our position away," muttered Herb Knowles, voicing the thoughts of every man.

"Sir, how about a pill to put 'em to sleep?"

"Okay doc, see what you can do."

"No dice, the bitches keep spitting them out. We tried to trick 'em by taking aspirin ourselves, but no go."

Bartholomew waited till the medic had gone, then leaned over, darker than the bushes and grass in the gloom.

"Look Skip, they're a danger to us, no two ways about it. I'll cut their throats if you like, we'll bury them, and that'll be the end of it."

"No thanks, Bart. Too many people have seen them, and the wheels know they're here. Gag 'em and leave 'em."

"All right then."

Later, Bartholomew wondered what had happened to him, that he could calmly consider cutting two throats when normally he would not abide swearing in the presence of women. Is it just the last few days or the whole thing? With a mind-chilling tremor, he realized he did not want to return to Australia; he would be happy, looked forward to, extending his tour and staying on with the next unit to come over.

Staring up at the clouds and stars, Bartholomew admitted to himself that he was enjoying the danger, looked forward to each operation, each patrol, each ambush, each encounter. He turned onto his side, wiggled into a comfortable position, and slept peacefully.

The useless probing continued, till "Red" Ryder lost three more men guiding another platoon along a track that had been cleared the evening before. As the explosion crashed out, the column halted.

"Oh, Jesus Christ," came a soft, resigned voice full of dread.

"Wait where you are," came up the line from man to man, Ryder grabbed the radio handset, called the HQ, and, frowning, set off back down the track.

Stan-the-Man Burrows sat with Bob Edmondson on the edge of the HQ pits. He looked up as Ryder halted before him, early morning sun on his freshly shaven cheeks.

"Sir, I've lost nineteen men for nothing in this area. The battalion has found nothing. I protest to you now about this waste and I'll take it further if I have to."

Burrows clenched his jaw, reddened, inhaled, and looked fiercely at the younger officer, then exhaled and said, "All right James. Bring 'em back. I'll stop this," turning to the silent watching signaler. "Get me brigade."

So ended the useless expenditure of flesh.

However, the god of war was preparing the dice for another roll on which depended the fate of the ARVN unit, now safely behind its walls.

Back in the base camp, the task of maintaining dominance of the area on the north continued between operations. Return from operations, out on patrol, in from patrol, out on operations.

The platoon was providing security for the mortars, who had gone out to the edge of the river and fired across at old known camps. Not a particularly exciting or dangerous task.

One man suddenly began to shake and tremble uncontrollably; tears streamed down his cheeks.

"Christ Jack! What's up mate?"

I d-d- dunno. I c-can't s-stop. It's th-the m-m-mortars," hands over ears, huddled up.

"But they're firin' into D-Zone!"

"Y-Y-Y-Yeah."

"Christ, Sammy—dive over and get the boss and the medic."

Back at the Regimental Aid Post, Major Prendergast, the medical officer, sat down and looked at the man's slumped shoulders, quivering spasms around his lips, teeth marks on knuckles where the soldier had bitten, downcast eyes.

"Okay, Private Brannigan. What is your job in the section?"

"Forward scout, sir." Eyes raised for a moment.

"How long have you been forward scout?"

"Since we got here—six months."

"How many operations have you done?"

"The lot." Fingers drumming on thigh.

"Hmm, and how much leave have you had?"

"Once to Saigon, sir." Fingers stop.

"All right. Do you want to stay in the company? I can have you given a job in admin. company, you know."

Voice trembles, but eyes raised to the doctor's "I want to stay with the section."

"Hmm-m. I'll see. I'll keep you here tonight, and we'll see. Okay? Now, wait in the next room, tell Staff Bowlinham I want to see him."

"Yes sir."

The soldier went out and Prendergast picked up the field telephone, ringing vigorously.

"Switch, the MO speaking. I want to speak to the CO. Hello sir, Prendergast. I'll like to speak to you about medical matters, please. . . . Very well, sir."

Later . . .

"Good evening sir." Stamping dirt from his boots on the steps leading into the tent.

"Ah, good evening Eric. Sit down. Drink?"

"Oh, thank you—that's enough, thanks sir."

"Now then," Burrows leaned back, legs clad in long trousers, sleeves rolled down as antimalarial precautions, "What do you want to see me about? Not VD I hope?"

"No," laughing briefly, "but seriously, if VD were a problem, this one wouldn't be."

"Oh?" placing his glass on the table top, both feet on the floor, his hands on his thighs. Stan-the-Man looked directly into the doctor's eyes. "What is it?"

"Today, I had the third case in two days of worn-out forward scouts—men who've been here for six months and have been on patrol after patrol, operation after operation. They are tired: yes, and frightened. But no man can go on forever. Lord Moran puts it very well in *Anatomy of Courage*. Each man has a 'bank account' of courage; every time he draws on it, the balance dwindles. Once it's gone, it's gone. The balance can be husbanded, or eked out, and can be replenished with leave, good food, rest, and general attention to his health and hygiene."

"Yes, yes. How serious is this in the companies?"

"Not really big, but that's why I'm here now, before it's reached the stage of affecting the battalion as a whole."

"So. I can't get more leave for us; we are part of the brigade, and only five percent can go on leave at any time, you know. More beer? films? books? sports? We have an infantry battalion to run here. We have to run ourselves, and mount operations and secure out there up to the river," waving toward the back of the tent. "We also are restricted to so many on the roster for the rest center at Vung Tau. Headquarters in Saigon and the logistic people over there," hand waved toward the tent front, "also get the use of the place."

"Well sir, I *would* like to see the man who does operations get precedence for leave and rest. There are people in BHQ and admin. company who never go on operations, who have vehicles, who are in town every day and have girlfriends there. Yet, they get equal leave or more leave than the rifleman."

Stan sat for a moment, sipped his drink, then, "Very well. Thank you Eric. I want you to work closely with your chaps in the companies—I know you do now," nodding, hand lifted to acknowledge the unspoken comment, "and keep me informed of this nerves business. We're approaching the period when it can be expected to become a problem, unless we catch it. Hmm? Finished your drink? Another?"

"Look uncle, you can't stop here. It will be very dangerous if shooting starts."

"I do not care! I want to fish!"

"What ya gonna do, Freddo, call 'im a cab?" grinned one of the onlookers.

Fredericks controlled his annoyance and wondered how he was going to get eighty-year-old Nguyen van Ngo to return to his home voluntarily. He took the old man's thin arm and gestured over the surrounding area: at the convoys rolling by, the artillery going into the position, and the soldiers walking past.

"Uncle Ngo, if the VC attack, you will be in danger here. If there is a battle, it will be a big one."

Ngo sat in the middle of the path, arm folded, a small, defiant figure in dusty black clothes and conical straw hat, surrounded by the mechanized war machine. The wrinkled face was set, the jaw stubbornly firm.

"I want to fish!"

They had come across Ngo and two woodcutters on the edge of an area abandoned to the VC, into which yet another search mission was being mounted. The woodcutters went quickly, but old Ngo, with the single-mindedness of the aged, decided he would fish, foreign soldiers or not, NLF, VC, Viet Minh, French colonialists, or river demons included.

Fredericks turned to Edmondson and gave a slight shrug, "We can't really force him to go, sir. And he's stuck on fishing."

Their problem was solved by the crash of an artillery salvo fired; Ngo leaped up, old man's stubbornness replaced by old man's fear. "Hai! hai!"

Fredericks seized the opportunity, "Uncle Ngo, you would be better at home alive with no fish, than here dead with fish."

"You are right, young man, you are right. I'm going." He swung easily onto his bicycle and pedaled quickly away down the red dirt road.

"Look at that old bastard!"

"Tell ya what, if I can handle a bike like that at eighty, I'll be okay."

"Eighty years old, ay? Jesus."

And where a battalion of ARVN drew only contempt, old Ngo was admired as he pedaled away.

"We couldn't have the old bugger around. If something happened to him, it'd be a shame."

"Christ, what a real bastard of an area! Everything creeps, crawls, or has thorns on it! Jeeesus!"

Father Tompkins lifted his sweat rag and wiped his streaming face. Prichard stood in the normal stance of the laden infantryman—bent forward slightly at the waist to relieve the weight of the pack on his back, rifle balanced on right ammo pouch. Their sweat had darkened their shirt fronts, leaving the pockets as lighter rectangles; it has soaked through the shirt backs, through the canvas packs, into the contents. Where clothing or towel was used to provide a soft layer against the spine, it was also wet.

"Talk about mad dogs and Englishmen! We must be trying to catch the bastards in their hammocks. No one with brains moves during the middle of the friggin' day, for fuck's sake!"

Tom did not reply; he was feeling too ill from the heat. He jerked his head forward, informing Father that the line was moving. So, in the blazing noon and early afternoon hours, they moved through an area consisting of patches of jungle—tall, green, vine-draped, cool—and areas of long grass dotted with clumps and patches of shrubbery and thorn bushes. The sun bounced off the grass wringing sweat from every pore. The thought of food from the tins of rations turned stomachs.

The distant roar of jet engines turned faces up, eyes slitted against the white, blinding sun—there, four silver F100s, flat oval fish-mouth forward-thrusting air intake, flat slab bellies, and rounded haunches from which rose the tall tapering tail. There they circle, silver against the azure sky, sun glinting off canopies, rolling in, level wings, diving, diving in arrow-straight line directly overhead, great flare of flame under the nose, smoke trails flick back under the silver bellies—pub, bub, bub, bub; pub bub, bub, bub; pub, bub, bub—out of sight over the tree tops. Wonder what the flying qualities of the empty 20mm cannon shells are? Because there are hundreds in the air over our heads, and they could cause more than a little consternation, arriving among us at a speed of about 450 knots and from a height of 2,000 feet. . . .

Thank Christ, moving into the cool gloom of the jungle: not very large, sunlight can be seen shining on the grass on the other side. Snapping fingers, the scouts pointing; section and platoon commander forward, "Who's that mob over there? The pricks oughta stay in their own area."

Green-clad figures with floppy bush hats are visible in the trees on the far side of the grass.

"Dunno, must be those mugs in Bravo. What d'ya reckon, boss?" turning to the lieutenant peering across the golden radiance reflected from the grass.

"Looks like Bravo over there; lost, ay?"

"Hmm, looks like it. Is that Corporal Macintosh near the red-flowering bush? He's the bloke who rides that motorbike back in Australia, isn't he?"

"I think it is, yer know," waving across the grass.

"Come on, we'll give them curry—can't read a map, the silly buggers."

"Looks like they're comin' over to us."

Both groups wade out into the waist-high grass, exchanging waves—hang on, we don't wave like that—their hats . . .

"Skip! They're . . ."

"Hai! Dich! Dich!"

"Look out! VC!"

A great burst of firing shattered the afternoon calm; bark, twigs, and leaves showered from the trees as both sides blazed away, moving back out of the killing ground of the grassy area, into the trees.

"Jesus, Skipper, that was close!"

"Too right. Quick, Section Commanders, anyone hit?"

"All okay."

"All here, Skip."

"We're right too."

"Good, good, Cunning bastards, trying to lure us into a trap."

"Comrade commander, no casualties."

"Ah, good, good. Very devious, the Australians, are they not? Trying to lure us into a trap by waving and making signs of friendship. Where there are some, we can expect to find more. We must leave quickly before their artillery and aircraft fall on us. Quickly, Ba Dinh's squad as vanguard, by the northern route to Camp 12."

"Yes, comrade."

As a rainy day closed in Sydney, Claudia Ryder put her key in the lock.

"Hello Mrs. Ryder, Claudia."

She spun around, key half turned; there he stood, in the shadows behind her, one foot forward, hands at sides, head down.

"You!" She froze with shock, at the same time trying to see him clearly through the gloom—nondescript dark trousers and jacket, dark hair, eyes shadowed, no accent, about five feet six.

"Yes, Heard from him? Tells you how he kills the women and kids, does he? And tells..."

"You worm! He's a man doing man's job! Unlike you."

"I'm gonna write to him and tell him you go out with other men. And that you go to bed with them."

"I don't go to bed with other men," she flared.

"I'll tell him different," and he was gone.

Knees trembling, she entered and dropped her shopping basket and handbag, sank into a chair and tried to regain control. What to do? At least write to James, telling him the whole thing, emphasizing that he must not worry. Tomorrow, ring the police and army security again. First of all, coffee and a cigarette.

The helicopter thrummed up and away, and the men on the ground began distributing the rations and letters that had been delivered.

Tom Pritchard walked around the perimeter of the platoon, dropping envelopes next to the prone figures.

"Father, two for you.... Nimbus, here y'go. Ya sheila's written to tell you that you're a daddy...Frank...Knowlesy ... Dwarf...Sir, one for you, one for Bart, here ya are, Les, the lucky last. Who'd write to you? None of the birds you know, can write."

Fitzgibbon tore open the white envelope, and a huge smile broke. "Hey, it's from bloody Smacker!"

"Yeah? What does he say?"

"Hang on, hang on. He's back in Australia. . . . out at Ingleburn; . . . he's okay, got everything he should. have. The Yanks wanted to cut off his legs, shit ay? . . . But he wouldn't let 'em. They did a bloody good job on him, according to the doctors at Ingleburn. . . . He's got plastic veins in his legs. . . . Christ, what can't they do now? But he's okay."

"Great, mate."

"Yeah. Good. The ol' bastard. Probably spinning war stories to the bloody nurses." Les began packing the ration tins into his pack, gone the dim weight that had been in his chest since that day outside the ARVN fort, when he stood watching the helicopter lights flitting away south.

Augie Bennett checked the platoon's location on the map, then slid it back into the thigh pocket of his trousers. Another forty minutes and he would halt them for a rest. Since Benson had gone to HQ in Saigon, he had been platoon commander, except for the ten days Lieutenant Harrison had been with them. Now, Harrison was on a light diet at the hospital, having fallen into a storm-water drain and smashed his teeth on the edge of the steel plate used as a bridge. Unkind souls in the mess said Harrison had been pushed.

Bennett nodded to the section commander of the leading section and made a forward sweeping motion with his left arm. The kneeling scouts rose and moved off under the tall dark trees, stepping quietly through the soft green light filtering through the leaves. The platoon strung out, moving slowly past the huge bushes, avoiding the thorns, prickles, and hooks on the leaves, branches, trunks, and vines in their path. The line curved to the right as the scouts paralleled a grassy clearing about seventy yards across—a pool of reflected molten yellow light seen through the curtain of green shrubbery.

The line halted as one man when the black-clad figure stepped out of the green curtain of the foliage at the far side of that grassy clearing. Invisible in their own jungle gloom, they watched as a second, third, fourth VC began crossing the sunlit patch, weapons slung or perched on their shoulder, faces shadowed under spherical-crowned cloth hats, chinstraps hanging loose to the base of their throat, checked scarves around their neck.

Bennett looked left and right and decided he had no time to alter greatly his dispositions: the platoon was already in a curve around the clearing, so he merely waved them forward, closer to the edge. Faces were determined, smiling or worried, depending on the outlook of the man. Bennett halted, extending both arms sideways from the shoulders, parallel to the ground, stopping the platoon; weapons came up as the firers remained standing, knelt or lay down, depending on the weapon and field of fire.

Number 3 Company of the Second Battalion, Q907 Regiment, was moving southwest to a Battalion RV, Number 8 Platoon leading. They were making good time. Platoon Commander Quyet Do estimated after another four hours' travel, they would be well out of the area where they might meet foreign troops. Then the battalion would attack their guns from the rear. Quyet Do grimaced as he stepped out into the furnace heat of the sun; in front, the backs of the two leading men swayed as they waded through the high grass: "Oh, it's so hot"; only a few paces, and they would be in the cool green shadows.

A wall of noise slammed out, and in the moment before, he was blown off his feet; Quyet Do saw many muzzle flashes in the gloom before him. He lay on his back, staring at the grass glistening before his eyes, curving away up to the blue sky. As he watched, several stalks were severed by an invisible scythe and toppled. He was aware of the roar of firing and screams and cries from his own people. Something was tugging at his pack; he turned his head and saw Be of the Ninth Platoon pulling him back by the pack strap. Quyet Do lay quietly, unresisting; he would have to conserve his energy for the hours' long journey by stretcher through the jungle to the hospital, with its white-gowned staff under the tall trees. Looking down over his reddened shirt front, he saw he was leaving a wet-glistening crimson trail in the grass; busy ants were already investigating it.

The return fire prevented any maneuvers by Bennett, and realizing he had hit a numerically superior force, he withdrew seventy-five yards to his left rear, went into all-round defense and began to call in artillery and air strikes before moving.

Meanwhile, Chinh Tien, the commander of Three Company, was organizing the evacuation of the many dead and wounded, and the retrieval of as many packs and weapons as possible. He decided to use one squad to fight any rear guard or decoy actions; everybody else would be necessary to carry the dead, wounded, and equipment. His aim now was preservation of his company; they must get as far as possible away from this place as quickly as possible. The enemy artillery and aircraft would be upon them at any moment.

"Mau len, faster."

For some reason, the enemy fire had slackened.

"Mau len!"

Tinh Phong, the political officer, knelt by one of the wounded, deftly fastening a bandage around the bleeding neck. Chinh Tien halted. "We must move in one minute, comrade."

Turning to the commander of Seven Platoon, "Comrade Nghiep, send three men as a vanguard; we are moving to Camp 31."

Beckoning the remaining platoon commander to join their little group, Chinh glanced around the scene: comrades dragging dead and wounded by, others bent under their loads of weapons and packs, yet others firing into the jungle across the clearing. The slaughter had been so great and so sudden that there had been no time to begin outflanking movements, and by great good fortune, the enemy appeared to have been a small group, but he had no time to pursue them now. Chinh addressed his audience of three, "Comrades, we are going to Camp 31."

Tinh Phong nodding approval.

"Three men of Seven Platoon lead the way, then Seven with the dead and wounded, Nine with more wounded and packs and weapons, then the rear guard, the remainder of Eight. Questions? Good, quickly now!"

The heavily laden groups moved away, swinging into the gliding, jogging, mile-eating pace of the Asian burden-carrier. Behind them the rear guard surveyed the scene: ripped and splintered tree trunks, reek of gunfire, crushed bushes and trodden down grass, empty cartridge cases, blood-stained clothing, a hat, smell of blood, a riddled and tattered pack, pools of blood, and a puddle of brains with eager flies swarming and busy disciplined columns of ants. On the far side of the now disturbed grass in its pool of golden light, the impassive green jungle stared back at them.

The first artillery round impacted with a roar 200 yards to their right rear: time to go.

The bus grumbled away down the street in a cloud of diesel fumes, and Jackie Myers trotted up the steps to the apartment block, inserted the small key into the door of the mail box, and withdrew a half-dozen letters. Crumpling the advertising blurbs, she dropped them into a convenient cigarette tray at the elevator door.

Upstairs, with coffee and a cigarette, she read the letters, keeping the two from Bruce till last. Instead of the written word, she seemed to hear his voice speaking, could see him smiling as he related the anecdotes, see his eyes as the endearments flowed.

Finished, she carefully placed them with all the others in the drawer of the bedside table and stood before a photograph of him taken at the Clifton Gardens Hotel, outside on the terrace: Bruce just beginning to smile at a remark, looking around at the camera, and in the background the sunny Harbor and a passing yacht.

With her fingertips, she gently touched the photo, murmuring, "Bruce, Bruce . . . please be careful, come back safe to me," a deep breath, "but until then I have to live. I'm not going to be a cabbage. I love you, but I must live while you're away."

Turning, she placed him in the part of her mind and soul she reserved for them both, where lived their happiness of bygone days and hopes for the days to come—the happiness when he returned; she drew the screen and opened the part for living today and now.

She undressed and went into the shower. Harry Brandon had an exhibition by a new South Australian artist at Jaralee, and she wanted to be there before everything was plastered with red dots.

10

"Wonder what training camp these leeches come from? Look at 'em, charging like screaming hordes."

"I've seen Malaya, Canungra, all the training areas in Australia, and I've never seen 'em like this, never."

Searching along creeks in the southern edge of the main mass of jungle, thousands upon thousands of leeches were encountered. Men would move along till the first one was seen on somebody—then the whole platoon began to itch and felt leeches all over them. Some men could not bear them, others ignored them completely; most endured them till the halts, then burned the swollen dark blobs or sprinkled salt, or mosquito repellent, on them. But still they came, with their obscene blind seeking, stretching, waving, sensing, and rushing toward the victim with the terrible sequence of stretch out, head down, tail forward to join the head in a loop, stretch out again. Where one found a place, others followed: entry through the rips in the cloth, the eyelet of a boot, the gap between trouser and boot top, on hands and arms, through trouser flies, waistbands, on necks, ears and faces, or even by penetrating the weave of cloth.

On the move, men's attention was on their surroundings; halted, they looked down to see the black monsters on exposed flesh or clustered in hideous clumps of six, eight, a dozen around their calves. In the gloom of the jungle floor, mates checked each other's heads and backs for the little beasts. Everyone dreaded having one crawl up to, or into, a body orifice, which happened but rarely. Men walked on with lower trouser legs, socks and canvas jungle boots stiff with blood where the leech clusters had sucked. Blood flowed after they had been removed as nature had provided the leeches with an anticoagulant to ensure that the supply kept coming.

"Dunno what we're fightin' 'em for over this part of the bloody country," whispered Father Tomkins to Pritchard at one of the halts.

Nimbus Farley paused, squeezing mosquito repellent onto a writhing mass on his left calf. "Wonder how the VC sheilas get on? How do they get on if these fuckin' things crawl up 'em?"

"Jesus, Farley, you think of the nicest things."

"Well, how do they?"

"Ask the next one ya see, don't ask me!"

"Christ, look at a man, will ya? If Christine could see me now!"

Pritchard stood up, hands and arms held out from his sides: sweat-blackened shirt, arms torn by thorns, filthy trousers and knees showing, green canvas jungle boots split from toe to heel and at the folds of each lace.

"These J-boots are a waste of time. I've only worn these on three ops—twenty days walking. Look at 'em. Soles good for a 1,000 miles, tops gone in a couple of weeks. Never again, mate."

"Saddle up. The boss wants to get to the LZ for tomorrow before we base up for the night."

All around in the dark, damp vine-hung jungle on the creek bank, men were shrugging into webbing, heaving packs onto backs, putting out cigarettes, standing ready to move in the soft mass of leaves and dirt, looking over and through the green palms and ferns.

Far away, muffled by distance and intervening trees, the artillery was booming without pause, a constant roaring like the crushing surf on a rocky coast; flight after flight of jets roared over, unseen, hidden by the many interlacing branches and leaves.

"There's something goin' on—listen to that."

"Yeah. Must be over on the other side of the river where the Yanks are. They're firing away from us—we can't hear 'em land, and the jets are fairly high when they're over us."

All afternoon the rumbling continued, like the ominous jungle drums of Hollywood.

Farther to the east, Morton's company moved through the dark dripping mass of trees, vines, and ferns, climbing over rotten trunks. The scouts knelt and gave the enemy sign. Ahead was a strange sight in the darkening jungle: benches and lecterns in areas cleared of undergrowth. No sign of life. The ground sloped away to a small creek before climbing to a hill top; the company ojective for the day. Darkness was forty-five minutes away.

As the lead section began to skirt the cleared areas, a lone VC carrying a weapon suddenly leaped from his hiding place and ran pell-mell down the slope. Two shots cracked out and he went down, rolling over and over. As the section commander searched the body, Moose Morrissey fingered his jaw with a huge hand and surveyed the area through narrowed eyes: the lecterns and benches, cleared undergrowth, creek and rising ground. Turning to the lieutenant who was examining the captured rifle, "Sir, we better be careful. This is a closed training area, set up for lectures an' all that. They're probably just up on the high ground across the creek," gesturing with one huge hand, "and in a proper camp, goin' by this."

"I don't think so, Sergeant."

"Sir, that bloke was obviously the sentry, trying to get back across the creek. Look at him—he hasn't been traveling today, he's not a courier. They're up there."

"Hmm," in a disagreeing tone. "We going across, it's getting dark."

The leading platoon quickly splashed across the creek and began climbing the slope in the failing light, front section spread out almost abreast as they clambered up, using saplings and roots as hand holds, to assist.

Leo Madison panted as he grabbed the huge root, one of a mass above ground around the base of the great trees, and pulled himself and his M60 up the last couple of feet. He stepped forward, placing his feet among the mass of roots, and looked up to see across the darkening hill top clear of undergrowth—frame shelters, log bunkers, cleared paths—in the second before the winking light on the ground slammed into his chest, and he found himself lying in the mass of roots,

Two grinning Asians jumped up from the pit five yards away and began to climb over the roots toward him.

"The M60 . . . you bastards . . ." With a supreme effort, unaware of the blood pouring from his mouth, Madison tilted his machine gun and, using the root as a pivot, riddled the two, flinging the bodies away with the impact of the 7.62mm rounds, before the light exploded in his head, as the VC machine gun fired into his prone body again.

Five other men had been hit and lay on the crest or at the top of the slope. The next sections reached the crest, firing at and throwing grenades at the bunkers in reach, but nothing could survive above ground on that hill top, and they were driven back, taking what wounded they could with them.

Two men still lay close to the VC guns, Madison and Vic Chalmers, ace snooker player of the company. He was behind a tree, out of reach of the VC fire, but badly wounded in the body.

"Hey sir," called Charger Seymour to the platoon commander, "get someone to cover us, and Pete and me'll go up after Chalmers."

"We will, ay?" from Pete.

"Yeah, why not? I've always wanted to get onto that good lookin' sister of his, now's the chance."

"Aw, thought it mighta been the $50 he borrowed off
ya to go on leave with. Glad to see it's not money ya
thinkin' of. Just yer dick, as usual."

"Well, you're gonna help me, aren't ya? You're my
mate, aren't ya?"

"Fuck you, Seymour."

With a section grenading over the crest, Seymour and
Sanders crawled up the slope and reached the wounded
man.

"We won't get him down with all this gear on—watch
those grenades, Pete."

Chalmers had been struck by several rounds, one of
which had passed through the side of one of his grenades
without setting it off. The yellow filling and notched spring
wire insides were visible through the rent in the olive
casing.

"Okay, that's his gear undone. Tuck his hands inside
his waistband, we'll have to keep his arms in. Don't worry
about the blood and dirt, the medics can have him later,
okay? We'll slide back down, pulling a leg each."

Raising his voice, "Okay you mob! Here we come!"

Keeping as low as possible, they slid feet first over
the crest, pulling Chalmers behind, amid a constant
showering of dirt, leaves, and splinters as the VC fired on
the spot but could not bring fire to bear into the shallow
dip.

Moose Morrissey had returned three times to try and
recover Madison's body, but his legs were tangled in the
roots of the tree. Each time Moose grabbed the pack,
entrenching tool handle or waterbottle, and pulled, the
VC put another burst into the body. Finally, Ryan, the
platoon commander, ordered Moose not to go up the slope
again.

"He's dead, Sergeant Morrissey. We'll only lose more
men."

Moose heaved a huge sigh, staring up the slope to
where the pitted tree marked Madison's resting place.

"Fuck you."

Ryan was not sure who the remark was for.

While the depleted platoon was trying to fight its way

over the crest, Morton was calling for artillery and sending a platoon around to the flank. As they moved swiftly around, climbing the slope, a platoon of VC appeared on the crest, and their fire brought the move to a stop.

The platoon went to ground, returning fire. These VC were good, they had reconnoitered the ground and preselected machine gun positions to defend such flanking movements.

Albie Grant's section lay behind a huge fallen tree, over four feet in diameter, which sheltered them from the machine gun sweeping the slope.

The lead section of Roger's platoon, attempting the second flanking move, came running around the slope through the green darkness, under faintly gleaming ferns and palms, and rested for a moment behind Grant's men. All seemed to be quiet here, though heavy firing continued behind.

Ernie Horton peered through the dim light up the dark slope, "Right, we'll go up here—hey Albie, what are you bastards hiding here for?"

"There's a fucking' machine gun right on this tree, that's why! Don't go over there!"

"Aw, bullshit! Come on my section, over this tree, don't worry about these cunts, step on 'em. Right? Over we go and up!"

The section struggled onto the fallen tree, sitting, kneeling, or straddling its mossy dark body, and the VC raked the length of the trunk with a long burst, driving the surprised and frightened but unhurt section backward in a welter of arms and legs, hats, weapons, curses, woofs of expelled breath as they hit the ground, flying splinters, bark, and lumps of moss. The two section commanders lay close together, Grant's men swearing at the second lot who had fallen back on them; Horton glanced down the wriggling mass of green-clad bodies and at the splinters flying from the trunk as the machine gun asserted it domination of the slopes, looked at Grant's annoyed face, smiled, "You're right you know, Albie."

The third and last platoon, moving behind the prone second one engaging the enemy on the crest, had hardly got beyond them when they too encountered VC trying to outflank. The darkness now was almost night, and Morton regrouped across the creek, having lost about 20 percent of his company in the battle, and having still not defined the enemy location or strength: night was upon him and he had wounded to succor.

No artillery had been provided: two gunships had buzzed over, spraying the area with rockets and 7.62mm machine gun fire, which was next to useless in the thick jungle canopy. During the night, two of the wounded died; Chalmers was the second.

Morton was ordered to leave the area before first light and make his way to the location by Ryder's company.

On the other side of the river, the American battalions were also searching, pushing their way up the jungle-covered ridges and creek banks. Preliminary airstrikes had gone in on locations reported to be held by the enemy. Unknown to the Americans, one strike had hit a rich target: the headquarters of Q902. Rescue work was still in progress as the Americans landed and began moving toward the HQ location. Quickly, two battalions advanced to engage the Americans, who were not sure the VC were there anyway. But the VC knew the Americans were and so had the advantage.

The Americans were strung out, three companies ahead of each other; the VC battalions sprang their trap, catching the Yanks in a dip between two ridges. The two US companies in the rear fought their way to the top of a ridge, waiting for the leading, surrounded company to struggle through to them. Forcing their way through the jungle, carrying their wounded, fighting off attacks by the assaulting battalion of Q902, the paratroopers fought their way back to the ridge top and then to the waiting companies and battalion HQ, the VC around them and now surrounding them all.

The US wounded and dead increased with every minute, but now they were able to bring their firepower to bear on an enemy who was at grips with them.

The artillery, from their positions on the other side of the river, poured an unending storm of steel onto the targets given by the forward observers. Jets streaked down into the smoke and dust of the battle delivering their bombs, rockets, cannon, and napalm.

With an entire battalion surrounded and fighting for its existence, there was no support to spare for the minor contact at dusk by the Australians.

As the dawn light seeped over the sky and drove the darkness back, the paratroopers stared at the shattered, riven, splintered, smoking scene of devastation around them; farther away, great blemishes on the jungle showed where the lightning they controlled had struck.

Among the splintered trees and ploughed-up earth, 400 enemy dead were found. How many were carried off and how many wounded was not known.

The brigade commander wanted to see results of the battle: a Chinook helicopter lowered a net into the shell-blasted area; sixty VC corpses were loaded into it, and the Chinook carried the dripping, unsavoury mass suspended under its belly and deposited it outside brigade HQ— proof of the most positive kind.

Then began the task of recovering the US bodies along the trail of their struggle up to the heights.

Ryder's company secured a grassy clearing for use by the helicopters. Morton's men were struggling toward them through the dense green-dripping mass, carrying their dead and wounded, except two dead left on the hill. The only helicopter that could assist them was a USAF rescue machine equipped with a winch; it hovered over the trees, lowered the wire, and winched up the wounded through the leaves. The silver "mixmaster" shuttled between Morton and Ryder, where the casualties and dead were evacuated by Huey.

To the same clearing the US dead were brought for identification and removal from the body of all ammunition, food, and items not of a personal nature.

Ryder's men, with "Baron" Lord organizing and encouraging, carried out their grisly task. The dead were brought in piled on the floor of the Huey, removed, and laid out on the grass; webbing removed, pockets searched,

dog tags checked, and details written on a tag provided by
the Graves Registration Team.

A huge green plastic bag, handles on the sides and
closed by a heavy-duty zipper, was laid next to the dead
man; he was lifted in, any personal items placed in with
him, bag zipped up, tagged, and placed with the others.
When six were ready, a waiting Huey lifted them to the
morgue.

Lying sprawled on the grass were blacks and Nordic
men, Mexicans, Nisei, Hawaiians, American Indians, and
all the races in the American mixing bowl; all had wanted
to be "airborne," the aggressive corps d'elite of the US
Army, and wear the paratrooper boot and the wings.

They had sweated and hacked their way through the
jungle time and again seeking the VC. Then climbing up
that small valley, they had found them. Fighting across
strange terrain in the heat, visibility not more than thirty
yards and usually only five or ten, carrying all their
wounded, holding off a greatly superior force, struggling
through the encirclements, back to their fellow paras on
the ridge, to hold the high ground against assault after
assault.

Now these lay in a jungle clearing. At the memorial
parade, an empty pair of boots would stand for each dead
man, mute symbol of the departed warrior.

"Jesus," said Father, wiping his brow, "it's bloody hot.
How many have we done?"

"Dunno," replied Pritchard, "about twenty that I
counted, but I guess twice as many as that."

"A man won't want to eat for a week, after this,"
moaned Nimbus; "these blokes have only been dead two
days and they're on the nose now, phew!"

The sickly sweet stench of dead men that seemed to
block the back of the nostrils hung in the air, mixed with
the smell of blood, entrails, sweat-soaked clothes, and jet
turbine fuel. The crushing heat removed the normal appetite; the task of identifying, searching, and bagging the
bodies removed the urge to eat from all but the hardiest.

Tom Pritchard stood, hands on hips, watching a Huey
climb away south.

"A man wants his head read, Father. Standing here with the knees out of his pants, boots fucked, sucked dry by leeches, standing sweating your guts out in a miserable patch of grass, searching dead men, in a country where one half want to kill you and the others want to rob you. Jesus ay," with a wry grin and shake of his head, as he wondered if he could spare the water to wash his hands covered in grime and blood.

Father looked up from under his hat brim. "Gonna transfer to admin. company, are yer?"

Tom stepped back as if stuck, "Fuck off!"

"Baron" walked up and stopped, looking at the pile of webbing and rations, "Well, how's it going, Private Pritchard?"

"Not bad, sir, Bit hot."

"Yeah, there won't be anymore for a while; stop for lunch now."

"Goodo, sir. I'll have a pick through these tins, there might be something good there."

"Yes, I'll be in that," said "Baron," kneeling and flicking over the tins, "though I don't think too many of the boys will be eating anything. Ah, here we go," selecting a tin, rising and fishing can opener from pocket.

Not to be outdone, Tom reached down and picked up a tin, producing his own opener as he, "Baron," and Father walked over to the recumbent forms in the shade on the edge of the clearing.

"Christ, dunno how yer can face food," from one of the prone sweat-soaked figures.

"Lunch time, isn't it?"

"Yeah, but fuckin' hell..."

"Bit hungry, ya know."

"Yeah, but Christ, yer been loadin' two-day-old bodies, ya know."

"So?"

Tom busily jerked the can opener round the rim, levered it open, and felt his gorge rise as he looked at turkey and noodles. White lumps of turkey in a coiling mass of noodles, all swimming in a strange-looking fluid.

Putting on his poker face, he got a spoon from his

pocket and picked some noodles out, glancing over at "Baron" who had thoughtfully picked out a tin of biscuits and was popping one into his mouth with obvious relish,

"Why didn't we go in to help Morton's mob?" asked Les Fitzgibbon. "We chase the little buggers for weeks, and when we find 'em, we have to let 'em go."

Ryder looked up from his map.

"You must remember that the brigade commander had a good-size battle over there with these blokes," indicating the clearing where the bodies had lain, "and getting that surrounded battalion out was taking all his resources. He couldn't have got involved in two battles, diagonally opposite the guns and HQ. Charlie Company had to look after themselves; it was just bad luck."

"Well sir, looks to me like the bastard didn't want anyone else to have a victory and get any credit. It's always 'US paratroopers' when they do anything and 'allied troops' when we do."

"Well, we're the junior partner, Private Fitzgibbon," in a tone of dismissal, as the signaler handed him the radio handset. He acknowledged the caller, listened, signed off, and tossed the handset back. With a brief glance at the surrounding men, he spoke to the other signaler on the set to the platoons, "Call the platoon commanders in; orders group in three minutes. We're going back late this afternoon. To camp."

Frank Gardiner climbed in the back of the Land-Rover and leaned his rifle against the partition between front and tray. "Where are we goin', Father?" to Rankin who was climbing into the front.

"Over to the logistic mob," patting his shirt pocket. "Got all the paperwork to pick up some plywood for the company CP."

The two chatted as the dusty Land-Rover rolled along the red-surfaced road, out of the brigade and along to the logistics unit. After the green gloom and damp of the jungle, it was a relief to be dry, free of leeches and thorns, and the eyes delighted in looking to the horizon, instead of peering and straining to see thirty yards. Sleeves rolled up, shirt collars opened, they rejoiced in the sun on bare skin.

They stopped in the visitors' parking area and climbed down, weapons automatically slung over their shoulders.

"Jesus, these bastards are well set up. Gravel paths, electricity—look, a bloody washing machine," thinking of the infantrymen sloshing through mud, using candles or lamps run off old radio batteries, and washing their socks and underwear in a steel helmet or ammo box. Showers were from a canvas bucket slung over a beam.

"Yeah. The closer to the infantry private you get, the less you have. Platoon headquarters are rear echelon pogos to us. Company headquarters are rear to them; these blokes regard Saigon-types as rear echelon pogos. Everyone regards the air force as pogos."

Father stood for a moment looking at the paths, overhead wires, and washing machine visible through the door of the building. "Come on. Let's get this plywood."

They walked around the nearest building and came upon a corporal sawing busily away at a sheet of plywood, He looked up, saw by their dress they were infantry or gunners, and adopted a truculent expression. "Whatdya want?"

"G'day. We're from the battalion. Got some paperwork here to pick up some ply."

"Yeah. Well, we haven't got any, mate. Go into town and buy it."

"Aw yeah?" Father looked at the sheet the corporal was sawing; stenciled boomerangs and kangaroos covered its surface. Figures that had already been cut out were stacked along the wall.

"Yeah, there isn't any," turning his back to his task.

Father felt a blinding light burst in his brain, then it cleared and he turned away, entering the orderly room. There he presented the request for plywood.

"Don't you know we want twenty-eight days notice for this?" asked the paunchy, sweating sergeant.

"I'm just bringin' it over, Sergeant," said Father.

"Well, we haven't got anyway."

Father walked outside to where Frank Gardiner waited in the sun, "No dice."

"Yeah. Aren't those battalion vehicles over there?" pointing to four Land-Rovers parked in a row.

"Looks like it. But the OC's driver says these bastards have a "normal wait" of seven days before they look at a vehicle."

"I hear they've got the new 25-set radio here but won't give 'em to us until the ten-sets are beyond economical repair."

"These bastards have never walked through the J with their arse out of their pants and their fuckin' boots fallin' apart, or loaded two-day-old corpses. Come on; I'll hit one of 'em if we stay here."

They drove back in silence, resentful of the gap between the infantry rifleman and the supporting services. They had nothing but their clothes, weapons, and friends, and were happy with a few beers and a film. The farther back from the front line, the more particular was the attention paid to privileges of rank, acquisition of the good things in life, and enjoyment of luxuries.

Father sighed, and half turned to Frank, "I know the bastards are necessary, but by fuckin' Christ, they make me wild."

"Yeah, fuck 'em. Say, did yer see that new rifle they got on the op? Russian, or something."

"Right, Chinese copy of the Russian AK47. The Intelligence Sections identified it. Thirty-round mag, full automatic, looks all right."

"Looks a bloody sight better than the burp guns and bolt-action rifles. Believe it was still in packing grease."

"That's what I heard."

"D'ya hear about the nog Ramsay's mob got on the creek? Tried to throw a grenade but got his guts blown out by it instead?"

"No."

"Yeah, apparently he was asking for a drink, but the interpreter wouldn't give him one till the nog told him his unit and what they were going to do next. When the nog told him, he gave him a big drink. He was gonna die anyway."

"Hmm. I heard Moose went up three times after Madison's body, to within ten yards of the machine gun."

"Yeah, must pay that, ay? How about those blokes in B? Sweeping the river bank and get shot at by a recoilless rifle. So they call up a chopper and piss off. Meanwhile, a mob of Yanks calls up, claiming some number of VC killed with a recoilless rifle from over the river. Didn't bother to check, just blazed away. Never hit anyone either."

"Old Smacker is up and about in Aussie. Les got another letter. Two broken legs will slow him down a bit, though."

"Yeah. Thank Christ for the Dust-offs."

Americans who worked closely with the battalion and went on operations with it were welcomed as members of the family. One had been at the gun position when the Australian battle on the hill erupted, and went with a winch-equipped Vietnamese H-34 to the scene.

"As we came over, we could see the pigs goin' backward and forward and tracer comin' up outa the trees. Soon as that mother-fuckin' slope seen that, he pulled up and turned away. He would not go on in, man. I poked my '16 in his face, called him a washerwoman, everything! He would not go down! Flew back to the fuckin' airbase. Then none of their ships was available to help and the 'mixmaster' had to go. I hope to see that mother-fuckin' pilot in town one day, I tell you."

"How ya gonna tell one from another, Dave?"

"I'll know that sonofabitch, man!"

"It's got me rooted, ya know. They're the same mob, yet the VC are a real pack of tough bastards. These others—I can't think of a good word for 'em. Why is it?"

"Got me beat, but ya right, one side can beat piss and pick handles out of the other, and they have rifles, machine guns and mortars against aircraft, tanks, and arty. They were runnin' riot over this place before we got here."

Fredericks walked in, a plastic-wrapped bundle in his hand.

"G'day, here's some things from the kills on the op. There's no Intelligence value in these, so we're givin' em back. See yer boss if yer want 'em."

"Yeah, all right. Want a beer?"

"You smooth-talkin' bastard. I knew you'd convince me after an argument. What ya got—Aussie or Yank?"

"Budweiser, or Budweiser?"

"It's drinkable."

"Listen Fred, just before ya came in we were talkin' about something maybe you can answer—you know about this country."

"Aw yeah?"

"Yeah. How is it the VC beat the livin' shit outa the ARVN, and they're brothers? One lot is so bloody good and the other is so piss poor?"

"Frank, if I could get that one sorted out, I'd have red collar tabs and crossed swords and batons on my shoulders."

"Well, ya must have some ideas, Jesus, ya speak the lingo, ya talk to both sides."

"How many beers ya got?"

"Why?"

"Well first, I don't want to spoil yer beer drinkin'. Second, it might take a while and we might get thirsty."

"Yeah, I can see why you're in Intelligence."

"Okay then. Why do the Charlies beat the ARVN all the time? If yer have a look at the history of this mob, it's one series of wars. They fought the Chinese, Laotians, Cambodians, Thais, a race called the Cham they all but killed off, and anyone else they could find. In between times, they fought each other; always the North fighting the South to see who was gonna be boss. When ya go to any town, the street names are the same everywhere—all military heroes. Always. They expanded south from the Red River Delta, creeping down the coast, killing every bastard in front of 'em. They only got here in the 1700s, ya know."

"Yeah, but what's that gotta do with now?"

"Hang on, hang on. They've always been fighting someone, if not the bastard next door, then punching up among themselves. The French had 'em for ninety years and got done. Basically, they don't like foreigners. When the French were here, the only ones who did well were the French and any Viet who became a Frenchman. They became more French than the real ones. And no one else got a look-in. The whole place was here to make a quid for the French and their Viet imitators. All public service jobs were held by Frenchmen or converts—everything: police, customs, postmen, clerks. The owners of anything were not Vietnamese. Wouldn't you buck if it were us? To get anywhere you had to become a foreigner. When the French left, there was nothing to build on. The people who fought the French were Vietnamese getting rid of a foreigner who'd never given them a fair go. The English trained and employed all sorts of locals in running their colonies, not the French.

"Of course, old Ho Chi Minh is a cunning old prick. He never gets slammed with the blame if anything goes wrong—Stalin got it for his purges, same as Hitler, and Mao wore it a few times for being hard on 'em, but Ho always has someone to cop it for him. When he was fighting the French, he got to be top dog by setting up all the other Viets, who weren't commies, for the French. The French got rid of them, and Ho was left as the only one. El Supremo. But he's never been saddled with anything. Always smiling, always patting kids on the cheek. Here, how about a beer?

"Well, when the French left, there was no one to head the South. The French had done 'em all in, or they were Frenchmen with Viet faces. Diem was the only one. He was against the commies and the French too. So he was brought in and did well for a bit. But he had lots of problems and got a bit tough to keep the jackals down. Then a bit tougher, and soon he was as bad as any of 'em. Or his family were, and they were running the show. So lots of people went out to fight Diem because they were fed up. They don't call 'emselves VC, they're the Liberation Front. Only a few are commies, and they control it and get their orders from Hanoi, there's no doubt."

"You're just here to drink our beer and practice for

politics. We only want to know why the bastards are so different, fuck ya."

"Les, as the actress said to the bishop, 'If you weren't so impatient, you'd find out all about it.'"

"Aw, come on Fred."

"Okay, if ya could tell it in a couple of sentences, it'd be bloody simple. If it was simple, we wouldn't be here, mate."

"Yeah, okay."

"Have a look in yer travels; you'll see all the building goin' on—schools, hospitals, roads, bridges, markets, wells, water systems, harbors, you can see it everywhere. And the government has to guard it all. The VC don't have to build a thing. They demonstrate their power by destroying things. And now—why are they so good? First, they only fight when they want to. Which is smart. Monty never let Rommel decide when and where the battles would be. Second, in the VC, apart from politics, promotion is on merit. A farmer's son can be a battalion or regimental commander if he 's got the ability. Not in the ARVN. Look at the kills we get. All dressed alike, perhaps a senior bloke has a satchel with documents in it, but otherwise they're dressed alike. Look at the ARVN. The officers are tailor-made—sunglasses, big watches, long fingernails—starched and polished. The higher up, the less time in the J. The VC are fighting for Vietnam, so they say, and their history is all wars against other people. They don't like the Chinese anymore than the next lot. The ARVN are the image of the foreigners—French and Yanks. They just beat the French; who's going to take a chance on the Yanks—another set of foreigners with Viets trying so hard to copy them, *and* hang on to all their privileges? All the VC have to do is promise, promise, promise, promote on merit, and point out all the bastardy from the Yanks. Wouldn't you fight? Frank, you remember Xuan. Father, Les? Xuan from La Popotte? How do you reckon that Yankee prick went making friends? Would he be a mate of yours?"

"No fuckin' way."

"All the VC have to do is let bastards like him do their

work for them. No one likes seeing their women turned
into prostitutes."

"Well, what in the name of Christ are we doin' here?"

"Tryin' to buy time for these people to sort themselves out. There is a quote from Greek history—'Tell
them for their tomorrow we gave our today.' Make no
mistake: there are good ARVN, otherwise the North would
have won. The ARVN have good men too. The Yanks are
trying to let people see democracy as we know it. But it's a
bit bloody hard in this situation—a rotten crowd running
it, a war on, and trying to get honest elections and a
decent government. And the thing is there's good and bad
on both sides."

"Christ, good thing you're in Intelligence or they'd be
watchin' ya."

"Well, remember this—the VC are the ones who murder schoolteachers in front of their classes, kill priests,
and put mines on the road to catch people going to
market, just to terrorize people. And I'm against that here
or anywhere. My job is to look at the enemy with two
open eyes, see his good and bad points. Otherwise, we'll
never beat them."

"Thank Christ I was born an Aussie."

"You can say that again. Look at the alternatives.
How would you like to have been born an African? An
Arab? An Englishman? A Yank? Hey? We're the luckiest
bastards alive."

"Fuckin' oath."

"There's good men everywhere—no doubt about it.
Those Yank radio and arty blokes who come out with us
are okay, and how about the helicopter pilots? The paras
did okay on the last op, when the chips were down. It's
just that they think too big—masses of guns, bullets, and
airplanes. That's all right in Europe, but what you need
here is lots of good infantry sections. They hardly think
below a battalion. Anyway, how's the Budweiser holdin'
out? Anyone goin' to Saigon tomorrow?

11

"Company!"

Shuffling of feet, silence, as CSM "Baron" Lord called the men to attention and handed over to the company second-in-command to call in the platoon commanders and report the company present to "Red" Ryder, who entered the cool, long dining tent on cue.

"Thank you. Company, sit easy, smoke," taking off his bush hat and pointing to the spot where he wanted the map board positioned.

The two soldiers carrying it set it on the easel in the front of the seated company and took their seat. By this time the shuffling, borrowing, scraping of matches, flicking of Zippo lighters, returning of packets to pockets, and rearranging of ash trays—as the smokers went through their rites—was over.

Ryder stepped forward, hands folded on top of the pointer.

"There aren't many secrets in this family, so you all know we're going out again in two days. Right. Over here, to the northeast," tapping the light-colored area amid the green splodges on the map, "is a rich rice-producing valley. The harvest is almost due. The VC want that harvest, so does the government. Our mission is to occupy the valley so the government can reestablish its authority there and farther east, and allow the harvest to be brought in. Enemy. There is a main force division here," tap, "in the mountains to the north. A local force battalion operates in the valley and, in fact controls it. Now, how are we

132

going to do it? We fly into this town, Vat Vo, the last
government presence, reorganize, and clear the VC from
these two towns along the east-west road, here," tap, "and
here," tap. "First, we secure the base at Vat Vo and go on
after that, depending on the situation. Now . . ." and Ryder
continued with the details.

After the briefing, there was the series of pre-op
tasks: drawing rations and ammo, packing, writing, and
posting the last letter.

The Hueys climbed to 4,000 feet, on course toward the
sun, gently rising and falling in the cooler air. The glorious
hues of Vietnam spread away as far as the eye could see: to
the south, the blue clean clump of mountains at Vung Tau,
and the sun-silver on the sea; to the west, the flat pale
green-brown of the delta fading into the haze; closer, the
dirty smudge of Saigon lurking under its shell of smoke
and pollution; ahead from right to left, the green carpet of
the jungle, broken only by the occasional river with its
flanking light-green swatches of cultivation. The Diggers
reveled in the height, the coolness, and the view. The
accompanying slicks stretched back in their scores. From
ahead and below another thirty or so Hueys appeared,
going back for another load. In that blue above-green
light, they appeared as a school of busy fish threshing
along under the shimmering circular veil of the rotor
blades reflecting the sun, the brilliant fluorescent orange
and green panels on the cockpit roofs bright as the markings of tropical fish swimming over a coral reef.

Fingers pointing ahead: up there, over the pilot's
shoulder, a lone hill humped above the green-blue carpet, the hill puffing white clouds, trying to draw a cool
veil over its head under the blazing sun . . . no, the jets
are pummeling it.

The local ARVN report a VC company on it; it
overlooks the town and airfield so is being "struck." To the
left, rising from the green, is a fluffy red cloud of dust; into
it dive the tiny shapes of a preceding lift, from the far end
pop out those of another in ragged formation, strung out
over the width of the cloud.

Descending now, out of the cooler air, the jungle roof becoming more distinct blobs of green and shadows; there go the silver F100s diving overhead, down the blue, smoke trails flicking back from cannon, bombs falling away; up he goes, effortlessly lifting away from the green, climbing into the dark blue, flashes on the hill, smoke...next one firing cannon...helicopter swinging onto the approach, swimming into the red cloud, trees now close below, red dust tendrils flit by, into it, sun a feebly glowing disc, helicopter in front the vaguest shadow. Settling in a suddenly clear bowl swept by the rotor blast, ground below, skids hit, rock to a stop; get out, kneel; helicopter huge in the confined vision range of this seething whirling dust storm, red dust in eyes, ears, nose, mouth, collar, shirt front, weapons will be filthy, bugger it! Dark helicopter shape lifting, moving past; over to the side of the LZ onto the grass, the others spitting red mud and grimacing in the red world at the bottom of this fish bowl; the next lot of dark shapes sailing by, one after the other, blind, only superb training and discipline allowing mass landing in this cloud with visibility no more than fifty yards.

Walk up the length of the airfield, into the town of Vat Vo, along the streets under the frangipani, mango, banana, and coconut trees, past the wooden houses with tiled roofs, stared at by the ever-present noisy children and the more reserved, dignified adults. The foreign soldiers: their objective is obvious—Tien Bien and Xo Ba, the next towns along the road. Even there the noise of the aircraft must be heard if the hundreds of helicopters and fat silver Hercules could not be seen in the clear sky.

Move through and camp in the jungle, out of town, for the evening.

Major "Red" Ryder spread his folded map on the ground, broke off a twig to use as a pointer—"only generals point with their fingers"—and glanced around his assembled platoon commanders, mortar forward controller, and artillery forward observation officer.

"As you know, the VC are in the villages ahead. The

population is Roman Catholic refugees from the North. The VC have controlled this area for a year. The ARVN have tried twice to take the places back but been done over each time. Our mission is to lead the assault, followed by C and A, with D in reserve. The ARVN went up the road each time. We are going to walk around behind them and get in over the fence. I think they'll be facing the other way," gesturing with the twig on the map. "Now, we'll move out at 0500, order of march..." and Ryder went on with his briefing, concluding with, "Any questions? Okay, ready to roll at 0500. Good night."

For all the following day, the companies forced their way south then east, keeping well away from any sighting by the locals. The night was spent quietly to the east of Tien Bien, preparing for the attack. Scouts had reconnoitered routes to the jungle edge so the approach could be made quickly.

Dark figures against the black trees. "Stand-to. Stand-to" hissed, shoulders shaken, feet tapped. Men roll to a sitting position, weapon in hand, and stare out into the lightening gloom, the drifting shadows of the patrol floating soundlessly past in their circuit. Pack, breakfast, shave, clean rifle, webbing and pack ready to embrace with their webbing arms.

"Saddle up," and begin the quiet, quick walk to the edge of the jungle. There, through the final fringe of leaves, branches, and vines, lies the town surrounded by a wall of bamboo bushes. Through the green tracery of the delicate bamboos can be seen the sheet metal, the thatched, and the tiled roofs. Along the road are people walking, cycling, or in their buffalo wagons—all oblivious of the Australians in the gloom.

A sunny, peaceful scene. The leading platoons, green clothes against green, move out of the jungle, cross the cleared area and move along the bamboo fence unseen by the people on the road. They climb through and under the 10,000 interlacing, entangled, hooked arms of the bamboo and are inside; the next platoon follows, then the HQ, the last platoon of the lead company, and suddenly the VC guarding the rear of the village open fire from the house where they are having breakfast.

The answering hail of fire silences them, and it is on: sections and platoons, "pepper-potting" up either side of the east-west road, never stopping, never allowing the VC to settle and become organized, bouncing him back, back, back. The companies following take up the chase, pivoting to clear up the north-south road, and in a couple of hours the town is cleared of armed VC, leaving behind their dead and weapons.

For no Australian casualties and one house burned, the town has been returned to government control, and mass can again be celebrated in the tin-roofed church.

Later in the day, the government reappeared—wearing sunglasses, starched, tailored, bemedaled in the figure of the captain district chief from Vat Vo. Trailing him, an entourage of clerks, information team trios, census takers, propaganda teams who began broadcasting and plastering posters, and assorted ARVN with tall crew-cut American advisers full of praise for the feat of occupying a town by force of arms, with only one house destroyed. Their method of air strikes and artillery preparation was not used.

During the intensely active house clearing, the people were sent to the rear. Ninety-year-old Tran Van Phuoc was ill, confined to bed; heavy firing and shouts in a foreign language convinced old Phuoc his last moments had come. A strangely dressed, sweating foreigner leaped into the room, saw Phuoc and pointed to the door, "Di Di Mau," thereby using one-third of his vocabulary. Phuoc shook his head and firmly gripped the side of the planks on which he slept.

"Di Di Mau! Di Di Mau!"

"Khong. Khong."

"Hey, there's an old bloke in here won't go!"

Slim Baker, the medic, trotted over hoping the Red Cross would have some beneficial effect. Phuoc shook his head and pointed to the crucifix and religious pictures of Mary and Jesus Christ.

"Ah! me too," and Slim pulled out his crucifix on a neck chain. Phuoc's old eyes lit up—a fellow worshipper! His thin hand shot out and grasped Slim's in a grip that could only be broken by hurting the old man. More a captive than a helper, Slim gestured to the rear, saying "Di, Di." Phuoc slowly got up, and together they shuffled down the road in the sun, past the follow-up companies, toward the assembly area where the civilians were held. Moving slowly down the road, away from the battle, Slim reaped the crop of witty remarks from the platoons lining the road.

"Takin' yer dad for a couple of beers, ay?"

"No, that's his bird's old man. Tryin' to get in good with the parents, takin' the old bloke down the club for a hit at the pokies."

A sniper some hundred yards away began to put rounds close to Slim's floppy bush hat, to the great amusement of the reclining wits.

"Wish I was a medic; get all the best jobs."

"Speed 'im up a bit, Slim!"

"Leave the old bastard."

"Captured Ho Chi Minh ay?"

The combination of heat haze, lack of training, lack of knowledge of ballistics and variations in Phuoc's rate of travel, ensured no sniper's round hit, though some snapped past with a loud crack.

Myers's platoon was leapfrogging along the row of houses on the south side of the road: section down, section moving, section clearing houses. Suddenly a racket of yells, thumps, thuds: Diggers running around corners and diving into doorways as a water buffalo went charging by, head down, great horns flicking, hooves kicking, snorting, dusty, invulnerable, one green-clad figure running just ahead of the great shape until a supreme burst of speed gained enough distance to dodge into a house and the beast went lumbering past, to be caught and led back by a ten-year-old boy.

An ammunition resupply Huey circled, awaiting landing instructions. The battle was by now at the far end of the town, and people were returning home along the road in chattering groups. The helicopter requested smoke to mark the LZ. "Throw smoke," said the company signaler; "Here it goes" in an unknown voice. Pop-fizz-zz-zz.

"Didn't know we had white smoke," said one of the company HQ.

"No, first time I've seen it." As the wind drove the cloud down the road, the first tendrils reached them— "Christ, it's fucking tear gas! Who threw that?"

Sneezing, coughing, eyes streaming, the group stumbled upwind, the signaler spluttering into his handset to warn the grinning chopper crew. The oncoming civilians were walking into the cloud, despite shouts and waves from the up-wind group. One matriach strode through the now dissipating mist; her bearing changing from old mother walking home along a dusty road, to discomfort when the gas enveloped her, to an infuriated woman who had lost patience with the stupid men of both sides who had disrupted her day.

As she came level with the group now distributing the ammunition delivered by the Huey, she gave vent to a stream of furious Vietnamese that needed no interpreting, reinforced by waving fists.

"Good on yer, lady."

"Hurrm, just like my bloody wife."

"You hook in, mum."

"Lady," pointing to the CSM, "he's the one."

But the old lady had no favorites. The skinny, gray-haired figure, eyes weeping from the gas, strode on up the road, the personification of outrage.

"Her old bloke 'll cop it," and the grinning Diggers went on with the ammunition handout.

"Red" Ryder's company was allocated the Roman Catholic church and yard in its sector. Ryder placed his CHQ in the church and his platoons in an arc. The one that had been led by Augie Bennett was commanded by newly arrived Lieutenant Guy Vernon, only three weeks "in-country" and on his first operation.

Fredericks walked over to Ryder, "Sir, you should get that new platoon commander to take down the flag he's got flying over his hutchi."

"Oh?" turning to look out the church door at the multihued flag hanging from a sapling over Lieutenant Vernon's small tent. "What is it?"

"Well, first of all it's a Buddhist flag, sir. He took it from the Buddhist temple. And we're in a Catholic church-yard. Just about the worst place in town to fly it. He reckons it's VC."

"Yes." To the signaler, "Tell him to come up here and bring the flag."

Lieutenant Vernon received a short lecture on religions, looting, and flag identification before returning the flag to its rightful place, with apologies to the shaven-headed bonzes.

Sitting behind the small fires, waiting for the brewing water to boil, Tom turned to Father.

"Hey Father, noticed how back in Aussie the battalion revolved around the CO and RSM? The CO was like God. The RSM *was* God. CO's parades, RSM's parades, battalion guards, RSM's work parties, Jesus. But over there, ya hardly see 'em or hear of 'em. They might be miles away. The company and platoon are the most important things, BHQ is," he shrugged, "out of sight, out of mind."

"Yeah. Yer world narrows down a lot. Also Stan-the-Man and "Razor" have a lot of other things to worry about now. Okay, water's boilin', Tom."

"Jesus, I've been waitin' for this brew all day!"

12

"All right, we've done well so far. Now we've got Xo Ba to clear." Ryder tapped the map before his assembled

officers and attached specialists. "We're leading company.
Mission, to gain entrance to Xo Ba and secure this square,"
pointing to a hand-drawn enlargement of the town. "The
other companies will come in and fan out along the roads
leading away from the square: A, B, C, D—tapping each
quarter of the town. "Now, execution. They will be expecting
us to walk in, probably from one of their flanks, and they'll
have to watch their whole perimeter. So, we're going to
bash straight down the road in the APCs, right in and get
out in the square. Blitzkrieg. Order of march . . ." and he
continued with the details.

Outside, the platoon commanders dispersed to pass
on the briefing to their men.

The morning was dim—a mist rose before dawn, and the
early activities took place in a gray world of muffled sound.
The APCs came snorting and rumbling up the road,
halting, muttering to themselves, bulking dark angular
shapes in the fog, the vehicle commanders erect in their
hatches, the dark machine gun and sloping shield combining with the man's figure to make a silhouette of a medi-
eval knight on his huge caparisoned charger.

"Mount up," but inside this time. Small arms fire is
more likely to inflict casualties than mines. Roaring, jerking
backward and forward in the rocking horse gait of the APC
at speed, the column sped down the red dirt road—the
forest a dark frieze on either side in the fog, the sun a
feeble glow. They would be on top of any enemy before he
could aim.

The sudden crackling of firing, rounds snapping past
overhead, faces inside the steel hulls turned toward the
open roof hatch where the infantry commander and one
machine gunner peer around the APC commander behind
his 50-caliber machine gun and sloping shield. Roar at
speed up to the gate, a contraption of wood and wire
between ornate concrete pillars—a herd of snorting ele-
phants ignoring the pygmies' tiny darts; lead vehicles halt
and pivot on the threshold, an infantryman jumps down
into the rain of small arms fire, runs over and checks the
gate for signs of mining—none, but the gate is locked. No

key, but a huge opener is snorting and rumbling to hand; it rolls back a few feet, then a modern juggernaut advances up to, over, and through the gate. The remainder of the herd bellow their triumph with a roar of exhaust and charge up the slope, through the pillars, up between the houses, spitting glowing tracer left and right through the fog at the dark cutouts, silhouettes, of running VC.

A thunderous arrival at the square, minor parts of the trumpeting herd charging into position all around the square, facing out. Ramps drop and the infantry spill out, sections welding into platoons, searching houses, securing the square for the onrushing following herds. And again, the enemy is not allowed time to stand and reorganize. Again, with no casualties and not a round of artillery or a single jet, no houses destroyed, the VC are bounced out of the town into the jungle.

Father came around the corner at the run, crouching, SLR slanted across his body, and leaped sideways, going down to one knee in front of the small prone group at the side of the well.

"Bugger me," he thought, "what's the world coming to when a man has to put himself between the guns and the women?"

Three women and a man, the man in front, all with hands held in front, fingers extended, palms together, jigging them up and down in the Indo-Chinese greeting, four pairs of frightened eyes watching him, the sweating foreign warrior. The women, two young and one old, all wore their hair bobbed, a sign that they were married.

His eyes and gun raked the small yard and clump of orange trees as Pritchard thumped around after him, automatically going to the next natural piece of cover, the end of the kitchen at the rear of the house. Tom went down prone and stared out along his rifle barrel, into the misty trees beyond.

No wonder the poor bastards look frightened, Father thought, they probably expect rape, looting, and killing, if not from what the VC tell them, from their memories of the French.

Back in Australia, someone in the platoon had got a paperback copy of Phillipe de Pirey's *Operation Waste*, and several of them had refused to believe that a cultured race such as the French would behave in the manner described. They were still under the impression that the reiterated and enforced British and Australian respect for the individual and his possessions applied to all Western nations.

He smiled at the four, and immediately parodies appeared on their faces, anxious to please the invader.

Jesus Christ, thought Father, what a bastard. Here's this poor bugger trying to look after these women—mother, mother-in-law, wife, sisters or whatever—every other bastard has got a fucking gun. All he hears is, "Give us some of your crop; Give us some of your crop: your sister, wife, daughter." Now and again, we get the odd medal for an act of courage observed by the wheels. This poor prick *lives* a life of courage every day, both sides pulling at him like bloody jackals.

He took his left hand from the rifle and laid it palm down on his thigh, shouting "Hey Tom, I think we're okay here," and turned to call back the way they had come. "Okay, down here."

Sporadic firing went on, rounds cracked past overhead, not worth worrying about. A breeze was sifting through the trees now, cool on the sweating cheeks. A wailing and howling grew louder from around the corner, and a group of men, women, and children appeared, pushed along by other section members.

"Hey Father, we're gonna hold 'em here till it's cleared. An hour or so. And they're yours."

"Thanks very fucking much."

The wailing groups stood making a tremendous racket, but Father noticed there was not one tear, and the eyes watched the soldiers alertly. The buggers are all acting, he thought to himself.

"Hey, papa, you," pointing to the oldest man. "Sit! sit! er . . . swoong! swoong!" going through sitting motions. The old man sat slowly, never ceasing his wails and hand jigging. Gradually, the others followed. After a time, the wailing died away and before long, animated conversation was cackling back and forth between the first four and the newcomers. All the while, cautious eyes regarded the quiet foreigners, now smoking.

The old lady, after low conversation with the man, suddenly began rattling off sentences to Father, accompanied by smiles showing black-painted teeth ("white teeth are the sign of animals to many Asians," said the briefer) and much pointing toward the clump of banana trees.

Pritchard called, "Hey, she wants to get some bananas. What ya reckon?"

"Yeah, okay, okay," with smiles and exaggerated nodding of head.

Soon, the whole group was munching on sweet bananas, with much smiling and nodding.

An outbreak of shouts from the square brought Father's head around the corner to see what was happening.

"What's up?"

"Fuckin' CS! Some stupid cunt's popped it up-wind and it's comin' down with the mist!"

"Tom! Some stupid prick has used tear gas up-wind. Some of these cunts shouldn't be trusted with a friggin' water pistol!"

As the white gas, indistinguishable from the mist, drifted with it downwind, the ancestry and future health of the man who used it were commented on in loud voices.

The happy picnic group became again a wailing mass, this time, with real tears and cries of distress as the gas worked on nostrils, eyes, mouths, and lungs. Father and Tom began sponging themselves with sopping sweat rags and were besieged by outstretched hands.

"It's only water. Water! Nuoc! Here," grabbing the bucket at the well, "Nuoc!" and until the invisible demons passed with the soft breeze, the bucket raced up and down, the water liberally splashed over all and sundry.

"Okay, let 'em go home."

"Thank Christ."

*   *   *

Jack Kowalski lead his four F100s north to the strike area, flying high in the clear blue under the blazing white sun. Arriving over the target, he swung into a gentle left-hand circle; looking back over his right shoulder he could see the other three stepped back, canopies glinting in the sun.

Below him the Cessna pilot transmitted, "Bantam Red Leader, this is Snapper Three Six, have you in sight; target is estimated company plus on the north side of the river bend over a mile to the east of the town. Watch my smoke, goin' in now, over."

"Red Leader, Roger, the eyes of Texas are upon you," as the tiny gray flea of a Cessna moved across the green floor below . . . a white spot blossomed into a tiny white flower on the green carpet.

"Snapper Three Six, Red Leader goin' down now," and as the sun moved behind in the turn, look up and around the sky, though God knows there are no enemy aircraft this side of the DMZ. Since he was twelve, Kowalski had wanted to be a fighter pilot; he had read everything he could lay his hands on about the great fighter aces—Bong and Barkhorn, Molders and MacDonald, Johnson and Jabara, and all the others. Then the USAF Academy. At last, "Fighter Pilot!" And here he was driving F100s around the skies of South Vietnam. If only he could promote the transfer to F4s, to the Eighth Tactical Fighter Wing in Thailand, flying up to the North, where the MIGs are. Goddam! Here he was digging instant swimming pools with 750-pound bombs. Ah well, left stick and rudder, sky and earth pivoting, blue sliding up and overhead, only green in front expanding silently, leaping up, up, sucking him down, down, down . . . select two 750-pounders, okay . . . wait—wait—wait—white smoke marker leaping up—go! F100 released of its load and drag bounds up, gently back on stick, climbing, "Red Two going down."

"Red Leader, this is Snapper; that was good, good! Red Two, put 'em in the same place."

Still climbing into the blue bowl, ease forward on the stick, look back—gray cancer obliterating the small fresh flower; Red Two streaking over, two flashes in the gray,

"Red Three going down," look up in front to the right, there he goes; Red Four—Roberts—still circling.

"Red Two, this is Snapper, right on the button! Red Three, put 'em fifty yards to the east of the smoke."

"Can do," from Three—Caprizetti—that sonofabitch can melt women with his eyes; formate on Four, up goes his starboard wing, the big silver bird falling away. Here comes Red Two up on the right, where's Caprizetti? There, climbing up, up.

"Red Leader, this is Snapper, let's have your twenty mike mike and napalm in the same area," and again the headlong rush down the clear glassy slope, illuminated gunsight pipper on the gray smoke stain, flashing over the town—a blur of silver in the bigger green presence below—pip on, squeeze trigger, rumbling under his feet as the 20mm cannon hammer away, myriad flashing twinkling stars on the trees ahead; wait, wait, go! Napalm away.

"Red Two going down, Red Three . . . Red Four . . ." until "Okay Bantam Red, a good result, good, 90 percent target coverage, I estimate 30 KIA. Pleasure to do business with you, okay?"

"Snapper this is Bantam Red, thanks, it's our pleasure."

Looking over his shoulder, Kowalski saw the gaping mouths of the air intakes echeloned neatly in the sky, three helmeted heads watching him and the next man.

"Okay you guys, don't get excited; back for another load."

Trailing their jet roar across the sky, Kowalski set course south. How long till he could strap an F4 to his ass and get up among the goddam MIGs? Goddamit!

Fredericks looked up from his book to meet the curious gaze of a man and his very pregnant wife. They gave nervous smiles, bobbed their heads, and indicated by pointing that they wished to proceed along the road.

Fredericks smiled to put them at ease, and said, "Hello, may I see your identity cards, please! Ah yes. Where do you live? Where were you born? When?" Asking questions about information on the card was a basic check; sometimes VC used cards from which they had not memorized details. However, Nguyen van Banh and Pham thi Nga really did live in Xo Ba and wished to visit Banh's sister and brother-in-law who lived some hundred yards down the street, past B Company HQ, near which Fredericks was standing. After a couple of minutes chatting about the weather, crops, the VC, and the imminent visit of an RC priest, Banh and Nga moved away with smiles much more natural than their initial nervous grimaces.

Fredericks turned to Bruce Myers, who was standing by his small platoon HQ that he had just established inside a grassy yard a few paces behind Fredericks.

"Bloody amazing the difference between the city people and the country ones, ay sir? In the cities all they want to do is fleece you. Out here, they're straightforward, good people like the country people back home."

"Yeah, the Diggers have noticed it too, Freddo. Definitely a better group of people. . . . Where did *they* come from?" as three ARVN strutted around the corner, with their sunglasses, gold watches, clean, starched, tight-tailored uniforms, and ignoring the Australians, bore down on Banh and Nga, who were still only four or five paces away.

"*You!* Halt! *Who* are you? What are *you* doing here? ID card! Where are you going? *Quickly!*"

With a "Back me up, sir," Frederick leaped forward and confronted the three popinjays, SLR muzzle coming up under the chin of the nearest. Vietnamese language includes pronouns that can be used for people or animals and is thus a great language for emphasizing the relative status of the people involved in the conversation.

Fredericks flared, "You! What are *you* doing here? This is an Australian area! You should not be here. You return in two days time, after the Australians as usual. Get!"

The three turned without a word, perhaps amazed by the presence of a foreigner fluent in their own language, and quickly disappeared around the corner. He turned to Banh and Nga, "Go and visit your sister now."

"Who were those little shits?" asked Myers as he, the signaler, and Bart Bartholomew placed their weapons down and resumed their seats on the low stone wall.

"Dunno, sir, but they didn't fight their way into Tien Bien or here with us, and even if they did, they have no right to talk to anybody like that. They make my blood boil, the bastards."

Edmondson stood on the edge of the verandah on which Stan Burrows had established his HQ.

Burrows looked up from his map, "Yes Bob?"

"Sir, I've got three Vietnamese in separate APCs, who say they can lead us to hidden VC dumps. They were forced to work on the construction of them and then carry the supplies to them. They are nervous and say there are many mines and booby traps, but they will lead us to the areas."

"What do you think?"

"I think they are on the level. Corporal Fredericks has done the actual talking to them, he will be going with them, and he will trust them. They are Roman Catholics, and the VC are here by force of arms and government negligence, not by acceptance of the general mass of the population. If we handle these blokes correctly, we can roll up quite a lot of the VC work here, sir."

"Yes; have they given you any idea where the stuff is?"

"Yes sir. Generally in this area here," indicating the spot on the map.

"Good, well we'll have to try in that area tomorrow so warn young Fredericks and the OC, but it will be dealt with in the orders group tonight. Thank you, Bob."

"Yes sir."

As the APCs rolled out along the road next morning, Fredericks watched the Vietnamese standing in the back of the vehicle giving him directions that he relayed to the APC commander. Huynh van Thong was dressed in a spare set of Australian greens, with a crucifix around his neck under the green shirt. Suddenly he began to wave his arms and point down a narrow side track shooting off from the dirt road they were following.

"There! There! Four hundred yards! Stop! stop!"

Fredericks grabbed him by the shoulder, "Okay, okay, we are going past, then coming back on foot."

"Ah," a broad grin as Thong understood the precaution of approaching from the rear.

Half a mile down the road, the APCs slowed, halted, turned about, and the infantry dismounted and swept through the trees on either side of the road but found nothing. Thong strode along the road with the sliding, jogging step of the Asian. He led them around the corner onto the narrow track leading away through the trees, carefully examining the road surface and edges, and the undergrowth clumps encroaching on the narrow cleared away.

He knelt and pointed into the trees: so well sited were the buildings that the casual observer would have had no indication that they were there. A careful approach and examination found no mines or booby traps. Thong sat under a tree while the quantity of rice was estimated and a report radioed to HQ. The APCs grumbled up and crunched and crashed their way around the camouflaged buildings. Made of wood and corrugated iron, with only the minimum of growth cleared to permit construction, they were protected from view by the bushes and trees.

For the next eleven days, dumps or caches were found all over the area. Each was approached with great care, and the contents removed for use by the government.

After the fighting that occured during the occupation of the towns, the VC had hardly been encountered. People had come forward and named the NLF personalities in the towns, and they had been picked up in a series of small actions by groups of infantry in carriers. The NLF members had then been handed over to the police. Of the armed units, nothing had been seen or encountered; they had withdrawn well into the hills and were waiting for the Australians and Americans to leave or for main force units to come to their aid.

The VC commander in Xo Ba was captured by a surprised and highly pleased group of government soldiers and dragged off to Vat Vo to be presented to the province chief. The fact that he had been captured while doing his reconnaissance alone, as none of his unit would come in and attempt to gather the information, was an indication of the state of the VC morale.

As the rice harvest was secured and the government reinstated in the area, the brigade moved south to sweep an area in which fleeting contact was made, and then they returned to base.

Fredericks and Frank Gardiner walked into the doorway of La Popotte.

"Hi Mai, hello Jenny."

Fredericks fell silent as he saw Xuan in her old place behind the bar. Beautiful ao dai, hair coiffed, but eyes hard as agate: cupid's bow mouth set in a hard line, deep furrow from nostrils to chin, and the tinkling silver bells silenced forever in the flat tones as she acknowledged his greeting.

He retreated to a booth, fingers drumming on the formica top as he waited for "garcon" to bring the beers.

Frank was the center of much excited chatter as he had brought Mai a small purse made of kangaroo skin, sent from Australia, and the girls ohed and ahed over it, while Frank, with a smirk, looked forward to reaping his reward from Mai in a few minutes.

For Fredericks, the day had been ruined by the new Xuan. He had seen men he had known for years, and whose families he had known, killed and mutilated as the two sides hunted in the green entanglements for whatever they believed in, be it politics, race, or money. With fire and shot they struggled as animals had never done, to bring their brand of peace; two great beasts struggling and trampling in the arena to prove one ideology supreme, while a girl, whose crime had been to be born into a society where elders came always before self, was brutalized by a man who more rightly could bear the title "vandal" than those who had done so originally. Fredericks could accept what happened to soldiers, that was the name of the game. But Xuan . . .

"Listen, Frank. I'll see you back at the truck, okay?"

"Hey? Yeah, mate. Mai an' me are headin' upstairs anyway. See you."

"See you later, Xuan," trying to show her by his voice and eyes how he feels, but to the hard-eyed woman he is only another foreigner.

Strolling despondently down Tu Do Street, ignoring the blandishments of girls in bar doors, cyclo-drivers, shoeshine boys, Indian tailor-shop touts, assorted money changers and pet sellers, Fredericks saw an American artilleryman he knew from previous operations.

"Hey Bergman, how ya doin'?"

"Hey there Fred. I'm right fine, thank ya. What about a beer?"

"Why not? How about here, the Sporting Bar?"

When they each had a cold-beaded Budweiser in front of them, Fredericks said, "Bergy , you haven't stopped smiling since I saw you there in the street. What have you done? Found the legendary young French virgin of Saigon?"

"Ha, ha, no, no, goddamit. Just got my own back."

"Oh?"

"Yeah, last time I came to this dump, I brought my Nikon. While I was standing right on gaddam Too Doe Street out there, some mother-fuckin' slope cut the strap and pow! Gone man! Shit. Waal, they don't mess with ol' Bergman. No sirree. So," leaning closer to Fredericks, "what I done was, I bought me another Nikon case; just the case. This mornin' I got me a grenade and put it in the case. Then, in town, I held the lever down, pulled the pin, clipped the case shut, and just walked around waitin'. Hey," at the look on Fredericks' face, "perfectly okay, man. Nothin' can happen as long as that lever is in place, you know that, shit. So, I just strolled around, real casual-like and let some bastard take it. Which he did, 'bout three blocks from here, over near the markets. So I just kep' right on walkin'. Yep," to the unasked question, "it did; 'bout three minutes later I heard a boom come up outa one of them little streets over that way. I just keep on grinnin' when I think of them laughin' in that dark little place, thinkin' they put it over another dumb Yank, then sprang! The lever flies off and them rats tryin' to scramble outa that hole in four to six seconds. Ha, ha, ha!" Eyes creased in mirth, "what a surprise!"

"Fuckin' hell, Bergy," was all Fredericks could muster.

"Yep, let's have another on me. A really happy day! Ha, ha!"

Augie Bennett ticked off the last item on his list of announcements that he had just made to the platoon, and looked over the top of the clipboard at the two dozen men in green clothes assembled before him.

"Right, one final thing. Those of you who were there won't forget the Iron Triangle. Or the ARVN mob who sat in the fort while we got the shit blown out of us." Mumble of agreement rising from the group. "Quiet down. Well, the bastards went on an operation in the Dau Dien rubber plantation—and got wiped out to a man—the fucking lot: Yanks, officers, everyone. Ambushed and massacred in the rubber. I might add it's the best news I've had all week."

"Fuckin' oath—too right, sarge—you're right there—serve the bastards right—couldn't happen to a better mob—the miserable pricks—mongrel bastards," rose as the men who had been there grinned or frowned at the news.

Tom Pritchard and Father sat with Nimbus and Les Fitzgibbon in a bar rejoicing in the title of the Yellow Canary, drinking reasonably cold Schlitz. Father and Fitzgibbon were facing the street and frowning a little against the glare bouncing in from the dusty sunny street. Suddenly into their view came two ARVN paratroopers, rolling into the street, obviously having been thrown out of the neighboring bar, the Pussy Cat, frequented by blacks who had made it plain that Whites entered only on invitation. And ARVN also, it seemed.

Father rose quietly and stepped to the door, looking along to the next doorway. Two burly blacks stood, hands on hips, regarding the two furious paras, who stood up, glared, placed their maroon berets on their heads, and walked off, skin-tight camouflaged uniforms dusty from the road. They paused at the corner, looked back and shook their fists; the blacks laughed and reentered the Pussy Cat, oblivious of the stares of the Vietnamese along the street.

Father returned and picked up his can of Schlitz.

"What's goin' on?" queried Pritchard.

"Looks like a couple of ARVN paras tried to get into the blacks' bar and got turfed out."

"Aw yeah?"

"Yeah, they got pissed off out of it."

"Ah, listen, how about a couple more here, then down to the beach for a swim?"

"Fair enough."

After two more rounds, Nimbus, who was facing the rear of the bar, leaned forward. "There's somethin' goin' on here, Father, all the girls are pissin' off, and the bar staff have disappeared—look."

"Come on, settle down Nimbus." But he looked into the long mirror along the wall behind the bar. Casually his glance flicked along; he frowned, and then carefully studied the reflection of every booth.

"You're bloody right. Come on, we're gettin' outa here."

They rose casually and began to walk out. Father stopped and touched Pritchard on the arm, "Hang on, I'll just have a look at the back. Give the blokes in here the word."

He turned and began to walk down the length of the bar, past the rear rooms, the store rooms, the reeking mildewed toilet, and into the weed-grown backyard that gave onto a narrow lane. Clustered in the lane were the bar employees, standing or squatting along the fence a few yards down. They were chattering excitedly but stopped when Father was seen looking out the gate at them. The inscrutable Asian masks settled, and he might have been looking at so many carvings.

He became aware of a presence on the other side, and there were the Pussy Cat staff, huddled up the lane away from their backyard. He turned back to the first group, and one of the girls frowned in warning, flicking her hands in a "go away" gesture. Father turned and ran back through the bar, now silent and deserted except for the quiet figures of the other three, standing back from the windows and staring out at the sunny street.

"Come on. There's definitely something going on here. They're all," hand wave to include the next-door staff, "outside and don't want to know us."

"Yeah," piped up Fitzgibbon, "I had a look next door and there's no nogs, only blacks."

"Time to go," said Father, and they walked out quickly, across the street and down to the corner, ignored by the strangely quiet locals. As they reached the corner, an approaching roar of engine turned their heads back up the street.

Around the far corner came a jeep without hood or windscreen, with four maroon-bereted ARVN. The engine noise quit and the low, squat vehicle slid to a stop just short of the Pussy Cat. The silent, unmoving Vietnamese along the street, those peeping from windows, and the four halted Australians saw one ARVN lift an M60 out of the jeep floor and climb out, followed by two others holding between them a long, sagging, gleaming rope.

"Fuck me! They're gonna brass up the blacks!" from Nimbus.

Before any of them could move, the gunner was standing outside the painted hollow-brick front of the Pussy Cat, adopting the correct braced firing posture, and shouted, "Yankee! Yankee!" to attract the attention of the Americans.

Then he began firing, moving the machine gun up and down, left to right, to ensure the stream of bullets covered the length of the bar. The rattling roar drowned all other noise in the street, nothing existed except the three camouflage-suited figures with maroon berets—incongruous in the sunlit street of bar signs—the brass cartridge cases gleaming in the rays as they spun out and rolled in the dust, the arms of the loaders held out from their bodies, elbows bent, feeding the gleaming snake into the black gun.

The driver sat immobile. The gunner carefully hosed his stream of shot down the length of the bar, not moving from his position. As suddenly as it started, the noise stopped. The silence was as crushing as the yammering burst had been. The gunner cocked the weapon, raised the feed-plate cover, brushed away empty cases and links in the prescribed manner, clicked the cover down, and the three remounted the jeep, made a U-turn, and drove back up the street, disappearing around the corner. Silence: no one moved. The Pussy Cat front was now a riddled mass of shattered brick, covering a scene of carnage from which no sound came.

As a siren noise grew in the distance, Tom Pritchard stepped back, shook the other three, and said, "Come on, let's get inside; your shout, Nimbus."

"It was my fuckin' shout last!"

"Yeah, but that was ruined; it doesn't count!"

13

Bruce Myers looked up from his map to watch the figures of Tomlinson's section spread along the edge of the high bank dropping away to the river. The sunlight flowed down the canyon, striking the leaves from the far side and turning them pale green, against which frieze the men were darker figures.

He mopped his brow, took the radio handset, and gave the platoon's location in code, "Four-two, locstat; Buick: up, two-point-four, left, three-point-seven, over."

"Four-two, Roger, out."

Snapping fingers jerked his head around; Tommy was moving carefully to Knowles's side. Knowles was staring fixedly at something on the far bank of the river. Then the remainder of the section was peering under or over bushes.

Tomlinson turned to look for Myers, a grin on his face and beckoned him forward. Walking a few paces to meet Myers, Tommy grinned and whispered, "There's a noggie sheila getting her gear off on the far bank, Skipper."

Myers frowned, then realized that it was no joke, "Hmm? Best have a look."

Gesturing to the remainder to halt and remain where they were, he quickly but quietly moved forward and under a branch peered toward the far bank.

Tuyet-Nga had left the other six members of the staff of the transit camp and gone down to the river for her afternoon bath. She knew no one of the six men would trouble her; such loose behavior was not tolerated and severely punished.

She sat for a moment, relaxing in the quiet, the chuckling of the water bubbling over the shallows, the blue sky and the sun on the glorious greens on the far bank. Then she rose and quickly stripped off her black pajama suit, tiny bra and cotton panties, took the small piece of soap and stepped into the river.

Balancing, carefully stepping from rock to rock she waded out to mid-thigh depth and sat in the flowing clear water. Rising, she thoroughly lathered—arms, shoulders, breasts, stomach, groin, and legs.

Up on the far bank, there was intense whispered competition for the binoculars.

"Come on Ferdy, you bastard, give us a look!"

"Piss off."

"A man knows who his bloody mates are, ay?"

The entire platoon lined the bank, watching Tuyet-Nga from the shadows.

"Good tits for a nog, mate."

"Yeah, not bad lookin' face either."

"Haven't got to her face yet."

"Aw Jesus, lady, don't wash yer box like that . . ."

"How'd ya like to be a piece of soap, Mitch?"

"Fuckin' what? My fur coat!"

"Keep it quiet, you mob!"

"Finished love? Gonna have a big sunbake now and drive all these randy pricks mad?"

"Nope. She's a good kid. Gonna dry off, get dressed, and go home."

"Wonder if she's got any sisters?"

"Brothers ya mean. Look at the track. Used every day."

Tuyet-Nga dressed and climbed the slope, making her way back to the camp. Phuong smiled and said, "Ah sister, any big fish?"

Tuyet-Nga laughed, hanging her wet towel to dry, "Yes, elder brother, but they only nibble appendages."

Phuong smiled and turned to the others, "Come comrades. Thai, bring the bucket."

The six strolled along, chattering and swinging towels. They climbed down the bank and began undressing, remaining in their underwear shorts.

Myers grinned and looked along the line of prone figures on his left and right, "Okay, here they come. Wait for my order."

Thai filled the bucket and turned to Phuong, "I'll take it back first, comrade, then return."

"Good, good."

Myers sighted on Phuong, drew a breath, said "fire" and squeezed the trigger.

Phuong was lifted off his feet by the three 7.62mm rounds that slammed into his thin body. The water leaped and foamed in white crystal frenzy as the rounds cracked in; the four already knee deep disappeared in the leaping madness.

Thai, terrified by the wall of noise erupting from the peaceful far bank, driven back by the snap of passing rounds, the white foaming where the other four were swallowed, and the sudden horror of Phuong picked up by an invisible string and jerked away, began running up the bank, bucket in hand, water slopping over the edge.

"Hey, look at the bloke with the bucket! Bet a dollar I can hit it!"

"Yer on!"

And almost instantaneously, every man of Myers's platoon was aiming at the bucket; round after round cracked past, over, under, and through it. Thai was carrying little but a handle and ragged top when some spoilsport blew his shoulder blades through his chest, and the riddled remnant of the bucket caught on a bush and swung gently to and fro.

Tuyet-Nga crouched behind a tree, frozen by the paralyzing blast of fire. She remained kneeling, staring eyes fastened on the lighted area of bush at the top of the bank; no one appeared. She huddled there until darkness settled and crept forward to move cautiously over and down the bank: there was—it must be Thai, and Phuong, oh, so terribly mutilated. Where are Chau, Nien, Nhu and Xanh? Oh, who has done this? There was no sign of any puppet or foreign troops.

She knelt in the night at the base of the path down the bank, dark waters gurgling past, but now their cheerful chuckle of the sunny afternoon was mocking, "we know, ha, ha, we know, ha, ha," and suddenly she was a twenty-year-old girl alone in the jungle with two dead men, four others gone, and an unknown thing that killed from a peaceful river!

She ran clawing and clambering up the bank, past Thai's stiff corpse, along the path, through the pitch black by instinct to Phuong's bunker. Seizing his M1, she huddled back in the underground section, the uncocked carbine pointing at the faintly lighter patch of the entrance, until the daylight seeped in and she nervously crept out, drank, and timidly, hesitantly, went to report the deaths at the next camp, nine miles away. Never again would Tuyet-Nga be able to relax fully, no matter how isolated or peaceful the scene.

Bruce Myers had left ten minutes after his last shot had been fired. For the remainder of the afternoon, exchanged glances brought grins and laughter muffled by hands across mouths, as the platoon relived the bathing beauty scene and the "bucket shoot."

Later in the evening, after rejoining the remainder of the company, and after the nightly routine of orders groups, stand-to, and stand-down, Myers lay back on his sleeping gear, head on pack, M16 a long darker shadow beside him, and stared up through the hard black pattern

of the trees into the softer night sky. What was Jackie
doing now? He concentrated his thoughts and tried to
bridge the miles and hours between the patch of dark
Indo-Chinese jungle and bright-lit Sydney. But the jungle
remained about him the same: dark, quiet, tropical warmth,
still.

While part of him was not greatly pleased that she
seemed to be leading an active social life with people he
did not know well, or know at all, his general feeling was
one of approval that she was getting out and not becoming
a recluse, tied to the radio, TV, and newspapers. They had
discussed the matter before he left, and in letters, and
Bruce had repeated that he did not want or expect Jackie
to sit and brood, waiting for bad news.

Her letters were bright and loving, so there was
nothing there, but sometimes, in quiet moments like this,
wishing so much to be with her, and longing for her
presence, separated by thousands of dark miles, a little
glow flared in a corner of his mind—what if? But he
doused it with a defensive move, the philosophical, "If she
is, you're too far away to do anything about it; there's no
sign of it, so stop worrying and go to bloody sleep."

He heard the whispering as the machine-gun picquet
changed and drifted into sleep.

Jackie sipped her Bacardi, watching from the periphery of
her vision the approach of the visiting Frenchman, Jules,
who seemed determined to seduce everyone among the
wives and girlfriends of the office staff, as well as compile
his report for the Paris office.

The girls dubbed him "de Gaulle's secret weapon,"
and every advance was watched by thirty pairs of eyes.
Marie-Louise, his languid wife, watched as well, and had
even approached one of the secretaries herself, stating
that Jules wished to go to bed with her, and she, Marie-
Louise, would not mind if Jennie did so.

Jennie swallowed her drink without choking and man-
aged a "This is very kind of you, Marie-Louise."

"Oh, eet is nothing serious. Ze experience, you
understand?"

Now, here he was, smiling, that Parisian "style" in his manner, while across the room Marie-Louise, head tilted while expelling smoke upwards, was observing with clinical interest as Jules spoke softly, "Ahh, Jac-ee," and she smiled at him, not hearing his conversational gambit, thinking, "Sorry, Jules. Harry Brandon is one thing, but itinerant scalp hunters quite another."

Marie-Louise met Jennie's eyes across the room, and she raised her eyebrows and moved her head slightly to say without words, "There, you have missed out, cherie."

Jennie raised her own eyebrows and gave a very Gallic shrug, before turning casually back to listen to the company secretary inviting them to a barbeque to celebrate his new swimming pool at his home at French's Forest.

The noon hush weighed the sunlit, shadow-dappled scene—quiet except for buzzing insects and the drone of a few low-pitched voices. The company was digesting its lunch.

Red Ryder consulting his map, "Baron" working out the rosters for the coming night's radio and MG picket at CHQ, the Diggers with ever-present paperbacks, letters, or dozing.

In one rifle section, a low-voiced argument on changes of nationality, "I was born in England and I'll always be an Englishman—and proud of it!"

"I was born there too, y'know, but I came out to Australia to be an Australian. My kids are Australians, they go to Australian schools; I pay taxes in Australia, vote in elections, own a house there—I've been naturalized, and now I'm an Australian, so is Phyllis and so are the kids."

"That's only paper! It's what's inside that counts. England! Always and forever! If you're born in Germany, you're a German, if you're born in Canada, you're a Canadian. I was born in England, and I'll always be English!"

"Oh, so if you're born in a stable, you're a horse!"

Silence.

* * *

Claudia Ryder hummed in time to Beethoven's *Pastoral* as she put the finishing touches to the tray of hors d'oeuvres. Rod and Diana would be here any minute, and good timing, she was ready. Ah, the bell. Humming, she danced over the floor, flicking off the chain, opened it with a smile.

"Right on time. Hel..."

"He's still killing women and children, and picking up diseases from the filthy har..."

The lightning flickered through her body, and one thought flashed before her mind—you bastard—and she launched herself from the stair top, knocking the small dark figure to the ground; as though she had rehearsed, she found herself stepping back up onto the step and jumping onto his body, all her 102 pounds behind the fashionable high pointed heels of her shoes. His breath gurgled out, rising to a shriek. She stepped back and sank her pointed toe into his stomach and back as he squirmed, hearing her own low voice, "You bastard, you bastard, you bastard"; as he rolled to his hands and knees, she grabbed his hair, turned his face up, and dragged her hooked nails diagonally across the still indistinct face.

He howled and struck out, landing one flailing fist in her side, pushing her away. Windows slid open, and a voice called, "What's going on there?"

Breathless, she could not answer, but advanced on the dark figure, who was clutching his face with one hand, the other holding the spot where the heel-tips impacted. Head down, he suddenly butted her off her feet. The voice from above was joined by others, "Hey you! Is that you, Claudia? Robert, there's a man attacking a woman down here!"

As she sprawled backward, the creature scuttled off with a moan into the darkness.

"Claudia! Are you all right?" Rod and Diana came running down the passage from the car park; a few other people from the building appeared from the doorways.

"Yes thanks. He got the worst of it. I thought it was you and opened the door instead of checking. Then I lost my temper and gave him something to remember me by."

When the neighbors had dispersed, the police and security men gone, she began her delayed dinner, laughing, sparkling, on top of her form.

"You know, it's marvelous! I feel tremendous! I was worried and afraid. Now, I've beaten the little swine, and if he ever comes back, he'll get the same treatment. I feel as if a great dark weight has been taken from my shoulders."

Two days later, the security officer telephoned.

"Oh, Mrs. Ryder, Lieutenant Bowers here, how are you? Oh good. Well, your caller was, as we now believe, a civilian who had been employed as a steward in the mess. Yesterday he appeared at the unit where he is at present employed on a casual basis, collected his money and left. He appeared to be in some pain and had bandages over a great deal of his face. Unfortunately, we were only informed of this today. He's left his lodgings, and at the moment the police are looking for him. However, going on past performances of that type person, I don't think he'll be back. Thank you. Glad we could help. Good afternoon."

And the creature crawled off to lick its wounds and wait for easier prey.

14

"See scenic Vietnam," snarled Nimbus as he hauled himself up out of the canal onto the bank. "Why do we always have to soldier in shit areas?"

The battalion struggled, splashed, submerged, and swam through an area of swamp, paddy, creeks, and canals, searching for the elusive Cong. After two days, and one known kill to the Australians, the neighboring Americans claimed 140-odd. Food supplies and weapons were found, but few armed VC.

For several days the brigade chased the enemy through the trees and bushes, along canals and over paddies; much ammunition was expended with casualties to both sides, but no decisive actions were fought. The overwhelming air power and artillery were brought to bear when possible, but the area could only be dominated by a long-term occupation with its attendant patrols, checkpoints, and denial of resources to the enemy. Time was what Americans begrudged: upward lines on graphs were the be-all and end-all.

Enemy killed, weapons captured, prisoners, surrendered enemy, munitions and supplies taken, refugees under government control, populated areas under the government flag—all were the subject of graphs showing "progress." Even the all-important battle for the minds had its "progress" reduced to statistics: so many leaflets dropped, so many lectures, broadcasts, and speeches delivered, so many enemy surrendered bearing the leaflet as a "safepass." Despite the USAF statistics of sorties flown, bombs dropped, trucks destroyed, and so on ad nauseam, the new Soviet material arrived in ever-increasing amounts: AK47 rifles, SKS carbines, RPD LMGs, 12.7mm DShK HMGs, RPG2 antitank rockets, helmets, webbing, belts, radios, mortars, mines.

Captain Frank Hartman drove the Cessna 0–1 "Bird Dog" right down to treetop level, peering under the low branches and the eaves of the houses. The little bastards had to be in there. The area was so wet and marshy that water was struck only a foot or so down. They could not have tunnels under the ground; therefore they must be above—in the trees, bushes, and houses. The amount of ground fire and ground contacts showed that the VC were ready to fight here.

The four Skyraiders circling above were waiting for Hartman to find a target. He was almost taxiing up to the doors of the houses trying to look inside. So far today there had been no ground fire, but on the previous two days there had been a great deal. He climbed and set a zigzagging course toward the areas being cleared by the ground forces; they might flush out something. At this early hour, the sun's rays shot in under the trees and house eaves making it easier to see in there, but it also bounced off the water's surface in the ponds, fields, and canals, in slabs of hard silver glare painful to the eyes, despite the sunglasses.

Flicking to the radio frequency allocated to the ground troops, Hartman heard reports of a contact and of a mortar or artillery fire controller passing a fire mission. Then the fountains of earth, mud, water, and leaves shot up. Ah, over there—climb, circle—nothing—bamboo—feathery clumps, trees, bushes, canals criss-crossing in long straight lines, scattered thatched-roof hamlets, orchards, tiny flitting figures along a canal bank.

Dive, pull out alongside, break over the top of them, height seventy feet, Asians pointing arms, guns raised. Okay then, the radio!

"Polecat Blue, this is Layback Five Three, estimated platoon of Victor Charlie on canal bank north of me, going in for smoke now, over."

"Layback, this is Polecat, Roger, over."

Never taking his eyes from the spot where he saw the VC, Hartman spiraled up, trying to keep between them and the sun. He could hear the firing directed at him, snapping over his engine noise—thunk! thunk!—as holes appeared in the wing surface. Is the fire coming from the VC he's watching? Thunk, thunk, thunk, behind somewhere, controls still okay, right—select rockets, here we ... thunk, thunk, thunk, thunk, Jesus, smoke in the cockpit—flames under the engine cowling—thunk, thunk, thunk, thunk, throttle back, stick and rudder—spinning—trees, water, roofs flicking past, growing larger ...

"Hey, they've hit that 'Bird-Dog!'"

Bart Bartholomew followed the pointing arm to see against the pale sun-glared sky the silhouette of the spinning plane—trailing a corkscrew of smoke down, down, down.

They had been following the group of VC flushed

from the cluster of houses just behind, seen the aircraft spiral up, drive, and climb again, followed by a crackle of gunfire in which a machine gun bopped out regular bursts.

"That nog gunner is on the mark, ay?"

Hartman watched the ground surging up—now—throttle, stick and rudder—power—straighten up, pull out—below tree tops—between these two—smoke and flames—field ahead, stick back, back, back,—throttle closed—switch everything off—grass, water—splosh! into the mud—everything gone behind a brown cascade of water and mud—stopped—door—M16 off rack—still flames—out out! Thank Christ into the open—over to that paddie bund. Chest heaving, Hartman lay.half in, half out of the water, keeping low amid the grass stalks. Who was around, VC or friends? Must move, the VC might get here first; the smoke is a good marker; roar in the blue—here comes Polecat, propeller disc shimmering, rolling as he flashes over—wave—Polecat Two . . . Three . . . Four arcing back up. Watch the ground, goddamit! Figures running along the tree line; stay low, M16 cocked; where's that blood coming from? Jesus, hit in the head and arm—anywhere else? Have to wait. Here they come, more cautiously, spread out. That guy is tall for a slope; and that one . . . Australians!

"Hey, you guys, here! Hey!"

"Bart, over here. . . . G'day mate. You all right?"

And Hartman slumped over onto his back, roaring with laughter.

"Am I all right Jeesus! I've just been shot down, blood running all over me and he asks if I'm all right! Ha, ha, ha," as his eyes followed the other green figures moving past the burning Cessna to secure the paddie. Above, four Polecats snarled in a circle, waiting.

"Hye, Aussie, you got a radio near? I got a target for them—the little fucker who put me here," as Myers came up with his radio operator trailing behind.

Vo thi Phuong stood on the edge of the canal and beckoned her mother and sister to her with a palm-down motion of the Asian. Anxiously, she peered at the sky visible through the trees lining the canal. For the past three days they had tried to get to market. Each time an airplane had appeared and either attacked or called others, circling while they paddled along, until the other screaming birds arrived and dived. Quickly, they climbed into the canoe, and the three set off paddling rapidly and keeping a keen eye on the sky.

Over a mile later Phuong's sister suddenly started, paddle splashing, and pointed to the east, "Hai! Helicopters! Look, look!"

The others' eyes flicked around, and there were the two aggressive bumblebees, soundless yet speeding nose-down along the intersecting canal.

"Quick, into the bank!" The three paddles flashed and the boat shot under the shade of the trees. The women grabbed onto the grass stalks, sitting motionless in the darker area, holding their breath, talking in whispers as if the distant monsters could hear them. The dark shapes followed the other canal, and as they passed the intersection, all three women released a collective sigh of relief. Then the dark death-bees began to circle a spot on the far canal; one climbed a little, turned, and dived. To the ears of Phuong and the other two, the machine guns sounded as a dull, distant moan; rockets flashed momentarily and slid down their trail of smoke, water spouts leapt above the trees. The circling continued while the three women held on, motionless, staring at the small angry shapes; then the two departed, following the line of the trees.

The three women remained in the shadows for several minutes, then slowly paddled along, heads turning continuously, eyes staring at the sky, small black-clad mice scuttling under the threat of the merciless, impersonal hawk.

As the canoe came up to the canal intersection, Phuong peered along to the right, in the direction the helicopters had been firing.

"Mother! Lan! Look!" pointing to the almost awash canoe drifting toward them under the shadows, splintered areas showing lighter against the dark wood, collapsed bundles of rags inside, an arm dangling from one huddled

black cotton pile, dragging in the water and trailing a
black rope—no, an eel feasting on the torn flesh!

The three women sat petrified as the sinking canoe
drifted downstream past their stern, trailing pink ribbons
into the murky canal water where blood trickled out of the
bullet holes.

"Who are they?" whispered Lan.

"I did not see any faces. Perhaps it was the people
from Ap Hoa Tien. They live that way."

Phuong turned to her mother, "Should we go on?"

Old Le stared into the sky, "They might come back."

"But we must get food."

"Yes, yes. If we are careful. We shall go on."

Paddling with the quiet strength of desperation, the
three continued on their way. Suddenly they heard a
muttering roar behind and turned to see silhouetted against
the light down the avenue of trees one of the dreaded
bees. The three women began a terrified paddling, trying
to outspeed a 100-mile-an-hour Horseman of the Apocalypse.

Specialist Four Ted Coszynski grinned behind his
microphone and dark green visor and spoke to the pilots.
"Looks like more up front, Lieutenant. They sure as hell
started paddling faster when they saw us."

"Okay, Coszynski, your turn."

The Huey climbed slightly, moving to one side and
paralleling the trees, the second gunship falling behind.

Leaflets, advising people to stay home for the next
few days, had been dropped when the operation began, so
anyone moving could be assumed to be VC. Whereas an
infantryman can take time to search a house, or halt
travelers and question them, a helicopter is not the best of
machines from which to ask a peasant his destination. And
as a distressed fish attracts sharks by its splashings, if the
peasants show signs of alarm, the pilot presumes they are
probably enemy.

The three women stared in terror at the frightening
beast thrumming swiftly up behind them.

"Quickly! we must get out of the canoe!"

They reached the bank and leaped for the top as
Coszynski began firing—waterspouts sparkled up, splin-

ters flew, Lan screamed as her conical straw hat was
plucked away by a snapping devil cracking past her ear,
the roaring engines and yammering machine gun overwhelmed their brains as the helicopter slowed and pivoted
overhead, hunter-hawk, eyes behind green visors peering
down for mice-people-prey.

"Where'd they go?" asked Coszynski, as they circled
tightly over the canoe.

"Let's see what rotor blast will do," as the pilot
descended using the whirlwind to buffet the trees, bushes,
and grass. Nothing moved.

Coszynski riddled the drifting canoe, taking pleasure
from his accuracy as the tracers streaked down into the
writhing leaping foam, and the shattered canoe drifted
apart.

"C'mon, no canoe, no carrying supplies. Let's go."

The Hueys thrummed off along the canal.

"Coszynski, you can have a canoe to your score."

"Holy shit, Lieutenant. I ain't gonna paint no goddam
canoe on this bird. We're here to zap Cong, goddamit."

The eight young men sped across the countryside in
their twin flying machines, looking for enemy to zap. Only
VC show signs of guilt when the government and its allies
appear, so anyone running is VC.

Phuong, Le, and Lan crept out of the holes dug along
the canal bank, eyes large with fright. "We must go back.
We will be killed."

Silently the three turned and began trotting the two
and a half miles home, keeping a careful eye on the sky.

For the next two days the entire population of the
hamlet huddled at home, never moving far from their
homes and shelters. NLF armed units moved past but had
no food to spare. Then Le saw the silhouettes of foreigners
down the far reaches of the canal bank.

"Quick! hide!" The men remaining scuttled into their
hiding places in canal banks, in paddies, sugarcane fields
or elsewhere. The women and children hid in the prepared shelters. Separate hiding places were necessary as
the government took men to be soldiers, the tax collector
accompanied soldiers and so did the landlord's man; and

perhaps these foreigners were like the French, who forced
men to be carriers of loot and ammunition, taking them far
from home and into battles, or perhaps they were like the
North African troops who sodomized everyone.

Phuong, Le, and Lan crowded into the shelter with
the five children. They shut the shelter and sat quietly in
the dark, gaining comfort by holding hands. Time passed
in the pitch black. Then foreign voices were heard. The
hands squeezed tighter in the dark and fear made the
silence and blackness into a physical weight pressing on
each pounding chest.

The cover was suddenly whipped away and light
streamed in. Nothing happened; then a Westerner cautiously
peered in and pulled his face away.

A foreign voice was heard, "Get Freddo, there's a
whole crowd of 'em in here."

"Buncha women an' kids in there. Searched the place,
nothin' so far."

"Okay. Hey in there! Come on out. We won't hurt
you. We do not hurt women and children. Come on."

"We are afraid."

To himself and the couple of infantrymen present,
Fredericks muttered, "Jesus. If something happens you
know what to do." Shrugging out of his webbing and laying
his weapon aside, he knelt in front of the shelter.

"Look, I have no gun. I will come in and talk to you,"
and in English, "a man must be bonkers."

Crawling into the shelter with a torch, feet poking out
into the house, he shone the light about and counted the
inmates, noting the fear in the eyes of the women and the
curiosity of the children. After some minutes coaxing, they
were persuaded to come out, and crawled blinking into
the kitchen.

As usual the children did most to break the ice and
bridge the gap. The sight of the biscuits offered to the kids
prompted Le to start the long story of their isolation from
the market. Halfway through the long recital, a droning
announced the arrival of a "Bird-Dog." The obvious fright
with which they all looked up and followed its passage
convinced Fredericks.

During the next couple of hours he observed similar signs in other people in the hamlet and pointed it out to Edmondson.

Edmondson watched their reactions to several passing aircraft then turned to one of his men. "Hop along to BHQ and see if the FAC is busy," referring to the forward air controller, "and ask him to come over here. I want to show him something."

"Hey, that's really interesting," observed the USAF captain, watching the nervous clustering inside doorways as the Huey throbbed over and settled near BHQ. "These people are really scared."

"They say the aircraft shoot at anyone."

"Well, hell, they were told to stay at home."

"This is a different society. They can't just phone for deliveries, you know."

"The idea is to halt unnecessary movement in the area and make it simpler for us. God knows, we don't want to hurt innocent people. If they aren't VC, they have nothing to fear."

"Have you ever thought how terrifying it might be to a peasant to be buzzed by a chopper? He gets frightened and runs. He runs and he's VC. This is the effect your air power has on people—look at them."

"How do you know they're not VC?"

"I don't. How do the pilots know they *are?*"

"Look Bob, we aren't getting anywhere. Our job is to support the ground forces. Interdiction is one part of that help. And ground fire *is* a big problem here. You know how many birds are downed in the south by small-arms fire alone?"

"No, I don't, but I know it's considerable."

"Christ, they're *told*. What more can we do? Let Charlie run free?"

When the FAC had gone, Fredericks stood up from where he had been sitting listening to the conversation, shook his head and said, "Well, there are two sides to it, sir, but how will these people believe the government, which is over the horizon and out of sight, is their friend, when all the planes are government?"

*   *   *

Battalion Commander Ba Thanh and Political Officer Bay Chieu knelt in the shade of a lantana clump and watched the buzzing gunships beating along the canals to the west.

"Comrade," said Ba Thanh, "I think we should remain here till dark, then move to the Two Dragons rendezvous. Puppet and foreign troops are on all sides," indicating the map case opened on the ground before them, "and 600 men moving are sure to be seen."

Two members of the reconnaissance platoon crouched under the next clump and listened carefully to the commerical model Sony radios they carried. From the radios squawked the voices of the foreigners; the two English speakers frowned in concentration as they listened to the transmissions of their enemies and tried to locate the positions referred to on their own maps. One started up and crawled through the grass to the two commanders.

"Comrade, an American unit traveling in APCs reports itself here," pointing to a canal line to the northeast. He crawled back to his Sony.

The two stared at the map; Ba Thanh for the first time felt worry stir in his stomach. "They might come right upon us," he muttered, tracing the reported locations and extending the line across the map: it went through their present position.

Puppet marines to the north and northwest; US troops to the northeast, east, and south. Aircraft constantly flying along the canals to the west, as well as above the enemy troops. Ba Thanh decided on a course of action:

"Comrade, we will bury the heavy weapons here; one platoon will move to the northeast and create a diversion while the reconnaissance platoon finds a way out to the southwest, west, and southeast. Rendezvous is the place of Two Dragons, referring to the junction of the large creeks. Bay Chieu nodded.

The diversionary platoon trotted off, camouflage of branches and leafy vines nodding with the movement. Ba Thanh trotted over to where the recoilless rifles, mortars, and machine guns were being tightly wraped in plastic and buried in the mud, hidden in shallow trenches under

bushes and covered over with dirt and leaves, or sunk in
the canals. The highly trained and highly motivated reconnaissance platoon had already departed.

Suddenly, the rolling roar of firing broke out to the
north. The hovering mechanical insects darted toward the
spot; artillery shells threw fountains of mud skywards with
the thud of slamming doors. The headquarters group
knelt, watching the diversion. Listening to the chatter
coming from their modified Sonys, the two reconnaissance
men were nodding and smiling as the diversion tactic
succeeded. Bay Chieu looked in the direction of the
reconnaissance platoon's pathfinding to see a gunship,
thrumming nose down in a straight line toward the artillery fire, suddenly break into a circling pattern, its attendant mate following, but always on the other extremity of
the circle.

"What are they looking at?" But all of them knew
what the helicopters were scenting. The Sony listeners
looked up and nodded. The gunships had seen men below
where they were circling.

Bay Chieu spoke up, "All they know is that there are
men there," pointing to the artillery, "and there," pointing
to the circling hunters. "We can remain concealed here
and do nothing to attract attention."

Ba Thanh nodded and sent for the company commanders. Quickly, he gave his orders. The five companies
dispersed around the two adjoining paddies, not on the
edges but in the field itself. Ba Thanh estimated that it
would be two hours till dusk. Then after dark the platoons
and companies could begin their creeping, crawling, wriggling, noiseless way out of the area.

Now the gunships were machine gunning the targets
they saw; a "Bird-Dog" flitted over and began dipping and
sniffing along the tree lines. Under the droning and thrumming of the plane engines, and the ripping calico sound of
the machine guns, came the deeper roaring of ground
vehicle engines. Suddenly the first M113 roared and
swung itself up onto the bund, wet flanks dripping
and gleaming golden in the sun, helmeted heads turning,
and rifles and machine guns pointing across the fields. It

turned and grumbled along the bund. Peering out through
the frieze of grass, Ba Thanh saw, one after the other,
M113s arrive on the edge of the paddies. Scattered firing
broke out as investigatory tracer flicked into the distant
trees. No reply; shooting stopped.

The first muddy monsters dipped their noses over the
edge of the bund and slid down into the flooded paddy,
wallowing their way across. Ba Thanh seized his own
hollow reed, preparing to submerge and breathe through
it when the huge threshing beasts came near him; deep
breath, reed in mouth, lie back into the blindness, the
roaring transmitted through the water to every inch of his
body. He felt the pressure in his ears as one roaring
engine went by; soon they will be gone, sweeping on, and
the battalion can go on to Two Dragons.

But the noise goes on. What? Very cautiously, Ba
Thanh raises his head. The riders on the M113s are staring
down into the water, pointing, one raises his rifle and
fires down; the other vehicles are not going away but
turning for another trip across. Men pointing into the
fields. They have found some of the hiding battalion. The
firing started as the Americans systematically ploughed
the fields with bullets, rockets, mortars, and artillery, then
drove back and forth across the fields.

Their weapons useless because of mud and water, or
the plastic wrapping, the battalion endured the slaughter,
buffeted by water pressure, pierced by shot and shell,
washed to the surface by the turbulence created in the
wake of the rampaging M113s.

As night fell, the flares popped continuously over the
scene; but the wavering lights created grotesque shadows
from many different angles, and the exhausted survivors
began slowly, carefully creeping out through the small
gaps in the ring of surrounding enemy who persisted in
talking, coughing, smoking, eating with rattle of cans, and
fiddling with weapons.

As the sun flared over the eastern trees, Ba Thanh
and Bay Chieu sat under a tree receiving reports from the
companies as survivors crept in. The surviving Sony
squawked, and the tired listener passed the information to

the command group. Muddy faces stared to the south where the tiny dots of circling aircraft glinted in the dawn sun. Soon the haze would make them invisible, but for the moment, in the freshness of dawn, the eye could cover the nine miles to the scene of the slaughter.

At midday, the administration officer had reported 340 comrades arrived at the RV; 260 were missing.

"Comrade," said Bay Chieu, "assemble the battalion and I will speak to them," pointing to the clump of bamboos to the rear.

Back at the scene of the slaughter, for a battle it was not, the young paratrooper major from brigade intelligence, S2, walked along the bund to the commander's Huey, which had set down on a higher, drier piece of ground.

Sitting casually on a small field table, with his trademark—the huge bowie knife—prominent on his hip, the brigadier general conferred with COs of the infantry units and APCs. The general, tall and lean in the paratrooper mould, took his cigar out of the corner of his mouth and regarded the waiting S2 through cold green eyes.

"Ho theah, S2, what yo'all got theah?"

The S2 suppressed a desire to reply in like manner. "Wha Gen'ril, yo wooden b'leafe thuh whole raft a dock-u-ments we'uns got from these heah lil'oh'Cong, suh, No-sirree Bob!"

Instead, he "popped" to attention and snapped off a springy airborne salute, "Sir, two full sandbags and these satchels," pointing to the pile at his feet, "all identifying individuals, companies, and headquarters elements of 808 Main Force Battalion. We have roll books, certificates, letters, and other documents of men in all five companies. Some heavy weapons were found," snappily pointing, "over by the trees. I'd say we got the whole battalion surrounded here. Body count so far: 210 KIA, plus eleven wounded here, and another eight KIA by body count in the preliminary contacts north and south. Total: 218 KIA, eleven WIA captured, plus 187 individual and crew-served weapons. What's in the mud yet, we don't know. Reckon we won't hear of the 808th for some time, General."

"Uh, huh. Good, good." Turning to the silent, grinning infantry and APC officers, "Very good. Let mah people have thuh names of deservin' ind'v'du-als foh deck-or-ashuns. Okay now. Ah'm goin' back to mah CP. Make shore thuh press people do get uh good coverage of all this heah."

Casual wave from cap brim to acknowledge the salutes, cigar flung into the paddy, and the general climbed into his Huey.

Bay Chieu stood to one side, watching the quietly assembling companies. His thoughts flitted back over the years—to his father, a very minor clerk but able to give his son five years of elementary education, which sparked a burning need to read so that he devoured every written thing in reach. With the reading, the questioning, "Why were the Vietnamese people partitioned and ruled by the French?" The first tentative moves into political discussions with friends. The fear of the French Surete. The growing hatred of the French and those Vietnamese who embraced everything foreign and rejected their own heritage. Then the Japanese came; the French masters were themselves subordinate to Asians! The puerile, badly planned, catastrophic French attempt to overthrow the Japanese in March 1945. The quiet Japanese struck first and soundly trounced the French, then gave independence to Vietnam. The heady days in power till the French and British arrived, post-Hiroshima, and the struggle since. The dithering, prattling socialists and democrats of every shade, so easy to outmaneuver and so simple to denounce to the French, who thus removed local opponents of the Viet Minh until only the men of the revered Ho remained.

When the French left, Bay Chieu went to the north; in 1960 he returned south to assist in the revolution. Now, with no family of his own, his parents dead, and uncaring for the fate of his brothers, Bay Chieu devoted every waking hour to the revolution. A party member since 1953, he had dedicated his life to the party. He never thought of his "old age," and in fact, did not expect such a period in his life.

Most of the battalion had washed their clothes, all had cleaned their weapons, and wounds had been bandaged. He caught the eye of several party comrades who were primed for their part in the coming address.

He stood, hand on satchel slung over his shoulder, looking around in the shady, pleasant place: so cool and green, so quiet—only the faint humming of a distant helicopter—and thought for a moment of other groups of revolutionaries who had gone into the wilds—Mao Tse Tung in the caves of Yennan, Ho and Giap in the mountains of the north—and his face firmed with resolution. The watchers noted the change in his features and muttered conversation ceased as he stepped forward.

"Comrades," looking around at the attentive eyes, "Comrades of the National Liberation Front. We have lost many comrades who have sacrificed their lives for the revolution: 260 brave soldiers have given their lives for the front, the people and the country. Comrades, why did they die, for what?" He held up one hand, palm down, encompassing the entire group in one wave, intense, penetrating eyes sweeping the faces.

"They died for unification! Our country! Freedom! Our people! They were soldiers to struggle for independence!"

Member Bi, "Our Country!"

And others, on cue, "Freedom! Our people! independence!"

Bay Chieu was astute enough to play on the Vietnamese xenophobia. He held up both hands and silence returned to the cool green meeting place at Two Dragons.

"Comrades, our departed heroes died to lift the yoke of the Saigon regime, to remove the burden of the greedy landlord, to destroy the police repressive measures, to allow our country to guide its own progress. They died for the children, youth, housewives, students, artists and writers, workers, and all the people of our Vietnam!"

In softer tones, "But for what do the puppet troops and the Americans and their lackeys die? They say 'democracy,' but everyone knows the Saigon regime does not represent the real people—the workers. The puppet troops die for the greedy, immoral generals fighting each other in Saigon. They die for the religious bigots and the landlords and money lenders! And the Americans! This is not their country! They fight for the 'American way of life' here, for their culture, and what is it?—the bars, the black market, the dissolution of youth, the destruction of morals: they turn our women and girls into prostitutes. That is all they want in our Vietnam—drinks and sex. That is what they die for—filth, corruption, and the yoke on our peoples' necks!"

Softer, intense tones, "But our men and women sacrifice their lives for the good of the nation. For our nation's future, development, and progress. Comrades, they," pointing to the south, finger stabbing the air, eyes blazing, jaw rigid, "they think we are defeated! Are we?"

Party members bounding up, "No! Never! No! No!" The remainder caught on the surging wave—arms and weapons waving over heads.

"Very well! Tonight we attack the puppet troops at Tra Quoc!"

"Attack! Forward! On! On! Assault! Down with the Saigon regime! Tra Quoc! Forward!"

Shouting now, "Comrades! Quiet! Comrade Ba Thanh will now explain our plan. Battalion 808 is a 'Determined to Fight, Determined to Win' unit. Tonight! Assault to victory!"

Twenty-four hours later, the brigade S2 puzzled over reports by ARVN that 808 Main Force Battalion had overrun the Tra Quoc post, killing forty-seven government soldiers, ambushing the relief column, and departing, for the loss of two bodies left behind.

"How the—? Hey, Top," to the top sergeant, "how can the goddam 808th *do* this? Jeesus, we still have bags of documents positively identifying the mothers twenty-one miles away, here, where *we* got 'em. They definitely lost over 200 KIV, yet next night, hit a GVN outpost. Goddamit! The general *and* the press think the 808th was destroyed two days ago. Keep this quiet, or you an' me 'll be checking movements of penguins in the goddam Antarctic."

"Hmm, okay sir."

15

Fifteen miles from the Place of Two Dragons, Stan Burrows glanced around the assembled officers: company commanders, arty and APC officers, FAC, brigade LO, intelligence officer, and helicopter LO.

"We all know the VC have been receiving information on our operations. This time, we moved down here and used the normal methods of planning and deployment; but while we were here, the brigade has planned another operation. We will be lifting off tomorrow and flying north to here," tapping the map. "The ARVN won't get their copy of the op. order until the choppers are on the way. This time, we might just surprise them. Now, the IO."

Edmondson rose and faced the assembled officers, "Sir, gentlemen. The enemy here," small circular wave with the pointer, "is the HQ for this area," larger circle on the map. "Everything is in there—the offices for personnel, operations, supplies, recruiting and propaganda, intelligence and reconnaissance. They are defended by the D603 Main Force Battalion."

The briefing continued until the "questions" period, and the group dispersed to conduct their own briefings.

Next morning, the waiting groups lay in the usual sprawled postures, some peering into the morning sky for the B52s that would precede the strike. Then, threshing on remorselessly came the slicks, shaking out into the long

rising and falling strings of ten with attendant gunships
buzzing along just behind.

They're down; over, climb in; here we go, riding up
that invisible glassy slope, wind pummeling clothes and
hair. Fingers pointing ahead—there, the giant footsteps
plodding across the horizon puffing up great clouds of
smoke: the B52s. Smoke fringing away, fading at the
edges; tiny midges diving, fresh smoke billowing from the
jet-fighters' bombs. There are the aggressive gunships,
beating alongside.

Ahead of the oncoming armada, one of Ba Dinh's
signals operators came running with a message, "Comrade, comrade! US B52s will bomb this area in fifteen
minutes and the Americans and Australians are to search
the area thirty minutes from now. From our agent at their
HQ. The order has only just been delivered."

Bay Dinh seized the message and scanned it, then ran
to Hai Quyen's office, situated in a small house. Hai
Quyen snapped out, "Quickly! Emergency move! Plan
Three. Send the battalion commander to me."

"Ah comrade, the US intends to attack this place.
Your unit has a high spirit and a famous fighting record.
They must hold the paratroopers until the headquarters
can escape. We will use Plan Three; north to the river,
along it to the west into the Flame Tree Camp, here."

"Very well, comrade. The 603 unit is resolved to
strike hard blows at the enemy."

While he had been speaking, Hai Quyen had been
packing documents into a metal trunk with handles for
ease of carrying.

He ran next door to supervise the packing of the
office and sent the first groups away with the maps and
most important documents; overhead the 750-pound bombs
were leaving the bomb racks. Hai Quyen ran next door to
pack his personal gear when the earth shook and dust
showered from the roof as the first bomb hit, then the
second, the third, and the world became a roaring, pounding
smoke- and dust-filled tray of earth shaken by the giants
above. With only a momentary pause, the jet fighters
began diving, bombing, rocketing, firing cannon, and

dumping napalm into the trees. The evacuation plan disintegrated as the shaken survivors, harangued by their leaders, picked up the dead and wounded, and ran under the smoke pall and diving jets, fleeing north.

As the assaulting slicks dropped lower and lower, the infantry saw the smoke and dust ahead and then to the sides, bomb craters fresh against the green, oozing gray spiraling smoke; uprooted trees, shattered trunks, jets diving overhead to release the slim pods that blossomed into the billowing red-orange-yellow flowers in the dark green mass.

And as the choppers settled, dust billowing out from the rotor down-blast, machine guns and rifles opened fire from the trees as D603 began its task. The snarling gunships threshed along the sides of the LZ, machine guns and rockets blazing.

The infantry leaped out cocking weapons, and attacked into the trees. The effects of the bombardment, gunship strafing, and assaulting infantry combined to make most VC fire inaccurate, but green-clad figures dropped here and there.

Then the real infantry work began: clearing the sides of the LZ and advancing on the HQ location. D603 could only slow down, not halt, the flowing mass that constantly outflanked and tried to encircle them. Carrying what dead and wounded they could, they retreated, buying precious minutes for the HQ staff to escape.

Lieutenant Phil Harrison halted and turned to his signaler, two paces behind; taking the headset, he began to transmit. Fifty yards away, the small man peering through the bushes realized that *there* was an officer with a radio, exactly what he had been waiting for, and touched together the two ends of the wires he held in his hands. The current flashed along the wires and the emplaced 105mm shell exploded at Harrison's feet, blowing him to pieces and propelling the shocked signaler back ten yards into the bush.

Tommy Tomlinson, running, crouched over, slid to a halt as he saw the black-clad figure from the corner of his eye. The VC was taking careful aim at someone—M16 up, sighting along its length, Tommy squeezed off three quick shots: the VC was flung sideways, rifle arcing into the bush. The section swept through; the man was dead.

"Here," throwing the AK47 to a rifleman, "hang onto this. Here are the mags."

Moose Morrissey halted behind the house, staring across the open ground bordered by shrubbery and trees. After the firing of the past minutes, all was too quiet. "If they haven't got guns covering that open space, they're not as smart as I think they are."

On the right, two dry creeks ran almost parallel a few yards from each other, before joining and running as one down to the far end of the clearing and through the forest.

Lieutenant Ryan beckoned his section commanders and Moose. "They won't have had time to lay mines, so the creek beds should be okay. We'll go as fast as possible down the left one, along till we get to the trees ahead, then go left or right, depending on what it's like when we get there. We might get behind them. Corporal Rutherford first, then you, Corporal Jones, and you Corporal Canning. Speed! Okay? Let's go."

As the platoon slid into the creek bed, inaccurate fire from the bush on both sides kicked up dust on the surface of the clearing. A machine gun firing from the trees ahead to their right beat on the left lip of the creek bank. The platoon hugged the right side of the bed and moved forward. The leading scout halted to scan the open area of the creek junction to his front as he reached the end of the intervening mound. A single shot cracked amid the machine gun bursts, and the scout collapsed. Ryan, already passing the lead section to see for himself the next leg of their journey, ran forward and knelt by the soldier. He noticed the wound was in the man's back and the cloth scorched by powder burns; he suddenly realized and began to turn as a hammer smashed into his head and a blinding light burst behind his eyes. The medic running up knelt by the bodies and was himself shot, collapsing next to the other two.

Rutherford turned to the men behind him, "Get Moose. Where the fuck is it coming from? How can they get fire down here?" He peered up the right lip of the creek bed where intermittent dust spurts leaped. Before Moose could arrive, a second medic crawled forward, keeping low, and, ensuring he could not be seen from forward of the creek junction, rolled Ryan's body over: the single shot cracked and he slumped forward.

"Where is that bastard?" Rutherford edged forward till he was almost at the bodies, looking up. He noticed a small irregularity in the creek bank and glanced in, flinching away as he saw the hooded front sight of a Mossin-Nagant lurking inside the small firing post.

"The bastards are inside the bank!"

Moose came stepping carefully up the creek bed as the platoon examined the face of the creek bank next to him. To step out and place a long-barreled weapon into the firing slots would expose the firer to the guns on the bank above. The slot was too small to allow grenades to be placed inside it.

With forethought, D603 had prepared the clearing and creek bed as a killing ground, and the four bodies—two dead and two wounded—were their results. Before explosives could be brought in, the VC had fled back along the tunnel so painstakingly dug down the center of the ground separating the creeks.

Meanwhile, battalion HQ was set up and the companies cleared the area. Small battles flared as the battalion secured its perimeter, groups of five and six enemy coming out of hiding and being shot down.

All during the nights and days, small, fleeting firefights flared when the enemy used their knowledge of the tunnel system to penetrate inside the battalion area and pop up to inflict what casualties they could. A diary was found in which the entry for the Wednesday before the landing stated nine hundred miles of tunnels had been completed.

Dwarf Palmer lay behind his M60, watching the area to his front. The gun had been positioned to fire down a long stretch of VC-dug trench.

"Psst!" Dwarf kicked his Number Two and nodded down the trench; around the corner fifty yards away

crawled two Viet Cong, their heads down, busily moving
forward on hands and knees, rifles slung, their eyes fixed
on the trench floor.

Tomlinson craned to see down the trench and grinned
at Dwarf. The big man snuggled the gun into his shoulder,
thumb depressing the safety catch, and waited.

The two zealous black-clad men swiftly crawled along
the stretch of the trench, never looking up. As the corner
came into his field of view, the leading man raised his eyes
and stared into the muzzle of the M60. Dwarf fired.

"That was bloody murder, Dwarf."

"I know Tommy. Wish it was all as easy as that."

"Aw, my word."

Tregonne stood looking over the fence at the mass of
men, women, and children who had gathered there, in
one large house, to keep them out of the way of possible
injury. He turned to Burrows, standing hands on hips and
frowning at the chattering mass of civilians.

"Sir, it would make our job a lot easier if all these
people were moved to town. We could back load 'em on
the empty choppers, and the civil affairs people could look
after them."

"Yes, I was just thinking along the same lines. We'll
do that."

Gradually the local people were flown out of the area,
despite their initial fear of the flying machines. After
repetitive and prolonged verbal persuasion, the simple
method was adopted: as the group approached the helicopter, the youngest child would suddenly be picked up
and placed inside the machine; the rest flowed in like
sheep. A soldier had to fly with each load to assist the
crew.

Frank Gardiner returned from one flight, and, grinning, walked up to Father, waiting with a group of local
people yet to fly.

"Hey, Father, saw a good one then. The woman in
charge of all the kids on that one got 'em on the floor
around her, biffed each one over the head, and made 'em
put their heads down and shut their eyes. After we lifted
off, I noticed one little bugger wrinkling his nose and

screwing up his eyelids. He put it on for a minute or two then must have thought, 'This isn't hurting a bit,' opened his eyes and had a good look around; gave a big grin when I smiled at him. He was really enjoying it. Then he nudged the kid next to him, and they both were taking it all in when the sheila woke up to 'em, looked up, saw them with heads up—biff, biff! Two great whacks over the head. They went back to the seventeenth century after seeing the twentieth."

"Yeah, well, I should be right for a job as an air hostess after a few more flights. Coffee, tea, or milk, madam? You Uc Dai Loi Number Ten!"

Fredericks sat near the edge of a large pit, sorting through the boxes, cartons, and satchels of books and documents brought from the houses, bunkers, and tunnels.

"How's it going there, Corporal Fredericks?"

He stood up as Stan Burrows approached with his small entourage. "Not too bad, sir. We've never seen anything like this before—the sheer quantity, I mean. All I've got time for is a very quick look at the top of each box or whatever to decide if it goes in the fire," gesturing to the smoke rising from the pit, "or is back loaded to Brigade S2. It's incredible, sir. Personal and unit dossiers, unit and headquarters correspondence, roll books, strength reports, weapon roll books, passes of all types, photos, commendation certificates, training pamphlets, tests, charts, maps—you name it, we've got it."

"And what are you burning?"

"School books, propaganda books, newspapers, novels, and so on. If it's not of Intelligence value, either it goes back to the Diggers for souvenirs or in here. I've lost count of what has gone back."

"Hmm. We've done well here. Keep up the good work."

"Yes sir."

Nimbus and Tom Pritchard dropped the new 12.7mm DShK machine gun, gleaming in its grease, onto the pile of its brothers.

"Jesus," muttered Nimbus, "look at all these fuckin'

weapons. They'd a murdered us if they had these 12.7s firing across the LZ, ay?"

Before them lay row on row of Chinese-made 12.7mm DShKs, tripods, AA-sights, ammo drums, US Thompson and M3 submachine guns, Czech ZB30 light machine guns, French M1929 light machine guns, Chinese-made 7.92mm PPS "burp guns," French MAT49 submachine guns, Mauser rifles still with the Wehrmacht eagle insignia, and MAS36, Mossin-Nagant, and US M1 carbines. Mortar bombs, grenades, ammunition of all types, and explosives lay piled around. Typewriters, uniforms, cloth, gym boots, telephones, and all manner of things lay at the sides.

"Those tunnels are fuckin' well incredible! They go down forty feet in layers. Rooms with telephones in 'em. Printing presses. Jesus," said Pritchard, "the work the buggers put in."

"Yeah. Notice something? There's no pistols and no money."

"Ya don't think they're gonna hand them in, do ya? Come on."

"Hey, did yer hear about the graves they found over in D's area? The VC were buried back in the walls, in the tunnel sides, way underground."

"Go on!"

As night fell, the infiltrating stepped up. The bright moonlight cast its impartial gleaming over friend and foe, betraying one or the other to his enemies and sometimes, his friends.

Nick Rutherford woke suddenly, fully alert. In the dark he tensed, listening, feeling with every pore of his body. Someone was creeping carefully past the place where Rutherford slept, moving toward the sleeping riflemen. The black form kept carefully to the darkest shadows, drifting soundlessly around a patch of moonlight.

Rutherford silently moved his hand in the dark, slowly grasping his M16, carefully lifting it, swinging it over, hand grasping black plastic foregrip, sighting down the length of the rifle, two quick shots, the enemy black shape against the moon-silvered grass slung into the soft light by the rounds.

The quiet, quick flurry of surrounding men waking, seizing weapons and lying alert, the soft voice of Moose checking his section commanders. Rutherford crept out and approached the moaning man, and an ice-cold douche ran from his hair over his body as he saw the Australian boots in the moonlight.

Kneeling quickly, with a cry of "Moose!" he rolled the shape over and recognized the face of his newest replacement, three weeks in-country.

The medic was kneeling, scissors gleaming, snipping. "Hell," rumbled the hulking shape of Moose. "What happened?"

Rutherford told him, in quiet tones.

"Okay," tapping one of the Diggers, "dive over and get the signaler to request a Dust-off for one, gunshot wound in the shoulder and arm, details to follow."

Bending over the wounded man, "What were you doing, young Jackson?"

"Sergeant, I just came off the gun," wavering voice rising from the shadowed face, breath hissing, "and I was goin' to wake up my replacement." Deep breath, "I didn't want to get sniped, so I crawled over to him. Someone shot me."

"Okay son, we have a Dust-off on the way, you're gonna be okay. It's only a scratch. Come on, let's get him to the LZ." To the waiting silent onlookers, "Back to your pits the rest of you."

But Jackson died in the helicopter. The M16 rounds had removed the bone from his arm. Next morning, the medic approached Fredericks, tossing papers onto his fire.

"G'day. Got a bit of stuff to burn here, mate."

"Okay, toss it in. An old shirt, is it?"

"Yeah, belonged to Jacko, the bloke who got Dusted-off last night. Have a look at what M16 rounds do to you. Just hold it, look here, the weave of the cloth—see all those little rough bits? Bone. His arm bone was fragmented and it's impregnated into the cloth."

"Fuckin' hell, ay. Hey, have a look at this," to a couple of Diggers sorting through the unwanted pile for souvenirs.

Nimbus and Fitzgibbon sat in the deep shadows of the bush, on the edge of the weapon pit, legs dangling inside, M60 a long, solid blackness protruding from the softer dark of the pit. Around them the battalion slept or sat alert behind machine guns or at radio sets. A small group huddled in the command post. VC crept along tunnels, up and out, cautiously moving about, waiting for a target. At irregular intervals a distant "chunk" indicated another VC mortar fired. Nimbus and Fitzgibbon took the broader view: they would be very unlucky to be hit by the occasional mortar round; better to sit up in the shadow and see more, perhaps zap a Charlie or two.

Miles away the artillery fired. The approaching shell roared overhead, then chung! The casing and flare separated, the metal container falling to the end of its trajectory with an alternate whistle-moan, whistle-moan as it tumbled end over end. By common consent, Nimbus and Les slid into the pit as the piece of ironmongery passed over, and the flare popped into light, swaying on the parachute, making a lurching grotesque shadow-dance from every tree, bush, and house below.

Back up onto the pit. Mortar fires, the slam of explosion, no movement from the watching two. Behind, the guns fire, chung! Overhead whistle-moan and the two are crouched in the pit. After the sequence repeated itself several times, Fitzgibbon grabbed Nimbus by the arm and hissed, "We're a couple of mugs! We sit up when the nogs fire and get down when our guns go."

"Yeah, but from that direction, we've got more chance of being hit by the fuckin' empty case than a VC mortar, ya know!"

"Uh, huh. How about when you're asleep?"

"Don't worry about it then, mate."

The long lines of laden figures moved silently through the early morning coolness to the large grassy area. The familiar chopping roar, and the long lines of Hueys appeared, sinking over the trees, to float down onto the grass, then rise up carrying the groups away in the cool air.

"Hope there's a beer waiting back there," shouted Father, against the engine noise.

Nimbus shook his head, "The bastards won't do that."

But they did.

"Hey Charger, seen this newspaper?" asked Pete Sanders.

"No, why?"

"Aw, I see here that 'senior army officers' say we are getting enough rest up here in Vietnam."

"Shit ay? How would they know? Haven't seen any senior army officers out on the operations sleepin' wet, carryin' sixty-pound loads an' the rest of it."

"Hmm. Well, what are they gonna say otherwise? That we're havin' our guts worked out? They never say anything's bad, do they?"

"Yeah, fuck 'em anyway. Who's goin' ter Saigon tomorrow?"

"Fergie and Buck, I heard."

Over in the company "boozer," built from timber purchased with Vietnamese money the soldiers "donated," but in reality from the satchel of a now dead VC tax collector, the postoperation "warries" were spinning...

"Went for a shit, put the shovel in and dug into a bloody tunnel entrance! No bullshit!"

"Looked through the window and there was this Charlie, just divin' into a tunnel; up with the M60 and let fly..."

"Jacko, the silly cunt, crawling to wake up his replacement got brassed up..."

"Anyway, we couldn't work out where these fuckin' grenades were comin' from. Finally caught a kid, so small he was hidin' in the smallest bloody place. The interpreter asked him if it was him, and he said yes. Only ten years old. Poor little bugger. Didn't know any better."

"Hey, did the interpreter tell ya about the hardcore VC they got? Yeah, in a bunch of civilians. If looks coulda killed, we'd a all been piled up, no worries. Bandy Bill was there when they were checkin' em all out—ID cards, you know. This old dame only snarled and spat. No ID. Wouldn't talk. Just spat. Freddo and Bill reckoned she was a hardcore VC, so they put her separate from the rest. Then Freddo asked a couple who she was. They all said, 'Dinky-dau, Dinkya dau.' Mad." Bursting into a roar of laughter. "The village idiot! Ha, ha, ha, hardcore VC!"

"Ya should a seen old Smithy there" (old Smithy being all of twenty), "takin' his grenades out to clean 'em; grabs one by the igniter set, lifts, and the set comes clean out in his hand. Sitting there white as snow, freckles standin' out like red paint, eyes as big as two bobs, lookin' at the fuckin' thing! Ho, ho, ho."

"You weren't too calm yerself, yer cunt," with a broad grin, from "old" Smithy.

"Well, while you pricks have been stompin' through the scrub, we been fightin' off the screaming hordes here."

"Yeah?"

"Yeah. One of the rear detail patrols got a couple of Nigels up on the river. Two canoes full of 'em tryin' to sneak over in the fog. Zapped one load, others got away in the fog."

"Aw yeah? Fair enough, ah?"

Hai Quyen, floppy-brimmed hat on head, blue and white checked scarf around neck, sat on the side of the path, among the others in the party, idly pushing mounds of dirt with a stick to disrupt a stream of busy ants. The group, all dressed in black cotton, was a portion of the headquarters, moving to a temporary camp with an escort of part of D603 Battalion.

He smiled at the closest comrades. "See the lesson here. These ants are all working for the same purpose. The dirt I push up does not stop them; it is a temporary barrier. And the blows I rain on them," crushing some dozens of insects that were immediately replaced by other hurrying fellows, "do not stop them. So do the imperialists and their lackeys try to halt us. But they do not know or understand us, therefore they push up little mounds before us, kill some of us, and tell themselves they are succeeding. But look," pointing down at the hurrying columns, "the work goes on. So does ours."

He sat back, waiting for the rest period to end.

*   *   *

Christine Pritchard sat back in the lounge chair, the TV movie flowing across the screen and slipping easily over her mind; she'd seen the film before, knew the story, and now relaxed, glad she didn't have to put any effort into watching the characters parade across the screen.

Her legs and back ached from a day of housework, washing and shopping, and now she wanted Tom to be with her. Wanted him for herself and the kids. The little devils were expert at reading human frailties and exploiting the weak moments in an adult. They were becoming a handful now, more and more as each week passed; they needed the presence of their father in the house. She found herself screaming at them more often and losing her temper more easily.

Tom going to the bush for two or three weeks on exercises was one thing, but away at a war for at least a year was another. There were even rumors that they would be there for fifteen or eighteen months. Oh God, if it was eighteen months, she would be a murderess—she would have strangled the little b's a dozen times over.

And how many times would Tom have to go back? There didn't seem to be any sense to it all. They weren't advancing or retreating or anything, just going into the same places.

Not for the first time, she began to review the points she would make to persuade Tom to get out of the army. He was needed by herself and the children; when he was away there was a huge emptiness, and the family seemed somehow to be marking time until he returned and his presence made the family complete. If he stayed in the army, he would be sent back to Vietnam again and again, and he was no good to them dead. She wanted him, needed him with her and the kids.

She had noticed that very few officers were named in the casualty lists: only NCOs and Diggers seemed to be doing the fighting. Tom explained in a letter that almost all the contact with the enemy took place at platoon level, which was one lieutenant and about two dozen men; so of course most casualties would be junior ranks. Christine was cynical enough to reply that she was sure the medals would be handed out in reverse proportion.

On the screen, the Hollywood stars embraced and the film ended. She switched off the set, and the light, and went in to that bloody big empty bed. Bugger the army and all politicians.

16

The drumming horde lifted off the grassy LZ as the infantry placed magazines on their weapons, cocked them, and dug out their bush hats from inside shirts or thigh pockets, flopping them on their short-cropped heads. After a couple of days of sweat, dirt, dust, rain, ants, leeches, thorns, prickly vines, and the ever-present heat, everyone favored short haircuts as being more comfortable.

A throbbing hum in the distance drew eyes to the long lines of Hueys, tiny dragonfly shapes, bearing an American battalion to a neighboring LZ.

Then the screeching roaring crescendo of artillery fire: the far side of the LZ erupted in smoke and debris.

"What the fuck's going on?"

"Dunno."

Heads turning, curious gazes toward the wall of smoke; another rising whistling roar—another crashing wall of smoke, closer this time.

"The bastards are firing on the LZ."

"Too many guns for the nogs."

"I mean our fuckin' guns!"

Stan Burrows turned to the gunner major, "Stop that firing, Greg," as another salvo crumped closer, shrapnel humming overhead or whomping into the ground.

"They're not our guns, sir," replied the gunner officer.

"Are you sure?" as another wall of explosions slammed down.

Looking up from his list of artillery fire missions, "Definitely not. The fire mission for this LZ has been fired."

Another rending crashing wall crumped down, the shrapnel now dangerous. A huge jagged chunk a foot long and four inches wide whacked into the ground a yard from Nimbus.

"Ah Christ! They'll be on us in a minute."

Men dived into old shell scrapes, artillery and bomb craters, any dip in the ground. Pritchard saw an old shallow scape nearly ten-inches deep. As the relentless wall crashed down again, he shed his pack, placing it on the side of the advancing explosions, and lowered himself into the protecting dirt walls. *Crash!* Another series of flashes, fountains of dirt and smoke, stones and shrapnel flung up closer than before. An unseen, implacable god pounding his fist into the soil in regularly spaced blows, ever closer, evenly timed. *Crash!*

Tom was surprised to hear himself praying, "Oh God, make it stop, make it stop, make it stop," as the inexorable, impersonal crashing advanced, nearer and nearer.

Suddenly, he felt himself pushed forward out of the shallow trench, his head and shoulders rising up into the shrapnel; looking back he saw Nimbus Farley and Les Fitzgibbon squeezing and wriggling into the narrow scrape, packs on the ground.

"You bastards! Go and find your own hole."

With no reply, the two unwelcome visitors burrowed deeper; Pritchard dragged the packs into a feeble barricade around his head as the earth shook under the giant hammer blows, and smoke and dust billowed toward them.

"Major!" snapped Stan Burrows, "I want that artillery stopped *at once!*"

"Sir, it must be VC fire. Our guns are firing in support of the Americans landing at 'Apple'!"

The artillery signaler made his own decision, lifted

the handset, pressed the switch, and said, "Stop, stop, stop."

Silence, the dust and smoke drifted down wind.

Burrows rose to his feet. "Obviously, they were firing the same serial twice. We'll speak later," to the crestfallen gunner major.

All around men were rising to their feet or knees, looking to the south.

"Righto, stop standin' around like molls at a christening. Saddle up."

The hand signal came back down the line of sweat-darkened green shirts: arms raised, forearms crossed—an obstacle—then one hand, fingers extended, held to form an angle with the other arm, in the basic shape of a roof—a house.

The platoon deployed and swept through, reorganizing around the corrugated iron building. Careful of booby traps, the men delegated as searchers quickly examined it. Inside was bag after bag of flour, each stamped with the handshake of friendship—"Hands over the ocean" symbol of the United States Aid system—and in Vietnamese, "Donated by the people of the USA."

"Look at it, will ya?" said Tom Pritchard. "Tons of it. Given to 'em for nothing, and out here in a VC cache."

"There's bloody truckloads of it. They didn't collect this a pound at a time. This is how it bloody well came off the ship," observed Father.

"Okay, Section Commanders, to me. Tommy, you stay here with Bart. I'll take the other two sections and see what else is in the next 300 or 400 yards. While we're away, do a quick count of bags here. Questions? Right, let's go," ordered Bruce Myers.

Later, Pritchard and Father sat looking out into the jungle as the cache was evacuated. This find had lead to others, and ton upon ton of rice, flour, oil, pickled cucumbers, and other preserved foods were removed.

"This is gonna hurt 'em. There's tons of it all along here, they reckon."

"Yeah. Straight off the fuckin' ship to here. There're some corrupt bastards somewhere, and I don't know if there aren't a few Yanks in it too. The sheer quantities of stuff found are incredible. They must be in it. Must be."

"Yeah."

Tom sat frowning, then asked, "Listen, do you feel sometimes as if it's another world, back in Aussie? Christine sends me clippings from the papers, writes about what's goin' on at home, the neighbors, all that you know."

"Yeah. And?"

"Well," pause, searching for words, "it doesn't seem important, know what I mean? To us, it's another world. We live out here, no family except the mob. Will we get a resupply? Will it rain? How many Charlies we gonna get? Are my trousers and shirt gonna last out? How many days to go? Really, I couldn't care less about the politicians, film stars, footy stars, and all that. Here, today, that's what is important."

"Yeah, yer right. We live for one thing really: catchin' nogs. And when we're back in that world, all those things will be more real. I guess, anyway."

"Hmm. It's gonna take time to get used to each other again. Apparently, the word's got around, all the wives checked with each other, and all the blokes want to have a kid when they get back. Bloody strange, ay? But they reckon it happens in all wars—the men want to breed."

"So I believe. All these 'baby-booms' after the First and Second World Wars. You'd think a bloke who's been in it would want to draw the line in case he gets done in and his kids are orphans, ay? But I guess the head shrinkers have got long names for it all. Looks like they're finished. Wonder if we'll prop here tonight? Might get a couple of 'em sneakin' back in for a look at what we've done."

Forward scout Herb Knowles ignored the sweat trickling down his forehead and peered into the sun- and shadow-dappled bush ahead, every sense alert, every nerve tensed to react at the slightest unnatural movement, gleam, or color. Partially crouched, M16 held firmly, Knowles moved from cover to cover through the grass under the trees. Not the dense green mass of jungle but a sparser growth that allowed plenty of sunlight through to make difficult the job of observation through the contrasting light and dark patches.

Suddenly, firing broke out on the right, some of the rounds snapping overhead. The company was sweeping with three platoons abreast. Ryder's company HQ moving with Myers's center platoon. The two commanders were only yards apart; Ryder gestured Myers over to him.

"They're heading this way. We'll go down here and wait—they could run right onto us."

Myers nodded and gave the "section commanders to me" signal; the watching corporals and Bart Bartholomew strode over—small group in the shadow-splotched areas under the trees. Myers spoke in the habitual low tones of the jungle soldier.

"Right, Mr. Gordon's flushed a dozen of 'em, got one KIA, the others are heading this way. We're going to prop here and wait for 'em."

Quickly the platoon and the HQ personnel sank into the grass, under bushes and behind trees, staring out through the now quiet surroundings.

Tommy Tomkinson indicated to Dwarf Palmer the arc of fire for the M60, moved back a few paces to where he could see his section, and went to ground in a patch of shade under a shrub.

Silence settled. Insects buzzed, birds chirped and chattered, the wind made the sunlight and shadow patterns jiggle.

After some twenty-five minutes, Tommy heard someone moving behind him. He looked over his shoulder and saw one of the company cooks approaching. When the company was in camp, they cooked; in the field, when everyone used combat rations, the cooks traveled with CHQ and provided an extra machine gun. The cook leaned over and said quietly, "Have we got anyone over that way?" pointing out where the firing had taken place.

"Only Gordon's mob and some Charlies. Why?"

Kneeling down, the cook murmured, "Well a couple of minutes ago, we saw a bloke out there."

"Well," hissed Tommy, "what was he wearing?"

"Aw, black clothes."

Tommy grabbed the cook's shoulder, "It was a VC! Why didn't ya shoot?"

"I'm not the Number One on the gun."

"Where's he?"

"He went for a shit."

"Well?" The clenched jaw, flashing eyes, lowered brow and tone indicated to the cook he was not popular.

"I didn't know if the gun was loaded."

"What?" in a strangled snarl. "Give me a look!"

Quickly, bent over, he moved to the machine gun. "What in the name of holy fuckin' hell are you pair of twits doing? Can't you see the fuckin' gun is behind a frigging ant-fucking hill!"

Silence from the two shame-faced cooks.

"Why didn't you use that?" pointing to the SLR.

"Aw, I didn't think . . ." mumbled the cook.

"Jesus fucking Christ! What the fuck do you think you're doing here?" Tommy hissed.

Silence resumed.

More and more caches were found and evacuated, until the battalion finally converged on the grassy clearing for extraction and return to camp.

Bob Edmonson sat with Reg Waterson, the adjutant, enjoying a cup of coffee.

"Well, here we are, pulling out in the middle of a fairly successful operation because the helicopters can only fit us into their program this afternoon," said Edmondson. "Far from being 'freed from the tyranny of terrain' as the American generals say, we are tied to the helicopter. We can't mount an operation unless there are a hundred choppers available. We can't walk in or out, go over the river by assault boats, do anything without helicopters. In Malaya we could be resupplied by one airdrop. Here we have to use helicopters that give the locations away. Complete misuse of the ground forces in counter-revolutionary warfare by tying them to the machines."

"I don't think any of these generals understands revolutionary warfare or its counter," said Waterson.

"I heard one Yank stating that the US Army does have a history of antiguerrilla operations—the Indian Wars! That's like comparing the War of Jenkin's Ear to Waterloo. They beat the Indian by not allowing him to live off the land—destroying his home, livestock, and family in winter, using railways, telegraph, and heliograph to provide communications for armed forces independent of the land. It doesn't apply here. They can't see that if you're fighting big battles then the revolutionary movement must be gaining enough members to provide the large units for the battles. You're winning when contacts fade away, no incidents occur, people don't support the movement. You can't force people all the time. Terrorism only goes so far."

"Well, all this military might must have some effect," interjected Waterson.

"Will it be the right effect? They'll provide any instrument of war, and they build roads, airfields, harbors, hospitals—but in the end, the Saigon regime and its cronies get richer. They got the contracts, they entrench themselves. What does the average person get to show him the Saigon government is the one to support? Nothing. He has his taste for the material things excited, but the police, petty officials, ministers, generals, and so on are the same group as always in power. Cliques fight for a bigger slice of the cake. The average person is quick to sense hypocrisy, and he can see it. The Americans in power don't understand the type of war here, and sometimes I think the Saigon regime doesn't understand either the VC or its own people, let alone Mao Tse Tung's writings."

"The Yanks have a great capability for looking at things and correcting bad techniques very quickly. They adapted to carrier warfare in the Pacific very well."

"True. I hope they wake up here. The caches we have been finding here are more important, with the documents, than the dozen or so kills we've got. Those people weren't important—it wasn't worth our effort to shoot them."

"Well, here we go. There they are."

Too far away for the engine noise to be heard, the tiny dots of the Hueys slid along the pale horizon sky. The first and second lifts departed, and the third appeared thrum-

ming along over the trees; the soldiers lined up in their
groups, hats tucked away, sweat-rag ends secured inside
shirt collars, weapons unloaded.

Then over the engine thrum crackled the firing of
many rifles and machine guns—the ten Hueys slithered
sideways and upward, like a school of disturbed fish,
formation gone, wobbling, but still threshing to the LZ.
They settled at all angles, scattered over the grass and
lifted off. As they flew low over the distant trees on the
way out, more firing broke out. The ten Hueys, some with
many bullet holes, zigzagged gaining height. The two
gunships circled and fired at the trees, before beating off,
nose down, after their charges.

"This is fucking nice! Shot at on the way in and out,"
grinned "Baron" Lord, taking a magazine out and clipping
it home on the rifle.

Four F100s circled, then the leader rolled over and
dived. Kowalski, acting as Shark Blue Leader, held the
bright "pipper" on the target area, ticked off two 750-pound
bombs, and pulled up into the sky, followed by the other
three. Circling, he looked down at the ragged gray stain
on the green. Far away he saw the shimmering train of
helicopter rotors. Rolling down, he spread napalm into the
gray smoke clouds and pulled the big F100 into a series of
climbing rolls.

"That bastard is enjoying himself anyway," grinned
Ryder.

"Yeah, showing off to the chopper pilots, I guess."

As the Hueys approached the shattered, smoking
target area, Kowalski lead his F100s over them as a
diversion. Scattered fire came up from the trees, but the
enemy had moved away and were unable to concentrate
on the slow choppers.

The F100s and gunships rocketed and machine gunned
the sides of the approach and exit routes to the LZ,
lessening but never stopping the ground fire. As the last
troops clambered aboard, a few flitting figures in the trees
drew the fire of the crews, an indication of how close the
enemy had worked in toward the sides of the LZ. Pritchard
saw, as the Huey lifted and climbed hard, two figures run

and drop to a crouch just inside the edge of the trees. He flicked his M16 to "fire-automatic" and emptied the magazine in bursts, correcting his aim by the one-in-four tracer he kept in case of just such a situation. The helicopter gunner watched his tracer fall and hosepiped a long burst into the area, imitated by several following gunners.

Looking back, the watchers saw Kowalski zipping low at right angles to their direction of flight, firing his cannon into the trees, then pulling up into another succession of climbing rolls.

Pritchard felt a tap on the shoulder, Fitzgibbon pointed at the cavorting F100 and mouthed, "show-off." Tom grinned in acknowledgment. Another op over. Another day closer to Christine.

The blinding sun beat down on the dusty street, driving all living things into the shade. The siesta hush sat over the town. The only people working were the bar staff; Indian tailors, with one eye open, dozed in their shops; cyclo and taxi drivers sat in suspended animation.

The dark cool interiors of the bars opened invitingly to the bar crawling soldiers, all seeking that never attained state of feeling "just right" in the bar: to drink, yarn, and come to a business agreement with the prostitutes. The bars were part of the system to attract foreigners and extract money from their wallets. Apart from the protection from sun and rain, the bars provided drinks and girls, and American pop music.

Generally, the Australians preferred to follow the customs of their own country: a group of friends sit together and yarn—women having little or no part in the traditional male gathering, much to the despair of women and overseas visitors, and the delight of womanizers and writers of denigratory journalistic pieces.

The Australian, being generally careful of his money, saw little reason to sit with a bar girl and indulge in trivial and banal pleasantries while buying her drinks of cold tea at two or three times the price of his own drink. If he was going to have sex with her later, then he'd pay her for that at the time. Why waste money on preliminaries that were not included in the eventual deal?

The Americans were more enthusiastic, sitting with a sloe-eyed damsel and buying "teas." The no-nonsense Australian was soon labeled "cheap Charlie."

Herb Knowles, "Dwarf" Palmer and a group from the company sat in a bar, ignoring the girls and drinking the overpriced American beer. Having washed away the dust of the journey, spun a few yarns, and relaxed, the normal male urges reasserted themselves.

"Jesus, Dwarf, look at that one in the blue dress. She must be half-French or something; what d'ya reckon?"

"Hmm. Could be. Gonna give it a go?"

"Well . . . feelin' a bit randy, ya know."

"Be careful Herb. Listen to yer old mate Dwarf. Pick an ugly one."

"Why?"

"Because everyone will be rooting the good lookin' ones. They're bound to have the jack. You've got a better chance with the uglies."

"Yeah, but fuckin' hell, Dwarf; six weeks since I was on leave, and yer want me to pass up a grouse-lookin' moll like that?"

The heat and beers had their effect, and Knowles's jaw firmed. "No; fuckin' hell, I'll try that one."

Rising, he walked down the bar and slid onto the bar stool next to the girl, who had noticed him in the long mirror behind the bar.

"Hey, how are ya?"

"Hello Uc Dai Loi. I am okay. You buy me one Saigon tea?"

"No, I don't wanta buy you a tea. How much short time?"

"You wan short time, hah? No buy tea?"

"Yeah, right first time, love."

Calculating eye sweep up and down Knowles, estimating in that second his degree of sobriety, degree of affluence, likelihood of believing a hard-line story and thence wringing extra from him.

"Okay, short time fi-hundred p. You have?"

"Five hundred? Come on love! I only want to hire it, not buy it!"

"What?"

"Five hundred no. Two-fifty." Hand delving into pocket.

"No, you cheap Charlie." Turning away to stare into the mirror, chin up, arms folded, "Four-fifty, okay?"

"Three hundred and some Salems."

"Salem? How many?"

"I tell you what—no money, three cartons Salem. Okay? Three cartons okay?"

"Hmm. Okay! Where Salem? You give first."

"Yeah, no worries. We got 'em over there."

"Your frien's also have Salem? They want girl?"

"They can look after 'emselves, love. How about it?"

"Okay." Speculative glance flicking from Knowles to the group. "I go upstairs, you wait, you follow. Room Six. Six," drawing a 6 on the bar surface.

"Okay, let's go."

"Wait, first you give Salem to man behind bar."

"Righto, righto. Here y'are, Nigel, Salems."

"Okay, Uc Dai Loi. Now I go."

Abruptly, she slid off the stool and walked out of the bar. Knowles, waiting for a moment, saw her climbing the stairs and followed.

Room Six lay at the end of a short corridor. The room was small and airy, with a washbasin, curtained-off bed, window giving onto the street, and a wardrobe. Pictures of Hollywood stars adorned the walls. Knowles shut the door gently and looked around. The girl was hanging her dress in the wardrobe and looked over her shoulder at him, smiling.

"Hey, you Uc Dai Loi. Why you pick me?"

Unbuttoning his shirt, Knowles grinned. "Because you're the best lookin' one, that's why."

"Oh? You think I am beautiful?"

"Oh yeah. You're all right." Unzipping his trousers.

"Why you no buy me tea? You like me, you buy me one tea, no?" Raised eyebrow.

"No."

Standing by the bed in the sunlight, she threw her

bosom out, head tilted to one side, regarding him out of her slightly slanted brown eyes. "Okay, what you like?"

"Whattya mean?"

"French, Greek? What you like?"

"French or Greek?"

"Sure. French," pointing to her mouth, "Greek," pointing to her shapely bottom.

"Oh yeah."

"Well?"

"Er . . . just plain and simple, thanks."

"Hah?"

"Like this."

"Oh, that nothing, Uc Dai Loi," as her hand slid down his stomach and began to stroke him. "Hey, you ver' big, Uc Dai Loi."

"That so? My name's Herb."

"Ahh? Herb, hah? Here, you let me . . . oh, wait Uc-Herb. Okay, now hah?"

"Jesus, you're right. You've got a good set of tits for an—girl over here."

"Yes," in agreement, "they very good. Here—no bite hard, Herb."

Afterward, Knowles lay feeling the breeze dry the sweat on his body. He cocked his head as a massed shout rose from the bar beneath them.

"Up the old red rooster—more piss!"

He grinned at the girl. "The blokes want another beer."

"Oh?" politely. "They are thirsty?" Rolling off the bed, she began to dress. "Okay Herb; I must go back to bar now. Come."

Overcoming his lassitude, Knowles washed, dressed, and followed her to the door. Placing one hand on her shoulder, he said, "You're not too bad, ya know."

At the bottom of the stairs she turned to him, smiling below speculative eyes, "You like me?"

"Aw yeah."

"Why you no buy me tea?"

"Whattya want—teas or Salems?"

"Tea and Salems."

"Oh Christ." He sauntered over to the booth, noting one less face. "Where's Frank?"

"Gone off with one a the birds. How was it?"

"Aw, not bad. Just a root."

"Hmm. What's her name?"

"Dunno."

17

Bartholomew lay in the noon hush, eyes sweeping the dark jungle depths, and wondered how long it would take to get the dirt of Vietnam out of his body. He doubted if the green clothes and socks would ever be clean again. He turned to Myers and softly said, "How many hours are you goin' to spend in a hot bath, Skip?"

Myers grinned, "About a week. Then surfing. Jackie and I go to the beach a lot."

Bart wrinkled his nose and ostentatiously sniffed, "Ever tried to work out what we smell of?"

"No. I'm not a masochist, Bart."

"Sweat, gun-oil, wet boots, wet clothes that have dried with dirt and sweat in them, wet socks, and plain Vietnamese dirt." Sniff, sniff.

"Yeah. No wonder they can smell us downwind. It's a wonder the leaves don't curl after a week or two."

"These bloody things aren't much chop," lifting a green-clad leg with canvas J-boot on it. "They wear out in a couple of weeks and your feet stink—Jesus! Canvas wet, dried, sweated, wet dried . . . phew."

Myers fanned his face, "You should bathe more often, Bart. You really are on the nose."

And they sank into the quiet noontime somnolence.

The company moved into the area they would occupy for the night and set about the quiet routine of eating and preparing their sleeping arrangements.

Charger Seymour and Pete Sanders were clearing an area about ten yards from the medic, nicknamed "Doc" as they all were. He quickly put on his rations to cook, placed a mug of water nearby, and called softly, "Sick Parade."

The word passed swiftly and the "sickies" made their way through the deepening dark green gloom to receive the best the medic could do with the contents of his satchel.

Ointments, powders, and injections. Brusque, no-nonsense, the medic dealt with the real or imagined aches, pains, and complaints. Last of all came the VD cases. As they made their way to him through the gloom, he prepared the injection.

The man halted, Doc asked "Which side?" as the green trousers were undone, "left" or "right" came the reply, the trousers dropped, white buttocks gleaming faintly in the light under the trees. "Okay, next." Fastening waistband, hefting rifle, the man made his way back to the weapon pit.

"See what ya get for touchin' those bar girls," hissed Charger.

"Yeah. What else do you recommend?" whispered Sanders.

"Wait till we get into gorilla country. We'll catch one and stake her out."

"Aw, come on!"

"Aw well, if you're particular, we'll put a bag over her head. Some of the harpies I've seen you with, there'd be no difference."

"Seymour, one of these fuckin' days . . ."

"Hey? You're my mate, aren't ya?"

"Sometimes, I fuckin' wonder."

"Hey listen—to show ya how much I think of ya, I'll give ya a tin of rations—here."

"Ham and lima beans, you mongrel! I wouldn't feed them to a dog!"

"No taste for good food, that's your trouble."

"Okay, that oughta do it," said Father, as he and Tom Pritchard put the finishing touches to their hutchi. Behind them in the shell scrapes, the rations bubbled on the solid fuel fires, bright in the gathering gloom.

A sudden, insistent rustling of leaves drew their attention; to their left, a sapling shook and trembled. In the gathering darkness, a sweat-strained green-clad figure was visible, standing legs apart, hands gripping the small tree.

"What the—?" muttered Father, frowning at the sight.

Tom grinned and punched Father's shoulder, "It's Johnny MacKay—pissing razor blades!"

The nearby figure, agony in every line of its body, gripping the tree trunk, head back, hung there in the gloom. Finally, the man shuddered, his head sank, he relaxed and wiped a green-clad forearm across his forehead. Still holding onto the tree with one hand, he turned and saw the two pale faces in the gloom. Mustering up a weak smile, he shook his head and muttered, "Whoo, it's enough to make a man take to drink."

The two witnesses chuckled in sympathy.

"Where'd ya get it?"

"Some bird in Saigon. Talk about pissing razor-blades! Fuck me! Medic asked me who, where and so on—all I could say was she had slant eyes, long black hair, and spoke fluent Vietnamese. Jesus, they're all alike, aren't they?"

"Yeah, too right."

After the shadowy figure moved off to its own hutchi, Tom said softly, "Bit rude sending a bloke out in the J with the jack, isn't it?"

"I suppose so. But it is a self-inflicted wound. And we're short of people. Whether they've got jack or not, doesn't matter out here. In fact, it's better. They can't infect anyone else, ay?"

The vehicles rumbled to a stop, ramps lowered, and the infantry stepped out, carrying their packs by the straps, and moved to the edges of the red dirt road running past the ill-tended rubber trees. The company commander and the artillery observer compared maps to agree on their position, then the platoons began sweeping though the rubber on the road sides. Suddenly, from no one knew where, an ice-cream and soft-drink hawker appeared pedaling down the road. Smiling, he opened his ice-chilled containers and waved bottles of orange drink.

"Where did he come from?"

"Fucked if I know."

"CSM—pass the word—no purchases. No drinking gifts of it either."

"Right sir."

The puzzled hawker sat in the shade watching the silent, green-clad men pass. The Americans, government troops, and even the French had been very happy to do business. Philosophically, he remounted and pedaled back to town to report on the number of troops and vehicles he had counted.

Major Red Ryder sat and looked around his small audience: his three platoon commanders, who sat with maps folded before them, the artillery officer, and mortar fire controller.

"Now then," plucking a blade of grass to be used as a pointer, "we've been doing well so far protecting this road construction effort. Tomorrow, we move 1500 yards to the east. Dispositions tonight for us and the Yanks are on this map—you can copy them later."

His voice rolled on with the remainder of the orders until the final "questions," and the group dispersed to pass on the information to their platoons, settling in around them in the thick scrub.

"Why dig so far? The fuckin' earth is like concrete and no bastard can get through this shit," waving at the tangled mass around them, "without waking us!"

"Come on, give it a rest," muttered Nimbus.

Les Fitzgibbon glanced over to where Tom Pritchard and Father Tomkins were sitting at ease behind their tiny fires, hutchi up already, bedding laid out.

"Yeah, righto."

Through the trees could be heard the grunting and

rumbling of the road construction machinery going into
the night laager 600 yards away.

Inside the American camp, Sergeant First-Class Elmer
Todd shifted his cigar butt to the corner of his mouth,
placed his M16 butt on his hip so the barrel jutted
skyward, and addressed his group of soldiers, standing
red-dirt stained before him.

"Okay now. What we're gonna do is go out front about
200 paces and provide security for the rest of the people
here. These engineers depend on us to protect 'em. We
got a radio, so we can call down fire on any Charlie we
see. We stay out all night, come in for chow. Right.
Ramirez, lead off."

The dirty infantrymen moved in single file through
the perimeter of their buddies surrounding the engineers.
Dark hulks of tanks and M113s stood like sleeping ele-
phants at intervals around the circle.

Arriving at the end of his 200 paces, Todd placed his
dozen men in a circle, himself and the radio man in the
center, gave his last instructions for quiet and alertness,
and settled for a long night.

Twelve miles away, the three battalions of Q910 Regiment began their rapid approach march through the night,
guided by local guerrillas into, through, and out of each
guerrilla's area. As they drew closer, the units fragmented,
until small groups of nine or ten were each guided by a
local along the paths and tracks toward the selected concentration point, where they would form up as battalions
and attack the US engineers, striking a resounding blow at
the Washington-Saigon clique.

Through the soft night, three main force battalions of
experienced soldiers, armed with new Soviet and Chinese
AK47 rifles and SKS carbines, and guided by their local
guerrilla force members, who were armed with older rifles,
flitted, jogging steadily toward the night camping place of
the engineers.

A burst of firing woke Stan Burrows. He raised himself on one elbow, peering toward the command post. He
could hear the low murmur of the radio operator. As he
was drifting off to sleep, another burst of automatic fire

sounded. He woke fully, waiting. When nothing happened, he sank back, but the firing flared again and again.

Elmer Todd lay peering through the bushes around him, one hand outstretched to grip the forearm of the radio man. All around his small group, dark figures drifted through the trees. They had materialized so rapidly and silently in the blackness that they were all around him before he realized what was happening.

The three battalions of Q910, minus those who had fallen before the guns of the enemy some 400 yards away, formed into their units, into their assault teams. Behind the first wave stood the local men, women, and children required to act as bearers of the wounded and captured weapons and equipment.

The US gun crews sleepily rolled out of their sleeping gear and closed on the guns before firing a harassing fire mission on a possible VC location six miles away. The crews swung into their long practiced drills, shells sliding into muscled arms, barrels rising against the velvet night sky.

Todd made his decision and whispered to the radio man, who bent and cupped his hands around his mouth to minimize the risk of detection by the deathly quiet, ominous figures all around them in the dark shadows of the moonless night, who now were streaming past them with the barest crackle of crushed twigs and clink of equipment—like so many black devils in a nightmare, the shapes trotted past Todd's men.

Realizing this was his chance to disrupt the assault waves, Todd opened fire, his dozen men putting forth a torrent of automatic fire. The radio message had given just enough time for the defenders to seize weapons and roll into the pits—time for the artillery to place the shells swiftly on zero setting, time for the tank crews to climb aboard—and the night was bludgeoned by a crashing outburst of fire, a Niagara that began and rolled on and on for four hours.

"Christ, what's that?" gasped Fitzgibbon, as the rolling thunder jerked them all awake.

"They're attacking the Yanks," whispered Nimbus, as though "they" could hear him.

Huge 50-caliber tracers streaked through the trees, and other invisible rounds snapped past or plunked into tree trunks and the ground, showering leaves, twigs, and dirt in all directions.

"This is no fuckin' good. If that Yank on that 50 twitches, we've had it. Shoulda dug deeper, mate."

"Shit, how could I know? We're gonna get hit by Yankee bullets!"

"Come on, fuck ya. There's that ant hill over here. We'll get behind that. Next time, Private Farley, I want you to dig to six feet before dinner."

"Get knotted, Fitzgibbon."

Todd's radio man was speaking rapidly, trying to give their location in the storm of noise and light. Groups of VC still pressed forward around them, and others moved past in the other direction carrying dead and wounded. The leading waves had been literally mown down by the sheer weight of the defenders' fire. The artillery rounds exploded almost in their faces; the tank cannon fired canister, and the tank machine guns added their fire to that of the wall of rifle and machine gun fire from the infantry.

Despite this, assault teams of VC reached the US line and overran it in several places, surviving only seconds before being cut down.

In answer to Todd's message, four US tanks and two M113s charged out into the night to try to find and rescue him. As the engines roared into life, underlying the drums of the guns, the VC reacted with the speed only disciplined, trained, and experienced soldiers could reach in the maelstrom of shot and shell before the American line, where the bush was literally being cut down by the gun fire. The recoilless rifle teams moved toward the noise of the engines, waiting till the engine note gave notice of the vehicles' movement, and then, closing in behind, fired on the ponderous, night-blind monsters from the rear. Two caught fire and burned; the others were halted, and the crews sat locked inside, listening to the enemy crawling and thumping over them, traversing their turrets and illuminating each other with search lights, hosing each other with machine gun fire to wash off the climbing, clinging black-clad figures, grostesque and evil in the light.

Todd moved his group, wriggling over the ground, deeper into a clump of bushes to await the daylight.

As the gray light seeped under the trees and bushes, absorbing the shadows, the defenders looked out on a scene of splintered trees, shredded bushes and silent bundles of rags—VC soldiers, men, women, and children, mown down in the attack.

The American commander turned to one of his staff officers, "Get the engineers to dig a mass grave. There's too many for individual digging."

"Christ, I hate getting up early," moaned Nimbus. The others made no reply, dark shapes doing final packing in the predawn gloom of the tent. One by one they carried the packs outside and plonked them on the ground at the entrance, then walked off through the soft night and gentle balmy breeze to the mess tent for the effort of swallowing food at an hour when the stomach would have preferred to sleep.

Water bottles filled last of all, and the dark groups assembled on the road, then turned and moved off to the trucks, boots shushing through the dust, raising a faintly seen cloud that hung at ankle height, separating the dark loosely striding figures from the more solid dark mass of the earth.

The sky was the faintest of grays on the eastern horizon and a deep, dark velvety, sensual blackness overhead. Bright against it flickered the blinking rubies of the helicopters, approaching from the south, moving into their long strings for the landing, drawing curving necklaces of sharp red flashes blipping against the blackness as they circled and settled on the helipad, a segment of beauty that had nothing to do with the ugliness revealed when the sun washed away the night sky and precise red lights.

To the east, a delicate pearl-shell pink seeped upwards, strengthening to a rose glow, then a red fan against which the distant fringe of trees and closer helicopters were sharp black silhouettes. Then the sun lifted the skirt of the night sky and, like an unwelcomed but determined visitor, shouldered its way up over the threshold, flooding the world with its ever-brightening light and ever-increasing heat.

The rows of helicopters sat mute, great blind staring perspex windshield eyes toward the sun, secured main rotors raised overhead in salute. The attendant crew men began their rituals: peering into the engine bays, freeing the rotors, checking machine guns. Then, the donning of bulbous helmets prior to linking themselves to the mindless inert insects, and transforming the silent things into whirring, throbbing, blinking flying beings.

The first engine whine signaled the climb into the belly. The rotor began revolving slowly, then faster until it skipped around as a dim blur, and the Huey shivered in anticipation of the flight.

A hundred roaring insects under the shimmering canopy of their mechanical wings, squatting in the early sunlight—the first row rises, dips noses, and threshes away; the second ... the third ... the fourth ... until the pad is empty.

The eighty Hueys raced low to the east into the blinding mass of the rising sun, then swung north, gaining height over the dark green carpet below, rising into the still cool air. Rolled-down sleeves and trouser legs fluttering in the wind, hair tousled, the infantry sat gazing down into the blue depths. Helmeted crew, impersonal in the green-visored bulbs, sat behind their control panels or machine guns.

The flight sank into the lower, warmer air trailing out into the line-ahead landing formation, lower and lower over the trees. The landing zone floated up in front, and the escorting gunships swam up abreast of the slicks—machine guns blazing, rockets hissing out—to flash ahead into the trees on the sides of the LZ.

The now familiar nose-up float down the LZ, crewman craning out to watch the rear, dirt and grass rising to

meet the skids, touch, bump, rock, crew waving the
infantry out, run, down, magazine on, cock, safety on,
there they go, off to the side before the next lot arrive.

Lieutenant Speed Gordon trotted his platoon, panting
under their packs, to their assigned location on the river
bank. He knelt and pointed out to each section commander his area. Toby Shaw waved his section after him and
walked swiftly through the grass, stopping to peer across
the hundred-yard gap of the river. He turned to the
section standing behind him, half raising an arm to point
out the machine gun position, pausing and glancing up at
a racketing gunship speeding overhead.

"Okay. We'll be here to secure this river bank till
they're across the other side. Tony, put the gun next to
that tree—" and ducked as the shots cracked from the far
bank. The section disappeared into the grass and bushes,
the M60 returning fire into the dark green wall on the far
bank.

Two of the section lay in the shadow of Shaw's bush:
one holding his thigh with red-weeping fingers, one held
by the pack in a half-lying, half-sitting position, head back,
eyes staring into the fathomless depths, small hole in shirt
front over the shattered heart.

"Hold yer fire. They've stopped. Get the medic.
Robbie's had it, Jack's hit in the leg."

The following lifts crossed the river unopposed and
secured a bridgehead; other battalions crossed and plunged
into the jungle.

Small battles flared as the opposing forces crept through
the green impartial veils. Once again, caches of food,
weapons, and munitions were found and removed.

Vy's platoon had evolved a successful tactic of creeping only as close to the foreigners as they needed to hear
their voices clearly, then emplace a large DH-10 mine,
quietly withdraw, unwinding the electric wires, and deto-
nate the mine from some distance away. As the DH-10
consisted of a concave mass of explosive studded with
shrapnel, the blast projected the shrapnel in the direction
in which it was pointed. Vy and his men had been most
successful against the Americans, who would not be quiet

and would not place small patrols out in front of their positions.

Vy and one of his squads crept carefully through the trees, guided by the noise of the helicopters.

Nam and Thieu went first, then Hanh with the Russian RPD machine gun, Chen with the DH-10 mine and battery, Tra, Dat, Vy, Le, Hai, and Vo. The quiet after-noon enveloped them as they moved under the trees.

Buck Norton lay, weight on his elbows, half dozing in the shadows. In a semicircle lay the other three members of the little patrol. He blinked awake as the movement to his front drew his attention.

"Psst. Wake up. Nogs in front," he hissed.

"Hmh. See 'em. Yeah. Right," from the other three.

"All right. We'll take 'em from left to right, as they come. Ready?"

Check rear-sight up, safety off, slowly raise rifle to shoulder, foresight on the oblivious black-clad figure framed by the rear-sight, breathe in—hold it—squeeze, and invis-ible strings jerk away the marionette in front.

The initial burst of firing was lost in a huge explosion—blast, dust, and leaves blinded the four ambushers who lay dazed as debris fluttered down around them. The enemy squad returned the fire, pinning down the four Australians. Then silence returned.

Cautiously, Norton surveyed the area; the dust cloud still hung, sunbeams striking a thousand golden motes through its drifting center.

"What the fuck was that?"

"Christ knows, but it certainly cleared the area. Look at that."

From behind, Myers's platoons swept in to investigate.

"What're you been up to?" queried Bartholomew.

"Saw about eight VC moving along here, opened fire, and this fuckin' explosion set us back on our arse. Dunno what it was."

"Right. The others are hooking around to try and catch 'em. Let's have a look."

"Be careful. Don't touch anything."

"Christ, look at the trees, will ya?"

"Like the inside of a butcher's shop. Blood running down the fuckin' tree trunks!"

"Look up there—guts hanging off that branch."

"Here's some electrical wire and a battery."

"Look at this ant hill. The bloody side is powdered! Shit."

"Blood trail here."

"And here."

"Piece of M1 buttstock here."

"Hey—here's the remains of a pair of pants—just the waistband. Musta blown 'im to bits."

Kneeling, Bartholomew examined the ground before him, then turned to Myers. "This is where they put something on the ground—a piece of plastic or something— put the pieces in and carried them away. You can see the flattened grass and leaves; blood trails lead up to it then stop. Only drops after that."

Myers shook his head, smiling. "It must have been a beauty. I placed it—thirty-five paces across, trees stripped of all leaves, ant hill powdered . . . Jesus."

Eight hundred yards away, Vy lay in the shade, clutching the M1 now without its stock. He had sent the surviving six on ahead, carrying the remains of Hanh, Trieu, and Chen in the plastic. Tra and Dat were also wounded. Vy would wait for a squad from the company to come for him. The explosion had been tremendous. How unlucky that the DH-10 had been detonated by a bullet. Vy sensed movement and held his breath.

A green-clad figure, black rifle at the ready, moved past his bush, the only sound being the grass brushing against the green trouser legs.

Vy gritted his teeth and lifted the shattered M1, aiming at the back of the man. He could not aim lying down, so with a great effort, he rose to his feet out of the shadows of the bush, next to a second soldier who also had not seen him.

Vy concentrated on the first man, still oblivious of the imminent shot: the third soldier swung his M16 around and fired the whole magazine into Vy, knocking him over, rolling him along the ground.

The two scouts dived to the ground, the third man began replacing the empty magazine, the fourth fired as Vy rolled to his knees with the momentum of his fall. The fourth man fired two shots—his machine gun jammed, and before their eyes, Vy rose to his feet, and stood, trying to raise the M1 again, a half-naked figure in torn black clothes, bones visible through flesh torn from them by the M16 bullets, blood gouting, shining, sparkling red in the sunlight, head lowered with concentration and effort, feet apart, legs braced, trying, trying—and crashed forward dead before he hit the ground.

"Jesus Christ. Who was that bastard?"

"Standing up after a full mag of M16! Holy fuckin' hell," wonder changing to grin, "he was after your bloody hide Frank."

Gardiner stood speechless, shaking his head.

Farther along, Tomlinson's section, followed by the rest of Myers's platoon, moved quietly through the green light of the trees, eyes alert for the lines, light, or shadow that might indicate another cache, or for the movement that might betray the presence of another VC. Dwarf strode along, M60 held like a toy, eyes sweeping the kaleidoscope of light and shadow presented by the trees, shrubs, vines, leaves, and branches before him. His eye caught something unusual. His brain flashed the message, and his gaze sharpened through the undersea-green gloom onto an Asian face, staring at something near Dwarf—his eye, alerted, focussed through the green, and with lightning clarity, he recognized the shapes of several VC, facing toward him, weapons ready.

"Down!" he shouted, thumbing off the safety catch and spraying the belt through the trees, as the answering fire snapped and crackled past, clipping leaves, twigs, and bark.

Myers's platoon dived down, saved from the imminent ambush by Dwarf's shout, and began to return fire. The VC shooting was a continuous drumroll of automatic weapons, and only a slight rise and dip in the ground gave the Australians the cover that prevented many casualties.

"Bart!" shouted Myers, "try and get around on their flank at your end!"

"Right!"

But the intense volume of fire made movement a matter of slow cautious wriggling. Outflanking was out of the question.

Dwarf, lying behind his M60, continued to put burst after burst in the direction of the VC; the gun stopped—automatically his hands flew through the actions—cock, raise feed-plate cover, and Dwarf hunched up onto his elbows to see the breech and feed plate, his head and shoulders rearing up as the burst from the VC machine gun slammed home, killing him instantaneously. The Number Two on the gun, Dwarf's assistant, unhesitatingly pushed the body aside, ignoring the blood and brains splattered over him, cleared the gun, reloaded and carried on firing.

The return fire from Myers's platoon was purely a self-defense measure; if it hadn't been evident, the VC would have been on them.

Suddenly they were gone. The platoon carefully checked to avoid a trap, then tended the wounded and prepared the dead for evacuation.

Bartholomew knelt by the side of the dead Dwarf, removing ammunition from the webbing and pack, while nearby a stretcher was made to carry the big corpse back.

Myers handed the radio handset to the signaler and walked over. "About ready?"

"Yeah Skip . . . notice something about their firepower?"

"There's a lot to it, if that's what you mean."

"Right. When we got here, they had a variety of old Russian, French, and American weapons. Now they've got the best new Russian and Chinese stuff, and aren't worried about ammo. They'd have had us just then, but for old Dwarf. The AK47 goes automatic, and I couldn't count the automatic weapons firing at us."

"Yes, Bart. They're as well armed as us, better in some ways."

"He was a good man," said Bartholomew standing up.

"Yeah, he was. Okay fellers," to the waiting stretcher makers.

They made their slow way back through the trees to the company position, where Dwarf's body was evacuated by Dust-off. A second Huey circled, waited, and settled.

The insulated containers with the fresh-cooked dinner were lifted out, and the Huey threshed away. "Baron" Lord organized the distribution of the meal. Compartmented paper plates were picked up by the individuals who queued, a platoon at a time, for chicken, peas, cabbage, mashed potato, fruit cocktail, orange juice, milk, or tea. The "Baron" stood to one side as the Diggers were fed, muttering about "good food, bully beef and biscuits, soldiering in my day, molly-coddling," and ending with a loud, "Milk! milk! They oughta fly in blood for *soldiers* to drink!" as the grinning troops went back to their pits, plate and mug in hand, rifle tucked under their arm.

The paper plates were simply burned in a trash pit, alleviating the need for cleaning camp pots, hot soapy water, and all the other necessities of hygiene in the field.

The Hueys lifted over the trees, closing into formation and heading south over the river. Bartholomew sat, rifle between his knees, wind buffetting his hair and clothes, looking out over the dark green carpet stretching as far as the eye could see.

Below him were the LZs of previous operations, the hills and valleys through which both sides hunted each other. With the battalion tour drawing to a close, he knew it would be unlikely that they would be back to the jungles below, and he was surprised to feel a faint whiff of nostalgia blow through his brain and heart.

Bob Edmondson sighed, placed his pen down, and looked around the CP. The eight-day clock showed 2 A.M. Another hour to go. He was about to fold the just-written letter into the envelope, when he noticed the plywood table top—covered in pencil and biro notes, grid references, times, radio call signs, compass bearings, and other jottings whose meanings were known only to those who had made them during the long hours of night duty since the battalion had established itself in the area.

In the corner, earphones on one ear, sat the signaler before his array of softly hissing sets, head bowed over a paperback. Down the table from Edmondson, Sergeant O'Malley, the intelligence section sergeant, breathed deeply and regularly, close-cropped head cradled in arms on the table top.

Before them on the table sat field telephones, message pads, pencils, map pins, and paperbacks. On the wall hung the various maps required to give an overall picture of the battalion's area, marked with the red and blue rectangles of enemy and friendly units.

Edmondson looked around, absorbing the night, the quiet, the underground room, the radio, the breathing sounds, the shine of the talc over the maps—this was a part of his life and career.

Augie Bennett flung the paper on the table top with a contemptuous snort.

"Don't know why I bother to read this crap. These reporters must have hair on the palms of their hands. They write absolute rubbish. 'Having a conversation in Saigon to the background noise of D-Zone.' Jeesus. Raving about how dangerous it is in Saigon—liable to have your drink smashed by a sniper's bullet."

Bartholomew grinned over his beer, "And we go there to relax."

"They're all military experts, though. Like the F111 nonsense. Overnight, every politician and wanker on a newspaper was an expert on aeronautics, military aviation, military strategy, light-crew training, and economics. Now they're all experts on jungle warfare, counter-revolutionary warfare, airmobile tactics—you name it, they know all about it."

"One bloke was complaining he'd never been offered a drink or included in a conversation with the officers. Why should they? Reporters have a bad name for quoting out of context; they have no loyalty except to their own fuckin' careers, and they're outsiders anyway."

"Yeah. They can drink with PR. They're paid to."

"I've been on ops and in contacts they've written about, but later when you read about it, you wouldn't know it except for the place names. They write all sorts of crap."

"It'd be the same as us going to write on a fashion parade. No training, don't know what you're seeing and its significance, so the people concerned think it's all crap."

"Yeah. The good thing is they only hang around for a day or so anyway, and ya don't have to talk to 'em."

"Yeah. Listen, how's young Corporal Markham turning out?"

"Oh, not bad, . . ." and the conversation turned to the important things of life.

The paper lay on the table, pages ruffling in the afternoon breeze preceding the monsoon.

"I think we're wasting our time here," said "Red" Ryder. "They obviously know we intended to operate here and are gone."

After several days of occupying and patrolling a very large rubber plantation, with plenty of signs of recent VC activity but no contact, interest started to wane. Then, when the Australian presence was established there, the search was shifted to the south.

The first company moved by helicopter and was engaged just off the LZ. The second company, seated on and in the APCs, galloped down the road to the new area, turning off to sweep through an overgrown patch of rubber.

"Keep your eyes open—B had a contact and got four kills. They could be here as well."

The untended rubber plantation had lost its cool, clear appearance—weeds, grass, and shrubs had sprouted in a dense carpet to a height of six and seven feet. The carriers cruised slowly and quietly through the growth, the crews and infantry peering about from their vantage point, ducking to avoid low branches, weapons ready. Suddenly, from under the tracks themselves it seemed, running, diving, dodging black-clad figures clutching weapons—the rifles and machine guns snapped, and the M113s roared like hunting beasts as the drivers jockeyed their huge charges around the trees, trying to run down the fleetingly seen VC. The hectic charge swept through the section of the plantation, the mounted pursuers alight with the sense of superiority and the spirit of the chase that the mounted man has always felt in battle with the man on foot.

"Christ," grinned one of the drivers, wiping his sweating face, "talk about riding down rabbits. The little buggers are like fleas."

"Which way did they go?" asked Knowles.

"Christ only knows—in all directions," answered Les Fitzgibbon.

"We're lucky no one fell off the APCs," muttered Nimbus. "They'd a been crushed, ya know."

"Is he cheering up or not?" Fitzgibbon asked a smiling Tom Pritchard.

"He'll complain about the dark when they put the coffin lid over his face. Here we go again," as the M113 roared and leaped forward under the branches.

"Any questions?" Myers looked around the silent group. "Right, let's go."

The fifteen men, faces and hands darkened and—except for the signaler—carrying only weapons, ammunition, and grenades, filed away through the darkening rubber avenues, feet "shushing" through the low grass. Shaking out into an arrowhead formation, they quickly but quietly reached the spot picked for their ambush—a junction of the slightly raised crisscrossing roads that divided the plantation into sections.

Night was just asserting its grip over the area— squeezing the last light from the western sky, cloaking all the figures with the anonymity of its gloom. The roads were visible as a faintly lighter band in the heavy darkness. The moon was just rising, its light silvery on the distant clouds that barred its beams.

Nguyen thi Lan her heart singing, her feet flying, as she moved down the jungle path. Ahead and behind strode the five comrades of the local guerrilla unit who had come to bring her home. Home! She had not seen her parents, family, friends, members of the Front or women's association for six months. How good it would be to be home again, and how good to be able to use her newly acquired nursing skills to help the people. For six long months she had studied and sat for exams in the school in the distant mountains. Now she was a nurse, with handsome certificates, notebooks, a nurse's long white gown, Red Cross brassard, gauze mask, and some supplies—all carried in the pack on Tran's back.

All friends, the escort had come to bring her safely from the mountains—two-days' journey away. They had chattered all yesterday as they walked along, exchanging news of the village and the school over the past six months, and at the transit camp in the jungle had sat up singing to Loi's guitar till quite late.

Now, so close to home, the youthful exuberance bubbled all through her limbs, body, and brain, and she wished they could run along the road, as they climbed onto it from the jungle. Glancing back, she saw the silver fringes on the clouds lit by the moon's glow.

The ambush party had settled into their positions under the rubber trees and, from experience, prepared their minds to last through the long hours of waiting.

Then out of the darkness came the pad, pad, pad of swiftly moving feet, and dimly seen shapes materialized on the road. So soon! Here we go then. Breathing held, the ambushers froze, weapons ready, waiting for Myers to spring the trap. Blacker, more solid against the soft sky, the dark shapes drew level and Myers fired, his first shot breaking the silence for a devastating burst that swept the road.

For a moment, Tran stood bewildered, then leaped sideways off the road and, flying away down the short slope, shedding Lan's pack, clambered across the creek and into the jungle, the sole survivor.

Lan became conscious of a terrible pain in her legs, and her wandering hand trailed through torn flesh and shattered bone. Unable to move and unable to control the pain, she began to moan, the only sound under the dark rubber trees. The silent watchers, waiting for further prey, stared into the darkness, fingers on triggers, as Lan's soft cries of pain bubbled out of her and rolled under the arches of the impersonal avenues of rubber trees.

Suddenly, one of the prone figures under the trees rose, took several long, leaping strides forward, and fired a long burst into the moaning body, and, as quickly, leaped back into the impenetrable shadows.

Silence settled, the only noise the faint rustling of leaves as the gentle night breeze stirred the leaves. The silver moon drifted calmly across its black velvet bed, its soft light reflected in the cold glassy eyes on the dirt road, and laying a faint misting on the still wet blood in the wounds.

In the distance, the quiet night was rent by bursts of firing as other ambushes were sprung. In the houses, the people listened and wondered who was dying.

The sun crept up, reluctant at first, then bounding full of zest into the sky. The ambushers swept the scene of their actions, counting bodies, collecting weapons and documents, pocketing souvenirs.

Lan and her friends, who had escorted her to the final rendezvous, lay sprawled in the untidy attitudes of death in battle. The successful ambushers searched the cold bodies, already reeking with the smell of blood and death.

"Hey sir, one of 'ems a woman. The one Frank put the second burst into." To Frank, "You fuckin' near blew her apart, mate."

"Sorry 'bout that," in casual tones.

"Found a pack down there, where that bloke musta dropped it."

"Bet the bastard's still running.'

"Wouldn't you be? Cure ya constipation, ay?" with a wide grin, looking up from the rent corpse he was searching.

"They were fuckin' early, weren't they? Hey sir," to Myers, "do you think they even knew we were in the area? They came bowling up the road without a care in the world."

"You could be right: they were early. That's a good ambush, isn't it? Slaughter the bastards before they even know you're around."

"These cunts never knew what hit 'em, that's for sure."

The roaring of M113s came out of the trees and

shortly after the angular hulks waddled through the avenues to pick up the ambush party after the bodies had been buried. The shallow graves were dug in the soft red earth, Lan and her friends thrown in and covered over, dirt thrown over the blood on the road—already the scene of industrious activity by ants and flies—and the ambush group climbed aboard the APCs, rolling back for a wash, a shave, cleaning of weapons, and breakfast. Behind them, the ants and flies burrowed after all that remained of a nineteen-year-old girl's ambitions of a medical career.

18

"Well, all a man's got to do is keep his head down now, and it's home in sixty days," mused Augie Bennett, staring out over the airbase panorama.

Moose tipped his can back, drank, sighed with pleasure, and grinned, "Yeah. On the final leg at last. Avoid bullet holes and a dose. We've about reached our POCD or whatever the Yanks call it."

"You mean PCOD—Pussy Cut-Off Date."

"Yeah, PCOD. How'd ya ever explain away the fact of arriving home with a load?"

"A man'd have to have the gift of gab, all right."

For the final weeks the battalion flew and landed on large sweeps through areas of jungle, looking for the elusive enemy. Contact was very light, resulting in a few wounded, and a dozen or so VC killed or captured.

Finally, the sure signs of going home were there for all to see—handing in of gear no longer needed, medical examinations that were as brief as, "How do you feel? How many loads have you had? Any aches or pains? Right, next," problems with pay being sorted out, and visits from people of the battalion that would inherit the tents, buildings, and so on.

Fredericks, the interpreter, strolled into the company mess for a drink with Pritchard and Father.

"How ya going, ya old bastard? S'pose you're stayin' on ay?"

"No bloody fear of that! I've got a gorgeous sheila back in Australia and I'm going! Anyway, I've just been over to one of the Yank battalions," jerking a thumb in the general direction, "and ya wanta see it. They've got a bloody big board up in front of their HQ showing all the medals they can get over here in correct order. Standin' in front are all these twenty-year-old Yanks with fistfuls—no bullshit—fistfuls of medal ribbons and all these little clips on a board. They get their medals clipped in the right order and then the tailor does his bit. Kids standing there with eight or nine different ribbons. We were fuckin' lucky to get one!" They all grinned, more in amusement at their own paucity than American largesse.

Finally, came *the* morning, that long-awaited "wakey." Men spoke of twenty and a wakey—fifteen and wakey; five and a wakey; oh my God, one and a wakey! Won't the fuckin' day ever go? Then, it's up, pack, breakfast, onto the buses for the final ride. Out past brigade HQ for the last time, along the road to Saigon. Where a year ago scenic rural Vietnam began at the roadside, now the US units crowded along left and right—hospitals, engineers, supply battalions, truck companies, repair shops—all with their identical low buildings of unpainted wood and identical Yanks in US tropical uniform and caps. Gone were the trees, flocks of cockatoos, thatch-roofed huts, buffalo, and figures in conical hats.

Still the same rushing, weaving, honking mass of wheels ridden by Vietnamese of every shape and size, still the blue haze of petrol fumes fogging the tree-lined streets. But who cares? We're going home, looking out the bus windows, with tired eyes.

The streamlined silver, red, and white Qantas 707 sat ready to roll along the runway and climb up out of the heat, smoke, dust, and smells, heading east to the Philippines, then south to Townsville and Sydney—and going far too slowly at 600 mph, rumbling through the night sky for the early morning landing in Sydney. And the air feels, smells, tastes, *is* sweeter.

Through customs—the mugs caught trying to bring in pistols and souvenir munitions have been well publicized in the battalion—and it's out to the relations, girlfriends, wives, and kids.

Father overwhelmed by a yelling mass of children, staggering back with a grin at his Alice. "Are these all ours?"

Muriel Burrows standing quietly to one side with a small group of officers' wives, a smile on her lips, calm eyes checking the approaching Stan for signs of change.

And in the gloom under the eaves, Phuoc called down to Binh, "60 UH-ID heading north."

Tom Pritchard lost in the bottomless sea of Christine's eyes, her soft voice registering on his brain—the kids are at their grandmother's till tomorrow. . . .

Les Fitzgibbon grinning at Sharon, and Leslie escorting a thinner but up-and-about Smacker, arms around their waists, "C'mon, you're late! I've been keepin' the Cross warm for ya."

Xuan looked up at the ceiling past the shoulders of the sweating American, calculating how much she would remove from his wallet when he'd expended himself in her and fallen asleep. Tomorrow she would be able to give 9,000 piasters to the collector for the Front.

Tiny Rhonda Morrissey smiling proudly at huge Moose, standing timidly before her. "Hello love, I'm back."

Bartholomew wondered how soon he could get back to Vietnam.

Bruce Myers embracing a radiant Jacqueline, all long tanned legs under mini skirt, soft lips whispering, "I've been waiting for you."

Hai Quyen handed back the message to the clerk, nodded, and resumed his reading of the directive from the central committee, smoke from the Gaulois curling thinly up into the dimness of the thatched roof, light from the kerosene lamp glinting on the talc covering the map. Outside the full moon shone silver on the river, and on the horizon the silent flares blossomed.